Praise for *Pack Men*:

'A landmark book in Scottish fiction. Disguising it as an archetypal tale of the educated working-class boy disdaining and admiring his unreconstructed mates in equal measure, Alan Bissett tackles Scotland's ongoing sore of sectarianism. With neither condescending sneer nor pathetic apology, he shows how it will always exert a pull on those at the bottom of the social pile. A big enough achievement in itself, but the overall impact is greater still; *Pack Men* is nothing less than a fearless dissection of contemporary Scottish masculinity' Irvine Welsh

'Bissett's ear for cut and thrust, for chiv-sharp wit and tinder-dry insult is incisive, pitch perfect, informed . . . the writing is subtle, well-paced, authentic and compelling . . . from the start the story transports you aboard its wheeled madhouse in the company of a colourful band of yahoos that Geoffrey Chaucer would be pleased to have invented' *Scotsman*

'Bissett writes subtly, intelligently yet also passionately about men . . . an outstanding novel' *Scotland on Sunday*

'Told with narrative flair and demotic brilliance, this is a hugely funny, ruthlessly honest and desperately necessary book' Sarah Hall, Booker-shortlisted author of *The Electric Michelangelo*

'If Scotland's father of working class consciousness James Kelman had a literary son it might be Alan Bissett . . . funny, irreverent and moving' *Gutter*

'*Pack Men* is a wry, entertaining and mature work . . . Bissett succeeds in making us root for the most unlikely of antiheroes, even as he implodes' *Scottish Review of Books*

'A blistering, adrenaline-fuelled romp' *The List*

'Bissett's best novel yet' *Scottish Sunday Herald*

'A pacy and fluid examination of masculinity, male bonding, sexuality and class . . . an assured and confident piece of fiction from a definite talent' *Big Issue Scotland*

Alan Bissett is a novelist, playwright and performer who lives in Glasgow. He was named Glenfiddich Spirit of Scotland Writer of the Year 2011. His previous novel *Death of a Ladies' Man* was shortlisted for a Scottish Arts Council Fiction of the Year prize. His play *Turbo Folk* was shortlisted for Best New Play at the Critics' Awards for Theatre in Scotland. In 2010 he wrote and performed his own 'one-woman show', *The Moira Monologues*, which toured Scotland to great acclaim and it is now in development with the BBC. The short film which he wrote and narrated, *The Shutdown*, has won awards at several major international film festivals and was shortlisted for a BAFTA.

Also by Alan Bissett:

Boyracers
The Incredible Adam Spark
Death of a Ladies' Man

ALAN BISSETT

PACK MEN

First published in 2011 by
HACHETTE SCOTLAND, an imprint of Hachette UK

First published in paperback in 2012 by
HACHETTE SCOTLAND, an imprint of Hachette UK

1

Cataloguing in Publication Data is available from the British Library

ISBN 978 0 7553 1943 5 (Trade paperback)
ISBN 978 0 7553 1944 2 (Paperback)

Typeset in Walbaum MT by Avon DataSet Ltd,
Bidford-on-Avon, Warwickshire

Printed and bound in Great Britain by
Clays Ltd, St Ives plc

Hachette Scotland's policy is to use papers that are natural, renewable and
recyclable products and made from wood grown in sustainable forests.
The logging and manufacturing processes are expected to conform
to the environmental regulations of the country of origin.

HACHETTE SCOTLAND
An Hachette UK Company
338 Euston Road
London NW1 3BH

www.hachettescotland.co.uk
www.hachette.co.uk

For the Falkirk boys

Ronnie
Moonie
Toby
Saunders
Allan 'the' Mann
John T.
Gary Black
Big Gilmour

Who's for the Martell?

F o l l o w
F o l l o w
B L U E
We will fol
R E D
low Rangers
here there
W H I T E
e v e r y
w h e re
Frannie
stands
at the
front
snake
char
mi

ng the minibus with its own song, fingers twirling. Everyone sings and stamps as the words spike the air, and I don't join in with the lines DUNDEE, HAMILTON, FUCK THE POPE AND THE VATICAN! They bring me up short, broken glass left on a beach that I *just* manage to skip over. Narrow escape.

But on this bus, does it matter?

Rangers sloshes out of Frannie each time he opens his

mouth. He bursts into a can of hangover Irn Bru, toasts the whole convoy heading south. His ego has flown from the cocoon of sleepiness it was wrapped in when we picked him up half an hour ago: blearily poking feelers into the pale light of dawn. Now he's on the wing. 'Sing up, runt,' he goes, slapping my back friendly/forceful. 'Mon the Rangers!'

Runt? *Runt?* That's a name I haven't heard in a long while. Harks back to a time when quotes from The Matrix were still cutting-edge currency between us. Nothing could be less futuristic than this actual future we've found ourselves in: a tiny fifteen-seater bus with rust sprayed up the side, the kind of tired dog used for Scout outings, bingo trips, or the transportation of labourers between sites. The seat lining is burst in places and a coffee stain does brown bygones. Now it houses our collective souls: me, Frannie, Dolby, and wee Jack. I swallow and wonder if mine is still intact. Jack sticks Rangers players into his book with dainty fingers, humming along with the song until Dolby taps a stern No.

The bus squeezes through the hustleandbustle of Falkirk town then – out! – tears onto the M8 by force of its own roar. Union Jack scarves trail from it like bunting. I glance back at my fellow passengers, pilgrims, their already sweaty replica shirts. Frannie had rung the bell of their names to us as they'd stepped on board, punctuated by a high-five or handshake: 'Bex', 'Jeff', 'Chaz', 'Sally' (a bloke), 'Rab', 'Wee Wife', 'Auld Alfred', and 'The Cage'.

The Cage had thudded mountainously past and taken up the whole back seat of the bus. I'd feared it tipping as he sat down.

His head looked like a cannonball with a smile welded onto it. He settled his arse into the seat and nodded once at me. I nodded back.

Dolby is gripping the wheel. Dolby is driving. Dolby is being a Responsible Father. Jack sits beside him in the front seat, sooking an orange juice, sticker book open on his lap. He's checking each team member in the same meticulous way a food critic reads menus. We slip in and out of motorway lanes like a fat wee jet, Scots on their hols wearing Here-We-Go hats. Rab and Chaz sway brotherly hands at each other, crooning,

No, no Pope of Rome,
No chapels to sadden my eyes,
No nuns and no priests and no rosary beads,
Every day is the Twelfth of July . . .

I'm not even Catholic and they make me feel Catholic. I'm already wondering how Frannie managed to talk me into this, during the phone call last month when I finally admitted how much I was hating Edinburgh/missing Falkirk and he'd dangled the juicy prospect of a Lads' Jolly to bring it all back. I was susceptible. I was weak. Forgive me, Father, for I have sinned.

At least the sun's out.

Wee Wife's rattling through a bag of Maltesers, puckered mouth working, savouring. She holds the packet up to me and I pop one into my mouth and she smiles, crow's feet creasing gently at the side of her eyes. 'Aye, ye cannay beat a Malteser,' she says. 'I liketay sook the chocolate aff ay them first and then—' She crunches down apocalyptically.

My tongue considers the Malteser. The Malteser considers my tongue.

'Sook,' she instructs.

The chocolate melts from the bald honeycomb centre and I roll it around. This Malteser is the highlight of my day so far; I want to make it last.

'Now crunch,' says Wee Wife. 'It'll no hurt ye.'

My teeth break the little planetoid and sugar dissolves on my tongue. She winks. 'Wee tip for ye there. That's howtay get the best outtay a Malteser, I tell ye.'

'If only I could do the same for you one day.'

Her mouth amuses itself with my accent. 'Posh yin you, eh?'

'Uh,' I say, 'not really. I'm from Falkirk. Same as the rest of you.'

She sniffs and nods. 'Aye, ye sound like it.'

I swallow another Malteser and turn back to Auld Alfred, who's been talking to me about the glory days of Slim Jim Baxter and John Greig with all the passion of a medieval seer. 'I wis sayin, son,' he croaks. 'See when Greig came oot that tunnel haudin that baw? Ye believed in him. Ye *believed* he wanted tay win that gemme.'

And, despite myself, I like the way his eyes spark-light when he talks about Rangers legends, warming by degrees. 'Wish I'd seen that,' I say, and briefly mean it.

'Souness. Greig. Struth. Smith.' His hands fan out in an abracadabra. 'These men were winners. Everythin a man should be. That's what Rangers are aw aboot.'

'Em, aye,' I say. 'We all like to . . . win . . . things.'

Frannie points down at the poly-bag snoozing between his feet.

'What?'

He makes a conspiracy face and draws me closer. 'Put yer hand in.'

My hand goes in, touches a glass neck, withdraws the bottle. 'Alvin's brought whisky!' he announces, and the whole bus roars.

Dolby wrenches round from the driver's seat like a Transformer mid-change. 'Hey. Telt youse nae boozin. No gettin points on ma licence just cos youse cannay go four hours withoot a drink.' He clicks his head on his neck, back and forth, and makes troubled breath, disliking the feel of this atmosphere on his skin. Some of the songs he's heard have filtered through the pores, formed dark sediment in his bloodstream. 'You've still got a power ay drinkin tay go, lads. C'mon, it's only nine in the mornin.'

Frannie shakes his watch at Dolby, as though trying to motivate a slacker. '*Nine twenty-four* and sixteen seconds, mate. That'll teach ye for no buyin TAG Heuer: "Pioneering Swiss Watchmaking For 150 Years".' He kisses it, gazes longingly at it. Two years ago, Frannie announced that the one piece of gentleman's kit he was going to make it his life's ambition to own was a TAG Heuer watch. All right, it was credit-carded, but it meant placing property on the Monopoly board of his wrist feasible at last. Now he makes damn sure everyone knows about it, parading through Falkirk High Street in his head, Ronaldo-smug, the TAG glinting time for the doomed drones. 'Gottay mind, mate, half the folk doon there will still be drinkin fay last night. We'll be like Buddhist monks tay them.'

Jack looks up from his sticker book to wag a tiny finger. 'Youse are big disgraces.'

'Whoah,' goes Frannie. 'Nae messin fae the wee yin. C'mere, pal.' He plants a rubbery kiss on Jack's head.

Jack burrows into himself, smirking with all the yuck of it. 'Aah. Get off me.'

'Hey,' says Dolby. 'Don't be cheeky to Uncle Colin.'

Jack seems to contemplate Frannie's aura for a second, until Frannie crosses his eyes and Jack giggles, light, breezy, easy as that.

This. My mate. My other mate. My mate's boy. When we were charging round Falkirk streets in a car called Belinda eight years ago, we never imagined that Brian (my *other* other mate) could be replaced so easily by a wee laddie (even if we all acted like one after a few Aftershocks), but there are no conditions to adoring Jack. He hasn't even learned how to lie yet, just hook question marks into the air and tug. He once told me I looked like Harry Potter. It was neither compliment nor insult, just statement of fact as Jack saw it, even if I'd wanted to tell him, get it straight, pal. I don't look a fucking thing like Harry Potter.

'So ye still support the Rangers, wee man?' says Frannie, in the same voice he'll use, no doubt, as he pushes Jack's First

Official Pint down the bar towards him ten years from now.

Jack gives the merest of nods, opens a book about dinosaurs.

'Good lad,' says Frannie, takes another scoop of Irn Bru, TAG winking on the up-down as his phone spontaneously plays My Generation and he takes it from his pocket. PEOPLE *TRYYYY* TO PUT US D—

'Yo,' he answers, before working a deep, satisfied nod and raising a hand to his troops. 'That's Stuart Storrie's train just arrived in Manchester, lads. Says the place is heavin.' The bus rumbles with satisfaction, then he listens to more Storrie stories and a smile breaks across his face. 'Whit's that, mate? Oh, aye, you tell her hello fay me. Naw, you just tell her I'm lookin forward tay seein her very soon.' He slides his phone back into his pocket, bunches his lips, kiss-like, Jagger-like. 'Wee honey. Right,' he adds, massaging a head-rest as he eyes Bex, Jeff, Sally. 'Lads. Listen carefully. Now, I am proud of every single one of yese. Course I am. Yese are Bluenoses. Rangers men. This football club stands for dignity and tradition.' He emphasises each point with Churchillian authority. They meet his stare with belief. 'But we have work tay dae. When Stuart Storrie tells me that a whole trainload ay us have just arrived in a city which – let's no forget, chaps – gave birth tay Oasis, the Stone Roses, Joy Division, New Order, the Happy Mondays, Elbow and the Charlatans . . .'

He lets the names dance like E'd up Mancs for a bit.

'Um,' I point out, 'the Charlatans are from the Midlands. And what about the Smiths?'

Frannie pings these crumbs away. 'Fuck the Smiths. Too

gay.' There are cheers at this and he returns to the task in hand. 'It all means that I, for wan, am not havin us turnin up sober as fuckin judges.'

'Calling Donald Findlay QC,' Wee Wife chirps, rolling a Malteser round her mouth.

Frannie stands erect and pretends to suck an extravagant pipe. Then his hands clamp my shoulders. 'Now, wee Alvin here . . . is a laddie who has forgotten his allegiance tay the tribe.'

The boos are half-hearted, but I can feel the stares on me, as though I've just been presented to them in a meal box.

'Well,' I cough, 'I, uh, certainly. Supported Rangers. As a wee boy. But, uh. Lately I've just become more interested in . . .'

'In whit?' Frannie says, like a quiz-show host helping a guest who's gone off-script.

'Other projects.'

They all pause to inspect this answer, before someone unseen at the back barks, 'Celtic?'

The sound of everyone sucking air through their teeth, as their arch rivals amble phantomly across the horizon.

'C'mon, son,' says the voice from somewhere, perhaps the universe itself. 'Ye a Rangers man or no?'

Frannie raises a hand. 'Order in the court.' This is overdoing it, even for him. 'Now, I hear whit ye're sayin, Mr Cage. But this boy does not kick wi his left foot.'

For a second I wonder if he's going to lift up my left foot to show them.

'Once a Rangers man, always a Rangers man.' He rubs my hair, before wiping the gel on his jeans with a frown. 'Ye're here, Alvin, that's the main thing. Int that right, everyone? Or should I say, every *Hun*.'

There's a gentle ripple of sectarianism.

Frannie, to my brief shock, hugs me and whispers, 'Glad ye could make it, mate. Gonnay be a great day.' He leans back, squints his phone at me. 'Buy a quick smile from the 99p shop, stick it on. There ye go. Click. Dolby?'

'Wheesht, Franman, I'm drivin.' Dolby presses his gaze to the road, Jedi-faced.

'Tell this peely-faced Edinburgh lab-rat he's gonnay have a great day.'

'Ye're gonnay have a great day,' Dolby Wan Kenobi instructs.

These aren't the droids you're looking for.

'Everyone's gonnay have a great day,' Frannie says, 'except that Zenit St Petersburg mob we're about tay *pump*.' He thrusts at an imaginary Zenit fan, makes porn-star faces, oohing and aahing. 'And I'm not talkin love-makin here, Alvin. The kind you usedtay dream about when ye were clingin ontay yer virginity for aw them years. I mean a right, fat, dirty pummelling.'

Zenit St Petersburg receives his load. Frannie's face does a long, slow orgasm. The bus claps the live floor show. Wee Wife is shaking her fist, going, 'Intay them!' like she's out on a stag night with us. Frannie mimes smoking his Donald Finlay pipe again, post-coitally blissful.

'You'd better wash your hands.' I laugh.

Everyone stares at me. I take out my phone and pretend to read a text.

How does he do it? The Franman has always just been so positive of exactly *who he is*. Even back when we were laddies hanging out in Falkirk on the boy-racer circuit or the chart-happy dance-floors, he'd be the advance guard heading towards the girls, sneaking through the raised spears of their stares. Me, Dolby and Brian would venture in to find him twirling his patter, forcing us to clutch at it as he jived the girls out from their corner. I'd just step from side to side, with all the grace of a newborn foal needing a pee, waiting for one of them to say, 'Aw, look at how *cute* he is,' and pinch my cheeks.

It's strange watching Frannie age in stages. The large gaps between actually seeing him make his evolution more pronounced. Lately, he seems to have become preserved in Mod, the look of choice for the hetero-male approaching thirty: Welleresque hair, Fred Perry tops, Harrington jackets, sarcasm tailored as part of Liam Gallagher's clothing range. Smart move, since Mod will always be modern, but not one I could pull off myself (today, for example, I'm in a Captain America T-shirt, since it's the only thing I own that's red, white and blue). Frannie was the first of us ever to buy a mobile phone, then an iPod, then an iPhone, and will probably purchase an iEye once they're invented, making us wait as a list of terrace-friendly bands scrolls down his retina. He's Q magazine's target demographic. He despises the NME as much as he does Celtic FC and students, his prejudices staggering and florid in full display, almost a thing of beauty, with elaborate, colourful insults and blooms of conspiracy theory ('How come the last three Lord Provosts of Glasgow have been Catholic, eh?').

He's not a bigot, he claims. He just fucking hates Celtic. 'Pantomime,' he once told me. 'You've got an arts degree, Alvin, ye should recognise theatre when ye see it.'

And here we are on the biggest day of his football-supporting life: the UEFA Cup Final. Rangers playing on such a stage is big enough to draw me and Dolby, who're not even that fussed about the beautiful/ugly game. Since it's only a short hop over the border to Manchester, looks like about a hundred and fifty thousand other glory-hunters (hey, I freely admit it) have thought the same thing. Means at least three out of the four Lads are on an actual Lads Trip for the first time since Brian emigrated in 2006. The Mann's probably rubbing moisturiser into his big nipples in the Californian sun right now. We've been getting his texts this morning at intervals, blasting out from across the Atlantic:

```
Mon the rangers
drink manchester dry
heddy haw
```

Ever seen a haiku with such intent? Brian Mann. Brian *the* Mann. All he needs is an umlaut – Brian Männ – and you hear it pronounced by Schwarzenegger. For years he was the head barman in Smith's, the pub in Baxter's Wynd just off Falkirk High Street, the sort of place you'd imagine Tam O'Shanter stumbling out of, burbling with drink. You'd find him in there, wiping the bar and listening to stories from Mark Baxter or Gary Bell, occasionally interrupting with, 'So did ye panel the cunt? Tell me ye panelled the cunt?' The story would end with one of them panelling the cunt. To which Brian would nod, satisfied. Good.

Cunts needed panelled.

But then he'd see you enter and his face would brighten, and he'd be sliding a Jack 'n' Coke your way and giving it, 'Pull up a pew, Alvin, pull up a pew. Tell Brother Mann the news from Poofworld.' And before you knew it, you'd been sitting there three hours, rat-arsed, and he was still wiping the bar, tutting at the lightness of your weight, and you were thinking about asking him to set you up with one of his spectacular barmaids, even though you were doomed to fail cos, let's face it, they all fancied Brian. It was why they worked there. According to Brian, it was why they had vaginas.

Falkirk.

This morning's as gorgeous as a catwalk in summer. The motorway's packed. More stamping and singing from the busload, their churning world of royal blue. Even Frannie can't believe how many cars fill the lanes with scarves and flags; he jags from one side of the bus to the other, his are-we-there-yet face pressed to windows. Dolby, rolling his neck in the front seat, tries to listen without prejudice, but winces each time he hears the words 'Fenian', 'Mick', 'Pape' or 'Tim' volleyed across the bus, and I mind that his mum was raised Catholic. Unease is oozing from him. He keeps rubbing his forehead with a wet wipe. He frowns and his eyes flick to wee Jack, who can surely hear all this but is making monster faces in the side mirror. Tricky biscuits. Unless Dolby acknowledges that these words are bad, Jack might use them. On the other hand, if he *does* acknowledge that these words are bad, Jack will want to know what they mean. This paradox creates static within Dolby: the brow-twitch, the finger-flex. Also, the texts he's been getting from Leanne have been sharp with teeth (whenever her name comes up, Frannie hums the Jaws theme) and I'm minding that awful night, last month, very late, when my phone beeped and he told me,

`shes shaggin that neil`

It's one of the reasons I've decided to move back to Falkirk actually, that Bat Signal going up. I mean, Edinburgh's not exactly been working out anyway (whose ambition was ever to be a bedsit-dwelling till-monkey?) but still I can remember the dripping smell of a fish supper, the opening guitar lines of 'Hotel California', as we sat in the front seat of Belinda eight years ago – overlooking Falkirk – and the words Dolby said to me, his rule for life: *Ye dinnay. Dump. Yer mates.*

Except I did.

Dolby's face is clouding now, the cauldron of his thoughts boiling, so I thrust a hand in and haul him back up with some good news: 'See Roger Waters is playin the *whole* of Dark Side of the Moon in the O2 Arena next week?'

'That right?' he says, brightening. 'Still tickets left?'

'Fancy it, likes?'

'The whole ay the Moon? I dae!'

'The Floyd need to get back onstage together,' I sigh, folding arms and leaning onto the headrest, 'like they did at Live 8. How good was that?'

Dolby measures this with a delicately raised eyebrow. 'Or as I like tay call it: the day Africa generously supported the cause of Pink Floyd.'

'A glorious cause. Well worth leaving that march in Edinburgh early for.'

The band pass in Floydian cortège, eradicating poverty before them.

'Speaking ay Edinburgh,' Dolby says, 'how's the bookshop workin out for ye?'

I cannot tell a lie. Well, I can, but not to Dolby. 'Prefer to be selling my own, likes, rather than fucking—'

'Let me guess: Harry Potter?'

'We should just rename the shop Potterstone's.'

'It's all right, though, eh?' Dolby says. 'I mean, it's a bookshop. It's no exactly toilet-cleanin.' He glances at me in the rear-view mirror. 'Unless ye actually do have tay clean the toil—'

'No, I *don't* have to clean the toilets,' I say. But I want to add, I have a degree, which has been doing absolutely hee-haw for the last three years except snigger at me from a drawer and remind me that I'm a bag of meat, bones and water like everyone else.

'Still, though,' says Dolby, 'it's how we got tay meet Clive Barker.'

Our eyes widen, electrified by the memory. Me ushering the streams of Horror geekazoids towards 'Mr Barker' – WE WERE TEAM BARKER! – who chatted amiably and scribbled things in their books, while Dolby stood beside me, rigid and impregnated with the thought that, once they all left, it'd just be us. And Him. Clive fucking Barker. The man who wrote Weaveworld *and* directed Hellraiser. Maybe he'd call upon us for advice about his new artistic direction. He didn't but, y'know, he should've.

When next Dolby looks at me in the rear-view mirror there's weight in it. 'You still aff the drink?'

'Aye.'

'Even the day?'

'Aye.'

He nods solemnly.

I was wondering if/when that'd come up.

Jack shows me a picture he's drawn of the bus, points everyone out. Bex, Jeff, Chaz, Sally, Rab, Wee Wife, Auld Alfred and The Cage are a general huddle with only a flash of blond, ginger or brown to distinguish them from each other. 'Look, Uncle Alvin, you're the one with glasses and lightning on your head.' Frannie is a blue scrawl with a smile, which actually pretty much sums him up. Daddy, at the front of the bus, is cross, eyebrows angled downwards and big upturned U for a mouth. When Jack is distracted, I'll hide it from his Dolby.

'By the way,' I say to him, 'I've nearly finished my book.'

'This the same yin about giant spiders takin over the toon?'

'Arachno Falkirk? Nah. Too unbelievable.'

'You never saw this thing in ma bath last night.'

'I'm thinking now the Ring . . . meets Twilight.'

'That's more believable.'

'Meets Goodfellas.'

'You'll need to take me through that.'

'Okay,' I begin, hands coaxing the tale. 'There's this group of friends, right, and they get this DVD out of Blockbuster on Grahams Road.'

'Grahams Road round the corner fay me?'

'Obviously. Got to keep it real. So if you watch this DVD once, that's it, you die. And there's these gangsters chasing the friends, but they're actually vampires, and they want to use the DVD to wipe out their enemi—'

'Just tell me the title.'

'*Grrrrr.*'

'*Grrrrrrrrr?*' Dolby says.

'Aye, but not with so many *rrrrs.*'

'*Grr?*'

'Few more.'

'*Grrrrr?* That's whit it's called? *Grrrrr?*'

'Yeah!'

Dolby takes a slug of orangeade, passes it to Jack. Jack wipes the top of the bottle and tuts. 'You get that look aff yer mother,' Dolby notes, then has to shout his response to me, as another chorus starts up and feet thud a rhythm:

Hu-LLO!
Hu-LLO!

'Alvin, ye ken I'd back ye in anythin. I mean, it's amazin ye've been through college an aw that.'

'University.'

'Whit's the difference?'

'Doesn't matter.'

'Well, either way, it's somethin I could never dae.'

'Course you could.'

He shrugs a galaxy in that pause.

'There's a recession on the wey, mind. Even I ken ye'll needtay come up wi better ideas than *Grrrrr*.' His eyes return to the motorway and focus.

Man, I think, looking at him, she's really done a number on you.

'*Sooooo*,' I say to Jack, 'excited about the game?'

He squints up at me, as though this is exactly the kind of boring routine question he's used to fielding from adults.

'Who d'you think will win?'

'Rangers.'

'By how much?'

Shrug.

'What if it's a thousand–nil?'

He stares at me indifferently. 'That's impossible.'

'Oh,' I say. 'Um, is it? Didn't know that. I'm sure I was at a game that was a thousand–nil once . . .'

Jack returns to drawing animals, now that I've proven

myself beneath contempt.

Behind me, so close it feels on top of me, Frannie and Jeff start a game of headlocks, arms grasping and comedy murder in their eyes. It's too fat and physical for this tiny bus, and I have to move the furniture of myself out the way. 'Shift yersel, runt!' Frannie yelps, through an adrenalin grin.

'Ho,' goes the big voice from the back, like a hand placed on them. 'Enough cerry oan.'

They instantly obey – 'Sorry, Cage, blame that dick' – smiling and doing mock head-jabs at each other. Dick. Dick.

The bus glides through the lanes of the motorway and Dolby leans towards me. 'Listen. How do ye feel about Frannie callin ye "runt"?'

'Didn't notice, to be honest.'

'Aye, ye did.'

I push my glasses up my nose. 'He's, um . . . He's just trying to make it like old times. Sure he doesn't mean anything by it.'

'Aye,' Dolby says, then shouts, 'Ho, Frannie.' The Franman stops singing and clambers towards us, skelping Jeff. At first I think Dolby's about to beast him for calling me 'runt'. Don't want that. No tension. Not today. 'Listen, if things go mental doon here, I'm takin Jack backtay the bus.'

'Eh?' Frannie says. 'Gonnay be fine, big man. Just a perty.'

'Aye,' Dolby says. 'But there'll be a hundred and fifty thousand pished Rangers fans at this perty.'

'Whit ye sayin about the Rangers, likes?'

'Okay, a hundred and fifty thousand *fans*. Just tellin ye. He's ma priority. We might needtay bolt if things get ootay hand.'

Frannie tries not to be insulted – 'Fair enough, man' – fails. 'But ye're worryin about nothin. See youse armchair fans?' He jabs a finger at us both. 'You two bastards. The *book-jockeys.* Youse are like ma mum, thinks fans cannay just have a drink withoot trouble. We're no animals, by fuck.'

'Language in frontay the wee man.'

Frannie bows towards me. 'Sorry, Alvin, I forgot ye're a sensitive soul.'

'Naw, no Alvin. *Jack.*'

Jack waves at another supporters' bus. They applaud, he applauds. A moment, like the top notes on a piano being played.

'Listen,' says Frannie, 'he's gonnay hear a lot worse the day.'

'Aye, well,' says Dolby, 'no fay you.'

'Tellin ye, mair likely tay get a riot at a Jay-Z gig than a UEFA Cup match. No that kinda vibe. This is the first European final Rangers have been in for thirty-five years. Every cu— I mean, everyone's just up for a good time.'

'A hundred and fifty thousand fans without tickets,' I point out.

Frannie turns to me so quickly that I flinch. 'Ho. Disnay matter.' Then, for some reason, he dons a pair of shades to conjure Manchester on a vast scale for us. He opens his arms, giving love to the world through the medium of swagger. 'These fan zones are meantay be amazin. Giant screens, entertainment. Gonnay be boss.'

'*Boss?*' said Dolby, 'You read the local phrasebook or somethin?'

Another bus draws up alongside us and Frannie sticks both thumbs up at them.

After a while I say, 'That's racist.'

Frannie frowns and looks at his thumbs. 'Eh?'

'The Jay-Z thing,' I say. 'Why not specify, like, a white artist?'

'Well, cannay mind the last riot I saw for Coldplay.'

'Crowd would be asleep, mate.'

'Alvin,' Dolby says, 'just leave it, eh?'

'Right.'

We stare at each other, as the years turn round 360 degrees.

I back down. Of course I do. The inevitability of it was carved by nightly jousts long ago. 'Sorry, man, I was a bit out of order there.'

'Aye,' Frannie says, gesturing down the bus, 'the *Orange* Order. Ye're fine wi me, pal, but ye'll needtay be careful. No everybody on the bus is so, eh, sensitive about these issues.'

'Aye, okay.'

'Partfay anythin else?' He draws his can towards his chest. 'I vouched for ye, Alvin. Ye dinnay get on a bus like this withoot someone vouchin for ye. So don't you show me up wi yer politically correct – em, how can I put this? – *pish.* Don't you dare.'

He bursts open his first Stella of the day, takes a swig, and lets it accrue interest on his tongue. Swallows. Then he raises the can to me, gentlemanly. Wee Wife sneakily checks out his arse as it squeezes down the aisle.

Dolby's looking at me as though I've just served Frannie with an eviction notice. 'It's cool, man. Calm doon. Ye ken he's no a racist.'

'I know.' Rubbing my forehead makes my fingertips oily, worry seeping between the whorls. The sun has charged its way up the sky like a horseman cracking a whip. 'Bloody hot on this bus. Geez a wet wipe.'

'Here.'

'Cheers,' I say, and try to articulate it, what's happening in my head, being here, among them again, after all this time. But what comes out is, 'Sorry, man. Having a hard time just now.'

'Think ye're the only yin? Dinnay take it oot on Frannie. He really wanted ye tay be here.'

'I know. I apologised, didn't I?'

Dolby checks Jack isn't listening, then proves he knows me: 'How about we save this for a mong night, bro? Fire up the bong. Get right intay it.'

'Yeah,' I say, nestling into the comfort of the thought. 'We'll do that. Cos this stuff's just coursing round my fucking head, driving me mental.'

'Uncle Alvin, you swore!' says Jack.

He doesn't hear 'mong' or 'bong' when they're knocked together, but the F-word shatters things.

'Good lad. It's not okay for Uncle Alvin to swear either, son.'

'Is that cos he's been through the clever door at university?'

Dolby's thoughts spasm for a second. 'Em, aye. Well put.' He half turns to me. 'Listen, man, let's not get wound up doon here.'

'Hearing you.'

'I'm no really interested in the fitbaw either, Alvin. But it's been ages since we had a big Lads' day oot like this. I think we aw need it.'

'Aye,' I say, staring at the motorway ahead, the scarves, the flags, the flags, the scarves. 'We do.'

Then I breathe in a bouquet of Scottish summer air. Hints of seat-leather, lager and men.

> Make her live inside you   scooped out hollow   a human-shaped machine   vacuuming   gathered together from spare organic parts ~~gases distended in her~~   When she reached out to touch an object kettle flowerpot slippers   it was like some hologram placed photo-realistically across space [once occupied] by her body moving synthetically   pre-programmed   with   futuristic hum   She said hello to people   neighbours but the emotion behind the utterance had vanished irrelevant data stray bits of binary   not the code her mind needed to carry out such tasks ~~such~~ as fill washing-machine answer phone pick up toys go to supermarket register sunlight on skin recognise scents shapes voices of her
>
>   dearlybelovedfamily how to interact she is she s

I'm halfway through reading Frannie's copy of Q magazine – cover features REM and Radiohead, so I'm stunned that he bought it given his aversion to both – when Wee Wife jams herself up onto the seat next to me.

'Hiya,' I say, wary.

'Awright,' she says, staring at me.

'Any more Maltesers?' I try.

'Ye'll get wan if ye answer me a question.' She pokes me in the ribs once, twice.

Frannie is on the phone again (to an ambulance, I hope, just in case there's damage to my ribs). 'Yes?'

'Some ay us back there were just wonderin. Whit you daein here, son?'

'What do you mean? The same reason everyone else is here.'

Her head sways a little, dancing with this thought. 'Just that ye dinnay talk like us, ken? Thought you'd mibbe be mairay a rugby man.'

'Naw,' I say, fully Falkirkising the word, but it sounds like a donkey braying.

'Ye supported the Rangers long?'

'Well.' I shrug. 'No really a supporter, as such.'

Her face does *You-don't-say* crossed with *Knew-it*. 'So whit are ye, then?'

'I'm just . . . Alvin.'

This is like sprinkling someone with toast crumbs and expecting them to understand the space-time continuum.

'Ye a journalist?' She peers at me, elbow knocking against mine. 'Writing somethin about how we're all just bigoted scum?'

'What makes you say that?'

'Just that I saw you were writin stuff doon in a wee notebook earlier. Wondered whit that was for. And ye talk like that Graham Spiers. And I fuckin hate Graham Spiers.' She's staring at me evenly, with a dusting of a smile. Beyond her shoulder, through the bus window: fields and farms. I could be tied up and bundled into a barn in any of them.

'No,' I say, leaning in. 'I write Horror novels.'

'Horror!' she hoots, clutching my arm, 'Like, Stephen King and aw that?'

My lips tighten. 'My stuff's more intellectual. More like Clive Barker.'

Her eyebrows lift. 'Barker, eh? Bloody good writer.'

This lands on my nose with butterfly-surprise and I shake my head. 'You know who Clive Barker is?'

She claps her hands together as though she's won a round of poker. 'Wee man. Ye dinnay believe aw that aboot how Rangers fans cannay read, dae ye?'

I laugh mechanically.

'Horror! Aye, I usedtay love aw that. Nee! Nee! Nee! Nee!' She mimes stabbing me. 'Wis that Halloween?'

'Psycho.'

'That Norman Bates – ho. Answer me somethin aboot that cunt. Why was he still steyin wi his mammy intay his thirties? Grow up, laddie! I will have ma boys right ootay there. Well. Jason's awready away. Aye. Em. Less said aboot *that* yin the better. Halloween, though! Went tae see it wi Boab Johnston, usually got the number nine bus fae Shieldhill whaur I wis steyin at the time. Cos I wisnay getting on wi ma mam, ye see. Fuckin boot. I mean, Godresther*soul*. But she wis a bitter wummin. And the thing aboot Boab Johnston wis he had a *car*. Oh, that wis excitin. Cos see in the eighties, before your time, likes, eh, finding a guy wi a car wisnay as easy as—'

'Were you a New Romantic in the eighties?' I say, to try and help her cohere, but her hands do a shooing motion at this.

'Och, son, I was just a party girl. Takin *sides.* I mean, it's just music. It's just *claes.*' She dances, demonstrating the eighties to me. 'Loosen up. That's boys, though, son, int it? Got tae be in some kinday *gang*. Cheers.'

She raises her can at me and gulps hugely.

'Tell me about it,' I mutter, looking at the buses threading through the motorway lanes. Redwhitebluewhitered.

'No you, though, eh?' She leans towards me. 'You're no that intay *gangs*, petal, are ye?'

'No . . .' I say, feeling medium-probed, '. . . I'm not.'

'Can tell just by lookin at ye. Now.' She taps my mouth. 'Open up for yer reward.'

With trepidation I obey and she very gently lifts a Malteser from the pack and places it in my mouth. It nestles there, shedding the briefest taste of chocolate, making me remember the very first time, back in uni, that John popped an Ecstasy pill on my tongue.

'Ye should know the drill by now. Crunch.'

My teeth crack the Malteser, then mash it. She's staring like a matron making sure it's done to her satisfaction. 'Good boy. We're gonnay get on just fine,' she says, patting my knee before clambering back to her seat. 'He's a Horror author, everybody!'

There are cries of disbelief and faces craning to get a look at me and I hold up a hand that I'm worried looks regal.

'A fuckin Horror writer!' says Chaz, applauding. 'Heard it aw noo.'

Soon the names of Horror icons – Ghostface, Pennywise the Clown, The Pope(!) – are swapped excitedly around the bus like banned kids' toys.

'Whit?' goes Frannie, raising his head above the seat with meerkat eyes. 'A Horror author? Is he fuck. He works in a bookshop!'

'Ho,' goes Wee Wife to me. 'You tellin me porkies, son?'

'Uh,' I say, 'No. It's uh . . . I'm just not yet . . . published.'

Frannie's enjoying landing me in it, smirking, and I remember that he didn't turn up for my graduation dinner in 2005. This memory singes my skin as he shakes his head at me, Pilate-like, denying me. Got a text from him as I was standing there in the changing area of the Albert Halls in Stirling, resplendent in my gown, while Dolby, Brian, Dad and my brother waited in the audience, wondering how the hell I'd managed to crawl through a thousand booze-soaked nights, scrawling notes on fag packets that turned somehow into essays, *all to get to that very day*, and the text said:

`No gonnay make it mate but have a good yin.`

Not

`Kent ye could dae it.`

Or

`I'm proud of ye.`

More like

`Fuck ye.`

The curiosity of the whole bus settles and there are tuts at the scale of my lie (it's not a lie, I'm just unpublished!). Frannie douses their ire with the fire-blanket of Rangers – 'Aye, so I reckon the year they've could've done it was 'ninety-two. That was our wan chance tay be European champions' – and I turn my face to the window to watch the motorway rolling past. Endless. Opening into mythical England. There'd better be something there.

There'd better be something somewhere.

The convoy has settled into a rhythmic, vague lull of claps, farts and car horns. Little Chefs wink lasciviously as we pass; we ignore them, disciplined as soldiers. There's the feel of everyone steadily making their way to war, like when Scotland and England had regular incursions over each other's border and, man, they'd actually *walk* there. Unbelievable. All that way, then being expected to engage in *hand-to-hand combat*? I can imagine (mainly from World of Warcraft) how tough that shit would be. Aye, that's right, missus, Rangers game, know? Is it fine for ma men to have a wee bowl ay soup, rest oor weary legs an that? It's awright, we're usedtay the marchin. Usually in July, right enough! Em, Zenit St Petersburg. Dunno, some Russian mob. Here's hopin they've no got heavy cavalry or archers, eh!

As the bus passes it, someone boos the sign that says, 'WELCOME TO ENGLAND'.

'Hoy,' comes that voice again, bass-rumbling from the back. 'Nothin wrang wi the English. Oor brothers in the Union. Show some respect.'

Jeff sniggers.

'Mean it, fucko.'

Jeff sniggers not.

I lean into the front seat and ask Dolby, 'Who *is* that guy? Helluva foghorn.'

'That's the Cage,' Dolby says quietly. 'Locks closed on ye.'

'Locks closed?'

'That's how he attacks. Just picks ye up and squeezes ye.' Dolby hunches wrestler-like, in imitation. 'Do me a favour, Alvin, don't be sayin, "Excuse me, that's racist," to him.'

'I'll be careful.'

'You'll be dead!'

We laugh. Uneasily.

'Whit's Frannie uptay back there?' says Dolby, popping a Starburst into his mouth. Jack yelps at the larceny. They were his. Dolby gives him a dad's-prerogative wink.

'Holdin royal court.'

'Big day for him, eh?'

'The biggest.'

But he is enlarging himself to fit it. Frannie sits jammed on the back seat, grinning like a hot-shot pilot in the movies, deep in the throes of game-talk with Rab and Chaz, hands shifting round a conjured pitch, predicting the future, all the runes of football-fan interaction. When I was wee, I was able to manage an interest in the game. You can't not. Like Star Wars, like superheroes, like soldiers and dens and gangs, football was as inescapable as the air we breathed. All of our dads were into it. All of the older boys were into it. So we were into it. There was no element of choice in this. But the further away from Falkirk my mind mutates – into Edinburgh, into *Grrrrr*, into World of Warcraft, into rejection letters from Jonathan Cape, Picador, Canongate *and* Penguin, into the daily, soft, amiable shop-drone of the Waterstone's Princes Street branch, beside the ranks of dreaming graduates stocking shelves and making book-pyramids and pretending to check the system when a customer requests a leather-bound first edition on the history of caravans or asks where the section for 'books about detonators' is – the more I need to know where I am with these guys, to check that Falkirk isn't just a hologram on Facebook, that plants are still growing there, insects hopping around as they should be. *That it actually still exists*. Because if it doesn't exist, maybe that means I don't exist.

'Any more texts from Brian?' I ask hopefully.

'Seven,' Dolby says, 'and they're aw potential hit singles.'

'The kind that Radio One would ban for obscenity,' I say. 'Must be loving it.'

'It's three in the mornin in California – he'll be like a bairn on Christmas Eve.'

'And he'll be missing Frannie.'

Dolby nods deeply. Brian and Frannie. Brian. And. Frannie.

w hat are ye sayi g mum?

w t re say n ? ma wee alvin

Falkirk! Falkirk! fa Fa lkirk! Falkirk! Falkirk! Fal f Falk irk!

Falkirk! falk rk! Falkirk! Falkirkfalkirk falkirk falkirkfalkirkfalkirk!

Last week I'd come through from Edinburgh for a meeting with Dolby and Frannie about the Manchester trip. That was actually how Frannie had pitched it to me on the phone – 'a meeting' – as though we were executives or gangsters. Dolby had augmented it later with a quick text:

`Bring mong.`

This was the first time I'd visited Dolby since Leanne had left him. Felt like Gandalf visiting Saruman, locked and fuming in his tower. I disembarked at Falkirk High station and walked down through the town, feeling it rear and solidify around me again.

When I was growing up, Saturday was the only day that Falkirk felt exciting, everyone charging into the town, released from work or school, for a stoat round the Howgate Centre with their pals, cup of tea and plate of Moscardini's chips with their gran, or a pint or nine in the Wheatsheaf or Aitken's or the Scotia with their neebor. As I strolled to Dolby's, Edinburgh shedding itself from me, I took in the Falkirkness of Falkirk, of the passers-by. Twenty years ago one of these people would've been Mum, pulling her two sons through the High Street for new school shoes, while they boxed and prodded each other, and I wondered what she would think of it now, were she to return to it all of a sudden, back from the mists of time and whatever happened to her. I saw the place through her eyes, and this made a gift of it. The soul of Falkirk is visible every day. Clothes, hair, facial expressions – even the way the people walk has a plainness about it that seems extraordinary if you know how to look at it. I was dreamstruck by the intricacies of life around me, teeming like an ecology. An old woman tottering with Lidl bags. A family clan gathered before Game, its consoles, screens, flaming posters for Tour of Duty 4. The father's jaw was rigid, accepting the challenge. The kids fizzed, fireflies. His wife drifted to his side, calmed his arm. They drifted on. Then: quick, quacking aunties, their chattering about Senga and Agnes. Neds. That square walk they once practised in imitation of the older boys, now natural and pantherlike. They prowled and possessed. They tested stares on shoppers. The airy hum of their consciousness, of quiet riches. The whole of Falkirk has stockpiles of thought kept hidden away, which the recession won't touch, the government can't raise VAT on, and their bosses can't quantify in staff appraisals before the inevitable chop.

On Saturday, people become whole again.

Falkirk flooded through me, burningly good, like a whisky. Even the buildings began to look beautiful. The neo-Georgian effort above the Argyl pub, the mock-Tudor across from it, the crazy-ass Gothic of the Catholic Church next to the library, and rising, massive, from all of this, like sleek plastic beasts, Tesco, Asda, Morrisons, breathing their synthetic fire and laying waste to the past, and when I look above the High Street, I see a rainbow strike the blue, and the Steeple becomes a huge Dark Side of the Moon prism in the sky, blessing me. Blessing all. Floyd Day in Falkirk.

TESCO
ASDA
RN BRU
BURTON

Aye, okay, I was off my tits. Of course I was. I'd had a wee toke on the way down from the train. Fuck knows, Falkirk doesn't feel like that every day.

Or ye wouldn't have left, would ye?

Jack opened the front door. There was a shy smile and he swung on the handle for a bit, more clarity in his gaze and sturdiness in his limbs than the last time I'd seen him.

'Hey, pal,' I said, clutching my hands in prayer. 'Gonnay let me in?'

He deliberated, then disappeared, fast wee feet making rubber patter in the hall. I gave chase and he screamed with terror when I whirled him up into my arms. 'Where will I see you, Jack?'

'The Dark Side of the Moon?' he cackled.

'Correct.'

Then Dolby came shuffling out from the kitchen with a cup of tea and a week's beard.

'You look like Chuck Norris.'

'Cool,' he said, and sipped his tea.

'You're giving the wee man homework, I see?'

'Totally. Jack, tell Uncle Alvin your favourite Pink Floyd songs.'

'Hmm,' Jack said. 'I like A Gnome Named Grimble Gromble. I like See Emily Play. I like I've Got A Bike You Can Ride It If You Like.'

'That's great,' I acknowledged, 'but I'm detecting a bit of a bias towards the Syd Barrett era here, Jack. Daddy hasn't played you The Wall?'

'I dinnay wantay give him nightmares.'

'Uncle Alvin,' Jack said, curling himself around the question, 'where do you live?'

'Edinburgh.'

His face clouded with confusion, and Dolby added, 'Where we went to see the castle.'

Jack turned his gaze back up at me, intrigued. 'Do you live in the castle?'

'No,' I said. 'I moved out of there. It was too small.'

He blinked and deflected my irony. 'I called it Castle Boring,' he said, and started a song, stomping and marching: 'Castle Boring . . . it's so boring . . . I was snoring . . . I'm in Primary Three now. Mrs Bateman's class.'

The name was a struck match, which memory coaxed into a warm flame. 'Oh, she was my teacher!'

'Mine tae,' said Dolby, his eyes mildly freaked.

'Mrs Bateman was great!'

Dolby nodded deeply.

I looked down at Jack and he suddenly felt like a wee Russian doll version of me, still inside me somewhere.

'She's lovely!' he said. 'She makes us all work out what our talents are.'

'What did she say your talent was?'

'Drawing! She told I could be an artist one day.'

'You certainly could.'

'What did she say your talent was?'

'Writing,' I said, remembering she'd once read out my story to the class. The Boy Who Loved Sugar was about a little boy (no?!) who loved sugar (really?!) on his corn flakes so much that just a spoonful wasn't enough. Soon it was two spoonfuls. Then it was ten. Then it was a whole bag of sugar. Then a lorryful. At the end of the story the little boy and his bowl of corn flakes were buried under a mountain of sugar, and when they found him years later he was just a skeleton with a spoon. Mrs Bateman had read it aloud to them all and I watched them smile and laugh, before the furrow of their eyebrows and then, finally, a spontaneous 'Eeeeew!' at the story's end, before they all turned their heads to look at me as though I was capable of throwing flames. At that moment I felt as though I probably could. Been chasing that moment ever since.

'Well,' Jack said, 'maybe one day you could be a writer, Uncle Alvin.'

'Maybe.' I sighed.

'What's your talent, Daddy?'

'It's certainly no findin the remote,' Dolby muttered, lifting cushions.

'I'm staying with my mummy tonight.'

I glanced at Dolby, who frowned over the top of Jack's hairshiny head, and it clicked: 'Oh, she's coming *here* to pick you up?'

'Any second,' said Dolby.

With *him*? I mouthed.

He indulged a smirk. 'He wouldnay dare.'

Just then, the front door opened and there came the awkward sound of a future ex-wife shuffling into her former home. There was spirit-clenching from me and a Where the

Wild Things Are excitement from Jack as he dashed past his dad to get to his mum. I suddenly saw, as though in infrared, what Dolby had done with the place since she'd left: moved his books defiantly into the living room, the philosophy and economics and history (all of it about twenty times cheaper than my education) and, of course, his vast rakes of David Eddings, David Gemmell, Raymond E. Feist, Robert Jordan, Stephen Donaldson, George R. R. Martin and Philip Pullman, a smattering of smiles from Jack captured on camera, and one of me, Frannie, Brian and Dolby, grinning Scottishly on a fishing trip way back, in a solid silver frame that said 'GOOD TIMES'.

During Leanne's stewardship of the room, it had all been gratuitous shots, dozens, of her in her wedding-dress, Dolby in his kilt, lounging in each other's arms and gazing with frozen love.

'Oh,' Leanne said, stopping short when she saw me. 'Alvin. Hello.' Her expression tremored slightly.

'Hi,' I said, in neutral.

She'd let her hair grow long again and dyed it blonde, her clothes that shade fancier, a scarf or shoe fancier, which I'd be able to go into more detail about if I knew the first thing about women's fashion. Basically, effort was being made. That much was clear. But for whom?

'How's, uh, how are things Edinburgh?' she said, remembering the conversational shorthand for her ex-husband's pals.

'Fine,' I said, like a child being asked how his day was.

'Good stuff,' she said, an airy pair of syllables which – given she had to shepherd her son from the flat of the man she'd cheated on while his best friend judged – meant she couldn't care less how things were in Edinburgh, which was fair enough. Jack started pulling on his jacket, trainers, gathering up his games and books, under the cover of which Leanne leaned towards Dolby and said, 'You two havenay been smokin already, have yese?'

'Don't be ridiculous,' he tutted. 'The wee man's here.'

'Just checkin.'

He shambled to the kitchen, growling, and her eyes trailed him. Then she turned to me and whispered, 'How's he been doing?'

'Um,' I said, hoping the fruit machine of my mind would triple-click some cherries, 'he's coping.'

'Copin?' she said, scrutinising this, 'Copin well or copin badly?'

Was she genuinely concerned for him or gathering ammunition for skirmishes over Jack? Alvin said ye're not copin. Yer own best pal.

'Listen,' I said, deciding to level with her. 'First I left, then Brian left, then you left –'

'I didn't leave, he kicked me out.'

'– and took Jack with you. It's only Frannie now, and he's out shagging, drinking and watching Rangers every weekend. Dolby's no in the right place for any of those things. He's *coping*.'

She bunched her lips and breathed. 'Alvin,' she said. 'Look. I know what ye must thinkay me, right. But see, Neil and me, it's no some sordid wee affair, we're—'

'It's none of my business,' I said, raising a hand.

'Right,' she said, and nodded it away. Then she glanced round and took in the sight of the books in the living room for the first time. Her hands threw exasperation into the air. 'Listen, gonnay stop him readin aw these politics books and smokin so much hash. His heid's wasted wi it. He's got too many ay these, like, weird *theories*.'

'Theories?'

She pushed her tongue into her cheek. 'Apparently the world's run by "dark forces". He's always bangin on about the *Thought Police* and bloody . . . *Newspeak* . . . and the "upper-class dictatorship".' She showed her palms and took a pretend step away. 'Whoah, too much!'

'I take it Neil isn't political?'

She cocked her head and lifted her eyebrows as if to say: what do you think?

'Right,' I said, instantly proud of Dolby.

She glanced to the kitchen, then touched my wrist. 'Just take good care ay him, Alvin. I'm worried about him.'

Does it matter, on this occasion, that she cheated on him yet still presumed to take his son with her? A woman who once loved my best friend is asking me to take care of him.

'I'll do that, Leanne.'

She gave a grateful nod as Jack came back into the room, all kitted out in back-to-Mummy clothes. The shortwave radio of my heart blipped when he gave me a cuddle, then his daddy saw the pair of them out, and I crossed the room and opened up the cupboard of dreams. There it was, among the toolboxes and Sellotape and old trainers. The bong. As powerful as the opening riff of the opening track on The Wall.

Seconds later, that bong was sitting in the centre of the coffee-table, an artefact recovered from a lost civilisation. I love the pageantry of weed-smoking. You sometimes need to clear a whole weekend for it, make phone calls to get it. Drink is too central within the culture to be exciting any more. Where's the poetry in cracking open a can? This is the reason why people like tequila shots and absinthe: they're the closest alcohol gets to taking drugs.

The front door shut. Living-room door opened. Dolby re-emerged, rubbing his hands. 'Right, fire up that bong,' he demanded. 'I wantay get OOT MA SKULL.'

MINUTES OF LADS' SUMMIT MEETING – 7 May 2008
VENUE: LIVING ROOM OF MARTIN DOLBY, GRAHAMSTON, FALKIRK **ATTENDEES**: MARTIN DOLBY (Chair), COLIN 'FRANNIE' FRANTON (CF), ALVIN ALLISON (AA)
APOLOGIES: BRIAN 'THE' MANN

Agenda

1. Welcome and thanks (Chair)
2. Recent text-messages from Brian
3. Arrangements for Manchester trip
4. AOB

1. Welcome and thanks

Chair thanked everyone for their attendance and remarked that it was good to see AA back in Falkirk. Chair noted that it had been too long but was pleased that AA had come all the way through from Edinburgh.

CF asked AA how his 'wee scribbles' were progressing.

AA replied that he didn't really want to talk about it, to be honest.

CF stated that he was sure it must be tough for AA, all those hours spent 'researching a book' in front of daytime telly with last night's pizza.

AA agreed that it was tough. *Actually*.

2. Recent text messages from Brian Mann

Brian had recently reported that the weather in California was 'hotter than a whore's drawers'.

CF commented that, according to the jammy bastard, it was always 'hotter than a whore's drawers' in California, unlike in miserable pishy Falkirk.

The group agreed.

AA reported that Brian claimed to have recently 'rode some bint raw'.

Chair and CF went heh heh heh heh.

AA wondered if anyone else was troubled by the blatant *sexism* in Brian's messages.

Action: Chair to text Brian saying they're with the cunt in spirit.

3. Arrangements for UEFA Cup Final, Manchester

CF reported that a fifteen-seater bus had been hired and that the price would be twenty pounds each. Chair and AA paid CF twenty pounds each.

Chair enquired about whether or not he could bring Jack.

AA asked if it was really the sort of event suitable for a seven-year-old.

CF replied that there would be a 'carnival, family atmosphere' and that Jack would be just fine.

Chair pointed out that Jack's mother wasn't too sure about the idea, but that she wasn't too sure about anything Chair did any more.

CF hummed the music from Jaws.

After some discussion it was agreed that, since Chair would be bringing Jack, therefore not drinking, he should probably drive.

Chair stressed that there would be no alcohol on the bus, and that he would not be risking his licence for anyone – got that? Boys? Ho! Got that?

The group agreed.

The group made plans to leave early on the morning of the final, as the motorway would be jam-packed with glory-hunters who'd never been to Ibrox in their nelly-puffs, *eh, Alvin?*

AA said that it would.

CF warned AA and Chair that there would be 'types' on the bus of whom AA might disapprove. AA and Chair expressed awareness that Irish political songs might feature and agreed not to make an issue of it.

CF said, well that was fine then, but that they were Northern Irish songs. Not Irish.

Chair noted that, tsk, such divisions were merely the work of a ruling élite who set the working classes against each other in squabbles over race, religion, territory and nation, to prevent them from realising their true enemy . . .

CF said, 'Eh? Whit?'

AA asked who that 'true enemy' was.

Chair replied that the enemy was capitalism.

CF sighed.

Chair added that it suits the Powers That Be if 'Papes' and 'Huns' are scrapping in Scotland and Northern Ireland, so they don't notice they're both being shafted from above by a British state that exists to prop up corporate greed.

CF objected – strenuously – to Chair's use of the word 'Hun' on the grounds of religious bigotry.

AA attempted to move the group to the next item on the agenda.

CF gestured towards the Politically Correct Brigade arriving to put out another Health and Safety fire, and enquired as to why it's not on to slag off Muslims, Catholics, Jews, gays or the disabled, but it's still respectable to call a Protestant a 'Hun' or to imply that they might be a knuckle-dragging meatheid who smells of hammers? CF demanded that Chair accord Rangers fans a little more dignity before he went on a supporters' bus with twelve of them. Seriously.

Chair suggested that perhaps CF chill the fuck out.

Action: Chair to pick up the bus the night before. Bus to depart from Chair's house at eight a.m. Repeat: nae bevvy, lads.

We're soon into the afternoon. The motorway chugs a sleepy rhythm as Dolby weaves between lanes. The songs have died down, the sun hammering flat our excitement on the anvil of time. Everyone is sprawled as the early start catches up with them; there are snorts and snores. The convoy around us is thickening, but the sunlight forces me to shade my eyes with my hand to look at it, like Lawrence of Arabia gazing to the horizon. Bus after car, car after bus, with the blue scarves waving and the Red Hands telling us, yet again, just in case it needed re-stating, that Ulster Says No. We pass fields, where cows stand and chew. Their sturdy, bovine souls. Summer light lacquers their backs, as they contemplate.

Frannie turns towards them. They watch back. Blank. 'Peaceful, eh?' he says.

'Aye.'

'I mean,' he adds, eyes vague and dreamy, 'whit have they got tay worry about, eh? They can just . . . disappear intay the herd. Any moment, they could be led tay the slaughterhoose, but they're content cos they're no even aware they're gonnay die.'

This is the most profound thing I think I've ever heard Frannie say.

'At least it's fair,' he says, for reasons beyond my understanding. 'Rich or poor, Pape or Hun. We aw needtay prepare those Famous Last Words.'

Fair? Aye. It's fair awright. Too fuckin fair.

He nudges me, smiles. 'Mind when we usedtay drive roond in Belinda, and we'd play that gemme: whit song wid ye have played at yer weddin?'

'Aye. Brian used to go for In The Army Now by Status Quo.'

Frannie snorts. 'He'll never get merried. One woman's gonnay be either too many for that cunt or no enough.'

'You know Brian,' I agree, even though neither of us really does any more.

'So whit song would ye want played at yer *funeral*?'

'Um . . .' I consider it, then say, 'Comfortably Numb.'

He rolls his eyes. 'Floyd. Typical. Well, I'll make sure it's the fuckin Scissor Sisters version.'

'You'd better not,' I say, 'or I'll be appearing in your bathroom mirror every morning.'

'You'd love that, ya wee poof.'

I attempt a smile, but it's a feat of magic I can't quite pull off.

'Anyway, what would you choose?'

'In My Life by the Beatles,' he says, 'for on the wey in.'

'And on the way out?'

He grins and opens his hands. 'The Entertainer.'

I can imagine me, Dolby and Brian trotting from the crematorium at Camelon dressed in waistcoats and carrying snooker cues, while Frannie lies in his coffin, chuckling like a dick.

The motorway slides past, doing its twenty-four-hour performance of a thrusting, industrious Britain. Cars. Lorries. Order.

Jack's scribbling in his notebook, singing under his breath. 'Sure it's old and it is beautiful . . . and its colours they are fine . . . *Fine wine*.'

'Son,' says Dolby, 'don't sing that.'

'How no?'

'Cos it's no a nice song.'

'I think it is a nice song, Daddy,' he says. 'I think it's a lovely song. The Sash My Father Wore.'

'I'm tellin ye, stop that.'

'I'm going to sing it at my school talent show.'

'I don't think they'd let you, pal,' I chip in.

'How not? They let people sing all sorts of songs. Fast ones, slow ones, sad ones, bimpy ones.'

'Bimpy ones?'

'Yeah,' says Jack. 'Ones that go bimp bimp bimp.'

'Maybe,' I suggest, 'you could sing one by Kylie Minogue.'

He scans the schedules of the Cartoon Network in his head. 'I don't know who that is.'

Dolby blows out a decade or so from his lungs. 'We're gettin old, man.'

Just then from behind us: thumping, polar-bear footsteps. An arm shunts into the front, drops a cargo on the seat. 'Whit's-yer-name. Dolby. Put this on.'

Dolby reaches down and takes the CD slowly, as though checking to see if it will erupt with spikes or not. 'Whit is it?'

'Superior bigotry.'

'Okay,' says Dolby. Inserts the CD. Care. Ful. Ly.

'Ataboy.' The biceps grimace before disappearing back into the bus.

'Cage?' I say.

Dolby nods. '*The* Cage.'

suddenly Derek s

twistin

jerkin

on the joystick Pac Man s goin

ma ma ma ma ma ma ma mamama ma
mama

ma ma ma ma ma ma ma ma ma ma ma ma

Dinnay stand behind me like that knobheid Derek goes
puttin me aff

sorry

step back just a wee bit tryin to see over his shoulder

bobbin aboot

He s really good at Pac Man but ye wouldnay think so cos
when Dad comes in to see how he s doing Derek scowwwwls

Dad leans over oh that s a great score son

Derek goes

Dad how come we ve still got an Atari?

Dad sniffs

looks at me

drops his voice

Ye ken the answer to that one Derek I am outtay work the
now

These game console hings are expensive

But every year I ask Santa for a better hing
and he never geez me wan!

Dad leans in goes
Eh well mibbe Santa s *also* outtay work Derek

think i dinnay ken whit they re talkin about

Dad s still tryin to get Derek to kid ontay me that Santa s real
but I ken he s no cos Mum telt me when she was skew wiff that
it was just Dad dressed up

(always does things like that
when she s skew wiff, spoils hings)

But everybody at school s got a Super Nintendo
or Sega Mega Drive

cannay afford it son

gotay ma pals hooses
got Mario
Legend ay Zelda
Sonic

but what ve I got for them to play when they come here?

Pac Man!

it s like the dark ages

Oh I think it s still a gid game   Seems pretty fast tay me
Dad chuckles

It s like playin wi a bat and ball!

Alvin likes it don t ye son

aye Dad I do

Well nae wunner

he s a baby

He is eight years old Derek Allison

Aye well we got this Atari when he was four!

. . . and even then it was fay the market . . .

Dad looks doon at the flair

Only sound in the room is Pac Man

ma ma   mamamama   ma   ma ma ma   ma   ma

Well I tell ye whit Dad says I never thought I would be raisin such an ungrateful son as this yin

Derek s eyes go big mental

aw look

ye just made me get gobbled by a ghost!

thought ye didn t like it anway

I don t! I m no playin nay mair

Derek throws the joystick
storms oot

Ho young man you ll no behave like that while you are under ma

Dad goes clumpin off to
SHOUT up the stair

bedroom door slam!

pick up the joystick

still workin phew

Start a new game three lives

theres Pac Man in his maze munchin his way round all them pills ma ma mamamama ma ma ma ma and oh no here s the ghosts bobbin up get oot the way Pac Man ! pull the joystick to the side round the corner phew see if ye can get the big power pill means ye can eat the ghosts

. . . Mum floats up behind me . . .

icecubes

tinkle Special Cola

leans overtay watch me play hic!

oh there s a ghost comin there son watch hic!

ken Mum can see it

tries to steer me through the maze but she s way behind finger just

tra ails aaaaa aaaa iiiii ls

across the screen then faws she goes that wey?

Em that wey!

Quick!

upstairs Derek and Dad shoutin she goes Christ will ye listen that pair never stop finishes the Special Cola

burp!

doesnay seem to notice she s done it

i notice though stinkin

here son I ve said to the doctor it s all right if you Derek and yer dad want to go and talk to him aboot these pills i m takin that s fine wi me son it s a new drug well I dinnay exactly mean *drug* Alvin cos it s no like a *drug* type drug mair like a like a

medicine?

ma mamama ma mamama ma ma mamamama mamama
mama ma mamamama mama mama mamama ma
goes Pac Man

aye medicine would be the word for it son like the Calpol when ye re no well son it s just like that except it s called *Pro Zac* it s for when grown ups aren t feelin well but it s no the sort of thing you get *addicted* tay Alvin ha ha it s just that well ye ken how sometimes I get stressed oot crabbit start shoutin at yese well it ll mean I won t *do* that cos what it does son is it *stabilises* yer moods ken how like
how like ye usedtay have stabilisers on yer bike to keep ye straight well all these pills will do is just keep *me* straight ma *moods* straight ken whit I m sayin son? they re a *good hing* for yer mum I m no gonnay turn intay a drug addict ha ha son that willnay habit I mean happen no gonnay go *freaky* in fact if anything it ll

Hang on Mum – Yes! Power pill! Run ghosts!

run! run! run! run!

run! run!

run!run! run run! run! run!

run!run! run! run! run!

There is no sense of irony about Loyalist songs whatsoever. Of course there isn't. This is why students don't hang posters of bowler-hatted parades and vintage clothes shops don't sell orange sashes. Even Frannie is rolling his eyes and shaking his head now, glancing out the window as though willing the motorway to rush by faster. The music sounds as though it could be from any maudlin country/folk record, except that, instead of John Denver or Tammy Wynette, you've got some Ulsterman intoning the names of the *glorious dead* or sweetly singing Begone, Begone, Ye Fenian Scum. Me and Dolby laugh, imagining the old codger in the studio – fisherman's sweater, big headphones – straining to get the right intonation into 'Fenian scum', just that *perfect* croon of contempt, while the producer tries to add more anti-Catholic reverb.

Frannie puts his hand paternally on my shoulder. 'I ken, Alvin,' he says, 'I ken this music's pish. But I'm just worried that if they see ye laughin, it'll offend them.'

'*I'll* offend *them*? Awright, how many Man Points for keeping a straight face?'

'Listen,' he says, 'a straight face is survival. Gottay mind, mate, it's their bus. You're the intruder here, like or lump it.'

'I'll lump it, thanks.'

'Well, ye're gonnay look like a fuckin camel by the enday this trip.'

When the CD gets round to The Cry Was No Surrender the Cage rolls down the window, blasts it to the family in the lane next to us, in what looks like a hired car. Mother, father, son and daughter smile and wave. Probably tourists. Gee, honey, listen to those Scots singing about their glorious dead. Probably something to do with William Wallace. Hey, kids, remember Braveheart? Give them a wave. Free-dom! We love you Scatlind!

Exhaust air from the open window is rushing into my face. *Cough!* 'Can I put this window down now, please?'

'Leave it open,' the Cage growls, from somewhere behind me, omnipresent. 'Whole motorway's enjoyin these songs.'

'Em, sure.'

We slow into a traffic jam and stop for the first time since we left Falkirk this morning. It's like an affront, for this whole exodus to be stationary, as though destiny itself has been shunted to a halt by a vast, unseen hand. Dolby looks up the length of the road: Rangers cars and buses all the way to the horizon. One draws up alongside us, the driver lowering the window to shout to Frannie, 'Ho, mate?'

'You rang?' Frannie bows.

'We've no brought music. Any Rangers CDs?'

The Cage takes charge. I'm amazed the minibus doesn't break in two as he makes his way to the window, yanks it open.

His fist tosses something. 'There ye go, burned it maself. Orange Glory.'

'Magic,' the guy says, and shows his bounty to the car, which applauds with a meaty delight. Sesame Street encouraged us to think about *co-op-a-ray-shin*, back in the day – Oscar the Grouch being taught a lesson about grouchiness, or Cookie Monster rewarded for sharing his cookies – but I'm not sure that the swapping of songs about the killing of Catholics was part of the remit. Yet everyone seems delighted to be part of the exchange, and no actual Catholics were killed during it. The sun's still out. The mood's still light.

Such a complex business, this whole common-humanity thing.

Frannie's iPhone. Every Rangers fan in the country has his number. He's so *present* in the world today, so filled and thrilled. 'That's Stuart Storrie again, boys,' Frannie reports, 'at the fan zone in Piccadilly Gardens. Says it's heavin.'

'Game's no for eight hours yet!' Dolby yelps at the wheel.

'Aye,' says Frannie. 'Already quite rowdy. Tesco have been discountin booze since half six in the mornin.' He muses, satisfied. 'A fine thing tay hear about one's employer.'

'I thought that was against the law,' Dolby says.

'Police have probably got a lot bigger things tay worry about the day.' Frannie shrugs. 'A hunner thoosand Tesco employees havenay just turned up in the city, have they?'

He's nine years in Tesco now. Frannie'll die with red, white and blue tattooed across his heart, given they're the colours of his two favourite institutions. But even he seems to have sensed the limitations of the place, as his mumbled complaints about 'arse-lickers that'll sell oot ony cunt tay get a management post' have been accompanied by a gob on the pavement. He'd started DJ-ing as a sideline a few years ago – had a couple of good slots in Austin's and Behind the Wall – but it didn't last because of his refusal to play 'Lassie Pish' in favour of good old-fashioned rock 'n' roll (Kinks, Who, Clash, Kasabian) therefore alienating most of the lassies in the place. And which respectable venue is going to deny its male punters lassies? 'If they're proper lads,' was Frannie's response, 'they'll stey for the music.' His disavowal of Lassie Pish is the flipside to his hatred of Intellectual Pish (also sometimes known as 'Alvin Pish') even though Beyoncé, Lily Allen and Goldfrapp have absolutely nothing in common with (a) each other and (b) Radiohead, Pink Floyd or Suede.

(Actually, I can hear traces of the Floyd in Goldfrapp. I could go into this.)

So the DJ-ing didn't work out for Frannie, which meant Tesco has had to.

'Half six?' Dolby says, and Jack glances up at his dad, somehow sensing the significance of this. The thought of booze being sold in huge quantities *since half past six in the morning* starts ticking in our brains, and there's a brief lull in which me, Frannie and Dolby contemplate Jack. Look at him there: a tiny, peeled prawn exposed to the world. His wide eyes. His simple trust in his dad. But when Auld Alfred croaks, 'That's the shout!' the whole bus cheers like a vodka-soaked bonfire going up, the embers of its laughter floating past Alfred's pale, proud smile.

'Get this shite aff,' says Wee Wife, crossing the Alps of the seating to tap Dolby's shoulder. 'Haw, whit's this pish we're listenin tay? Whit's wrang wi some eighties music?'

'I'm with ye right there,' Dolby replies, clearly relieved, 'but ye might needtay talk tay Mr Cage.'

She spins round instantly. 'Ho. Gordon. Dae we really needtay listen tay this?'

Cage sighs a little, as though being handed a gas bill. 'Chrissie, it's gid music. This is the day for it.'

'It's no the fuckin day for it,' she says, hands on her hips, making a shield of herself between Cage and the CD player, 'It's never the day for it. Music about killin fuckin Fenians isnay music. Whit's wrong wi a bittay eighties?' She swivels her hips to show just how good the eighties were. Cage shakes his head at her. 'Stick it up yer arse,' she says, then tries to rally the rest of us, 'C'mon. Jeff. Bex. Rab. Eighties!'

There are smatterings of Naw and Aye, awright, and she clasps the Aye-awrights in her fingertips and raises them out of the air, draws them together. 'That's it. Mon, Frannie. Wee man. Whit's yer name?'

'Alvin.'

'Chipmunk, aye, c'mon, whit about some eighties?'

'Um,' I say, scanning the faces on the bus. They're all staring at me to see which way I'll go: Cage or Wee Wife. 'Well. Uh. I'm not so into the eighties. Before my time.'

'Thank you!' says Cage, licking his finger and marking a score on an invisible chalkboard.

'But I do have this,' I say, bringing out a CD I'd made just in case, which now feels as mighty as the Ark of the Covenant. 'Manchester Greats.'

'Who's on it?' says Wee Wife, snatching it from me.

I get halfway into the list – 'Oasis, the Stone Roses, New Order' – before my voice is smothered by roaring and clapping and Frannie is wringing my shoulders as though it's moments of genius such as this that he wanted me on the trip for. I feel like the doctor who's just told him his baby is healthy and the mother is doing fine.

'Okay then,' nods Wee Wife, deeply. 'Looks like a result. That awright wi you, Gordon?'

'Democracy rules,' Cage grunts, staring right at me, and his gaze is hard enough that I hear Robert Shaw in Jaws say

> Thing about a shark is he has lifeless eyes, black eyes, like a doll's eyes. When he comes at you, he don't seem to be living.

The Cage looks away out the window of the bus, and the shark retreats, slowly beating its tail.

'Let's rescue this perty,' Wee Wife goes, jigging her way towards Dolby before delivering the CD as though it's a Valentine. 'There ye go, son. The people have spoken.'

Dolby lifts his eyebrows at me in the rear-view, and as the first notes of Waterfall by the Stone Roses chime, smiles are lit all over the bus. Everyone who isn't Auld Alfred (croaking weakly for some Elvis) sings along, and I do as well, and Manchester gives us

Step On   Happy Mondays
    Don't Look Back in Anger   Oasis
                                        Panic   The Smiths
                        This is How it Feels   Inspiral Carpets
  A Day Like This   Elbow   Blue Monday New Order
                        The Only One I Know   Charlatans

Aye all right, I know they're from the Midlands.

We sing the lot of them. Frannie's holding his Stella out of the window, letting his throat feel the words as they come blasting from his mouth. Dolby's whistling along in the front seat, and Jack is nodding while he plays his DS game. The songs rollick around our throats. Northern swagger. Us and them: Scots and Mancs. It's just rock 'n' rowwwwwww! Chaz and Jeff disco-point at each other, bouncing along the lyrics. Sally slaps a tempo into the seats. When the CD ends we're exhilarated. The whole purpose of the journey has been forgotten. We're sweating and happy and lads and a lassie, manchester-united.

'Ho,' Wee Wife says, as the CD is popped out of its slot, 'Manchester Greats? Whaur wis Take That?'

'You're not . . .' I say, and almost laugh. 'You're not serious, are you?'

'Damn tootin I'm serious, son. Best band there's ever been. Int that right, Gordon?'

'Aw nay doubt, Chrissie,' says Cage, staring at me, before turning his big gaze back to the the window.

Friday Friday Friday Friday Friday don t think there s anything in the world as good as friday man stretchin itself all over
Thank crunchie it s Friday !

Fidget fidget

just want oot hame get the uniform aff hoo the weekend !

Ye could see it in Mrs Bateman Friday just flowin throo her voice She was readin us The Last Battle by C. S. Lewis it s one of them narnia books if I get a girlfriend when I am older she ll havetay be intay the narnia books
I ll just go uptay her and say sooooooo what s your favourite narnia book? and she ll be like Oh Alvin! it s The Last Battle!
Then I take her to meet Mum Dad Derek who will totally think she s great

and we become king and queen

THIS WILL BE WHAT I M GOING TO DO WHEN I FINALLY GET OUT OF THIS CLASSROOM!!!
right
Dad will take us tae Carnegie Park (that s in Dunfermline) in the Glo Buggy (that s our car cos it s bright green) and just before we leave Mum will say to me and Derek have you had a pee? and we ll both go aye totally but halfway there Derek ll need a pee *tsk* Mum ll go I TELT YOU TAY GO BEFORE WE LEFT i ll be readin

goosebumps
point horror
five go to smugglers cove

and Mum ll say alvin son don t read in the car ye always get carsick honey
but it s BORIN when you don t read but then oh no i ll be like

Mum i feel sick

Derek ll be like

Ha ha ha ha ha ha ha ha

i ll be like

Shut it you

Mum ll be like

Jesus Christ Duncan i need a drink see these boys

Dad ll be like

Probably a pub or somethin near the park

Mum ll be like

Sall right i brought a hip flask

Dad ll be like

Ye brought a hip flask?

Derek ll be like

I m needin the toilet

Mum ll be like

Look can we just get there ! left late cos youse were muckin aboot even
though i telt yese tay get a move on Look at yer wee brother there Derek
he went tay the toilet like i telt him but you obviously didnay cos that s
twice now ye ve hadtay go TWICE do i make myself clear Derek Allison
do i ? cos see when i tell you tay go tay the toilet
you make sure ye f_in well go !

Dad ll be like

Aye all right there s no needtay swear at the boy Calm doon

Mum ll be like

I AM F_IN CALM !

Now *that* my good friends is called a cliché.

A cliché has a fancy wee french bit on the end called a "cute" Miss Bateman showed me howtay find them she said

a cliché is a well worn phrase that people use too often such as

raining cats and dogs or i could eat a horse

then she striked out like this bits in my stories that went

~~it was a dark and stormy night~~

~~and then I woke up and it was all a dream~~

~~or *was* it?!!!~~

cliché alert!
get detective Alvino of the San Francisco police force on the hunt

I m going to strike out some clichés that Mrs Bateman uses

~~ok finish the sentence you re on~~

~~it s your own time you re all wasting~~

~~the bell is a signal for me not for you~~

~~do you think that s a sensible way for an eleven year old to behave~~

~~you re supposed to be setting an example Primary Seven~~

strike oot wans that Dad uses

~~your eyes are bigger than your belly~~

~~less haste more speed~~

~~always taste your food before you salt it~~

striked oot wans that Derek uses

~~you go in goals alvin~~

~~shut it muppet~~

~~that is cos i m class in a glass~~

striked oot wans that Mum uses

~~I AM F_IN CALM~~!

that gets a double strikethrough

cos see when someone says that to ye? never ever means they re calm

The bus enters Manchester city centre, roaming through the ebb and flow of blue-shirted men all around us. Shades and flags and laughs bob up and down, washing towards cashpoints, off-licences, bars, cafés, sandwich shops. Hands are raised to each new bus that passes. Foam hats float, Union Jack flags billow like sails. Tight fists in the air. Air tight in the fists. Frannie's arm is round my neck and he shakes me, and for a second it feels like we're in that book I read in my first year at Stirling University, Three Men in a Boat, when a wee bunch of toffs decide to escape the daily routine and punt off down the Thames together. They meet people. They argue (but ever so mildly, you understand). They are dazzled by the brilliance of everything, by the slowness and beauty of life when you stop to look at it, and it made me think of the Lads back in Falkirk.

Frannie points towards a policeman wearing a Rangers scarf. 'Check it oot. He'd never get away wi that in Scotland.'

The Cage dismisses it with a big hand. 'Just a laugh.'

'I'm only sayin. Imagine a polisman wearin a Rangers scarf in Glasgow? There'd be an uproar.'

'Aye, well,' Cage harrumphs, 'I'm sickay this "Scotland's Shame" business. Ye're allowed tay rip the pish out the English all ye like, but the minute it's the Old Firm there's a steward's enquiry. I'll stop singin The Billy Boys when them Tartan Army wanks stop singin Floweray fuckin Scotland.'

I chuckle dutifully and Cage grins at me. 'Ye like that yin, wee man?' I try to smile back. He narrows his eyes and I shrink in his gaze. Frannie tries to lead Cage back into banter, but the gravitational pull is too strong. No more of Frannie's cheeky eye-rolling at the charged patter, Cage is all for stoking coals of hot bigotry now. The rest of the bus are unresponsive, either too woozy or weary for it, but Cage is thudding up and down the aisle, slapping shoulders and rubbing at necks, hissing, 'Let's get intay these Russian Fenian bastards,' before Dolby points out that, 'I think the national religion of Russia is

Orthodox Christianity not Catholicism,' making Cage cackle as though appreciating the gag.

'Baws tay that. They're fay *Saint* Petersburg, eh. Sounds Papish tay me, eh, wee man?' He tugs the sleeve of my Captain America T-shirt. I try out another laugh, but it's a hard sell to the rest of my face. 'Tell ye whit, Alvin, we'll stuff some Catholic intay them, then shag it back oot them again, how's that?'

Can hear Auld Alfred muttering, 'Wish he'd gie aw that a rest,' his face made granite with dignity, and I realise he's probably one of these old boys who just loves his team, but hates all the pish that comes with it, and Cage turns his head towards Alfred, before choosing to ignore him and starting another song, jigging his bulk from side to side and commandeering the party, before throwing a finger in the direction of Celtic Park.

Why don't you go home?
Why don't you home?
The famine's over.
Why don't you go home?

The bus judders through the streets. Manchester's trying to go about its business, in suits and shirts and shoes around us. It is bustled. It is jostled. It is no longer Manchester. It's just telt: Ho. You. Manchester. You are oors for the day. Hear us, boy? Listenin?

Manchester says: We love you, Scotland, but we just want to

be a northern English city again – pleeeeease?

Enough ay the 'Scotland' cerry-oan. We are 'Rangers', super Rangers. C'mon ye just needtay get intay the party spirit. Stella for me. In fact, make that Stella for a hundred and fifty thousand. Tay go.

Cage has hauled any reluctance into his fist and pulled. The song is ripped up from the floor through everyone's lungs.

Hu-llo! Hu-llo! We are the Billy Boys.
Hu-llo! Hu-llo! Ye'll know us by our noise.
We're uptay our knees in Fenian blood, surrender or ye'll die.
Cos we are the Brigton Derry boys!

'We'll needtay be careful doon here,' Frannie whispers.

'Aye,' I say, 'we've got Jack.'

'Naw, I mean us. Rangers.'

'How's that?'

'We were fined last year for "sectarian" chants at a UEFA Cup tie in Spain. So, for the first time, it's no just Scotland but the European governin body that's asking questions ay us.'

I clear my throat lightly.

'Don't geez that.' He tuts. 'Aye, there's bampot Rangers fans.' He allows his brow to lift towards Cage. 'But there's bampots in every support. Ye ever listened tay some of the sexist, racist, homophobic pish ye get at grounds up and doon the country?'

I open my mouth to speak, but am too stunned by Frannie's

sudden conversion to the cause of political correctness, and he barges his way into my reply.

'Did anybody listen tay Aberdeen fans sing about how wannay theirs shattered wee Ian Durrant's knee? Did they see Celtic fans chuck bananas at Mark Walters? Aye, and let's no forget the first black player in Scotland wis a Rangers player, by the way. Maistay the racist jokes I get sent tay ma phone are fay guys that support the Holy Tic. Immigrants who hate other immigrants. Get yer heid roond that yin.'

He's away now. Oh, boy. There's an actual finger in the air.

'They greet themselves sair defendin the Catholic Church and the Pope, who's in chargeay a Vatican that no only encourages the spreaday AIDS in Africa, but *still* thinks shagging before marriage is a mortal sin, thinks abortion makes women murderers and thinks the likes ay me and you deserve to burn in a fire for aw eternity for no going along wi it. They bang on aboot Brother Walfrid starting Celtic Fitbaw Club tay help the poor ay Glasgow's East End, but dae they ever stop tay remember the Holy Father's no exactly sittin on a milk-crate ower there in the Vatican?'

He's Hurricane Katrina taking 9/11 on a date.

'That bunchay posers at Celtic Park sell this "oppressed sufferin Irish you'll never walk alone" shite. Aye, the Rangers support's got its problem element.' He drops his voice. 'Exhibit A's chargin up and doon this bus the noo. But we dinnay pretend tay be angels either. That lot cannay face uptay the fact that they're as prejudiced as every ither cunt.'

'Aye, but—'

'Tellin ye, Alvin,' he goes, all that trapped Old Firm-fan paranoia bursting into full glory, 'ye can jump up and doon in a pub in the Gallowgate glorifyin IRA atrocities and folk'll pass it off as "the craic". Ye're allowed tay insist yer wife dress as an armoured tank if ye're a Muslim. But the second anyone sticks The Sash My Father Wore on the karaoke, a folk ballad aboot their ain family and community, ye're as popular as Freddy Krueger in a primary school? We no got a right tay celebrate *oor* culture?'

I throw out, 'Em, a culture that wants to be up to its knees in the blood of another race?' but it's like a crisp packet being chucked at him.

'C'mon. Dae you believe Ozzy Osbourne is actually a Satanist?'

'Em.' This flummoxes me. 'No, of course not. What are you talking about?'

'Listen,' he goes, 'everybody on this bus works nextay Celtic supporters day in, day oot, and we're no aw kickin fuck oot each other every break-time. But on Old Firm day it's yer bog-standard, let's-kid-on-we-hate-you-hate-us fitbaw rivalry wi the stakes just that wee bit higher.' He squeezes both my shoulders, excited as a kid who's heard a rumour that the fairground's coming to town. 'That's whit makes it so *gid*. That's how folk who support their pishy wee local team, fuckin Fawkurt and St Mirren and Arbroath, dinnay *get* it. Celtic supporters love it tay. Dae ye hink everybody on this bus actually wants tay round Catholics up and shoot them?'

I fold my arms. 'Well, I dunno, do I? They seem to like entertaining the thought a bit too much for me.'

It's said a person looks most like who they really are when they're approaching orgasm: unleashed, uninhibited. Frannie looks most like who he really is when he's demolishing the delusions of Celtic Football Club and the outrageous indulgence of their grievances by the media. He didn't even go down the obvious 'kiddie-fiddler priests' route. I find myself leaning back in my seat with the intensity of it. My mind fumbles at left-wing concepts I hold dear . . . em, brutal British imperialism . . . um, monarchy worship . . . subjugation of Irish people . . . but spasm in the face of Frannie's Rangers-infused politics, and can't hold any of them for long enough to wield them. They clang back to the floor to be kicked away by Cage as he thunders past.

'That's better,' Cage roars to the party, like a coach to a team of slackers, 'Hu-LLO! Hu-LLO!'

'But still,' Frannie says, glancing around himself, 'we'll need tay be careful doon here.'

He pops in some chewing gum and watches Cage, as though aware that his own patter's been forced onto the subs' bench.

Dolby stops the bus, then covers Jack's ears until Cage finishes the song. After the applause he says briskly, 'Right, everybody aff,' and we ease ourselves out, stretching legs drowsy with drink.

'Heddy-*haw*,' says Frannie, first off the bus into Day-Glo May. He pops his shades over his eyes, surveys the streets as if through a sci-fi visor. 'First stop: Rovers Return.'

Jack steps off the bus, Neil-Armstrong-carefully. 'Is this Manchester, Daddy?'

'Stick close tay me, son.'

The Cage grunts and can't help himself: 'Tellin ye, boys, I'm in such a good mood I could fuck a Fenian.'

The city of Manchester is sound and mass. Victorian banks and soot-infused industrial buildings and flashy style-bars and modern, clean city-centre apartments, the same kind of things you'd find in Glasgow, but a Scot always experiences England through the faintest layer of strange. The same but not the same. Eerie. We shuffle through the streets, Jack in the middle of us gasping round at it all, like Dorothy in Oz. Men are thick about us. The air is stippled with their shouts, the buildings daubed with sonic graffiti. I look at Dolby and Frannie and remember them beside me with Brian, in the years when we raced around Falkirk in a car named Belinda. They were nineteen-year-old Goliaths towering over me with turn-of-the-millennium clothes and hair, and here we are now, trailing a bairn and invading an English city with a hundred and fifty thousand of our countrymen as though in some bizarre Dr Who time-travel story: the Scottish episode. What am I doing here?

Let us blame nostalgia. I was born in 1984, two years before Graeme Souness took over Rangers and caused a sea-change in Scottish football. Rangers were thinking big and spending big, and the rest of the Scottish league trailed in their red, white and blue wake for well over a decade. I had a phase of Rangers-supporting, which lasted from about the ages of eleven to fifteen (until *I grew out of it, y'know, like proper adults should*) coming just at the end of the Nine In A Row era, when Rangers won the league year-upon-year and the only thing Celtic fans had to cheer was Ireland winning Eurovision, and when they were still challenging to be a major European club. That kind of thing leaves a mark on a boy, which even the deep mental cleansing of an arts degree can't quite wash away.

Let us blame: Colin 'Frannie' Franton.

WhoHasBeenWaitingForThisDayAllofHisRangersSupporting Life

AndWhoHadtheBusBookedtheMinuteNachoNovoScored

ThePenaltytoPutRangersintotheFinal

That'sRightAlvin

TheUEFA!

C U P!

FINAL!

Let us blame: wee Jack. Neil took Jack to a game at Ibrox last month, and Dolby, incensed, demanded of Leanne that he, as the boy's own father, should be the only one permitted to take Jack to a football match. This is despite the fact that Dolby can't even stand football, let alone Rangers, and that Jack described his Ibrox experience with Neil as both 'boring' and 'weird'. So how does Dolby top Ibrox? Manchester. Father and son are official Gers supporters for the day. All to get back at some other fucker.

Aye well that's men for ye, son

Leanne only let Dolby on the condition that Jack wasn't going to be subjected to drunk men pishing against buildings. 'Never mind the songs,' she'd said. 'He cannay understand whit they're about anyway. It's the pishin in public I cannay abide. *Dirty*.'

Let us blame: given Dolby's a father, I've been working like a pharoah's slave on the pyramids of books at the front of Potterstone's, and Frannie's out spinning his patter in Falkirk bars most weekends – fuelling his dream of swapping the early-morning shift in Tesco for the Radio 1 Breakfast Show, ignoring the playlist with a crisp wink and a thumbs-up to the webcam – *we just hardly ever see each other any more*. Trying to get the bastards twenty miles from Falkirk to Edinburgh requires the summoning powers of the One Ring. We have to take an opportunity for Lads' action where we can, especially with Brian gone, the same way everyone rushes outside when there's sunshine. I didn't want Dolby being the only poor, lone, not-that-fussed-about-the-Gers refusenik on the bus, so I came with him. Why not? It's the sort of thing we would've done, way back, when both Brian and I were still in Falkirk and all four of us were presuming our eternal presence in each other's lives.

Kids. Jobs. Wives. Soon to be ex-wives. Emigration. Working our way through the greatest hits. How had everything become so *adult*, so *friendless*? Who could account for the sudden explosion of comfortable nights spent alone in front of the telly or Facebook? Where the fuck had the last eight years disappeared to? Could we all please have a look round for them? Careful where you stand: you could accidentally crush a banker.

On second thoughts, everyone, get your heavy boots on.

'Watch Jack,' Dolby says, bending at the knees and holding

his groin. 'Just gonnay nip over for a pish.' With that he takes a quick glance round and leaps a mid-height wall, ninja-fast.

Jack stares up at me, made timid by the sheer number of strangers who swarm gigantically around him, strafing the air with Weegie banter and swear words.

'Dad'll just be a second,' I say.

Jack nods.

I nod.

I scratch my cheek. 'Juuuuuust a second.'

Jack looks around. Jack sniffs.

'Look, Uncle Alvin,' he goes, and holds up a picture he's coloured in of a blonde woman wearing a red, white and blue dress. 'Barbie's on her way to Ibrox. She's going to marry . . . em . . . Barry Ferguson.'

'I'm sure that's what she's always aspired to, pal.'

'They're going to live in Ibrox and have tea parties and roller discos.'

'Then she'll be Barbie Ferguson?'

This catches him, and he grins and jumps up and down. 'Barbie Ferguson!' he hoots, and I feel that singular glow of pleasure you only get when you've just made a child laugh.

'I'm going to show Barbie Ferguson to my pals at school,' he says, admiring his handiwork.

'What are their names?'

'Um . . . Jodie, Emma and Sophie.'

'You play with the girls at school?'

He nods. 'Girls play better games. They're not so rough as boys' games.'

'What do the girls do at playtimes?'

He turns his little cow gaze up to me and says, 'We just talk.'

'Talk is good,' I say, feeling – for some odd reason – the same small thrill I used to get at university, halfway through writing an essay in the middle of the night, when it would all *make sense.*

'I'm not a boy anyway,' he says, smiling with mystery.

'Oh, really?'

'I'm a *girl-boy.*' His lips are tight and his eyes wide, as though announcing the name of a cool new dinosaur he's just discovered. 'A boy-girl.'

'I thought you supported Rangers?' I say, leadingly.

Jack shrugs this away. Rangers clearly cannot compare to the fact of being a *girl-boy* or a *boy-girl.*

'But Neil takes you to the games at Ibrox, doesn't he?'

He contemplates this, but the answer comes with silence, a diluted nothing, a mere flicker downwards of the eyes.

'Jack, do you like Neil?'

His answer is to stare into Barbie Ferguson's smile, and there's something too curled-in about that response. He lets his eyes drift upwards and I follow them towards the blurred shape of Dolby leaping back over the wall, Spider-Man exiting a crime scene. He sees Jack shuffling mutely. 'What's up wi the wee man?'

'Oh, nothin,' I say. 'He was just tellin me Barbie's a Rangers supporter. Weren't you, pal?'

Dolby takes the picture from Jack. 'Barbie? Why are ye drawin pictures ay Barbie?'

Jack doesn't even blink. 'Cos she's beautiful.'

'Right,' says Dolby, looking at the picture, then at Jack. 'O-kay.'

Before he can probe this, however, Manchester is calling: Dolby's phone rings and soon Frannie is asking where the fuck we are. We catch up with the rest of the boys, moving our limbs swiftly, the blaze of summer on our skin, dodging a group of guys with their arms round each other, walking down the street like the Monkees. Dolby swings Jack up into his arms, and the boy giggles and seems to have all the lightness of a dandelion head. The Cage's bulk and baldness come into view, and a flag draping his shoulders reads

WE ARE
THE PEOPLE

this is yer best face son

whit yin Mum?

See This yin Like this

like this?

Naw ye re daein it wrang Alvin !

You re hopeless !

whit s ma best face for Mum?

Yer best face son is the face ye want tay have on when ye re deid like

clean pants or

polished shoes

an i mean shoes ye ve done wi actual *polish*
no spit

(or just went roon
them wi a bittay
toilet-paper?)

See when they pack ye intay that box?
Ye ll want tay have yer best face on so they ll
huddle roon ye an bawl their eyes oot and say ye were a

special laddie

an at the school they ll have an assembly
an the teachers ll be there havin a wee sniff
and the heidmaister will be sayin that ye were a

fine young man

That right Mum?

and aw the lassies will admit that they fancied me?
and the boys will agree that I was in the top five at fightin?

and probably in the top three at fitba?

(and how are they gonnay
fill that hole in right midfield?)

(and I d have played for Rangers
if I d lived long enough?)

that s certain son

that sortay face?

Exactly ma wee Alvin Stardust

That sortay face

Mum?

Whit?

Why ye talkin to me about death?

best prepared son

Manchester is really quite impressive. I mean, I live in Edinburgh, so it's hard to compete with an actual castle, but still. There's Gothic and Modern and Victorian frowning down at the blue-bodied ants swarming through its streets, as though history, art, architecture were passing judgement on sport: You are beneath us. Do you understand the revolutions in thought that we have produced? When you are gone we will return to the spirit of the imagination, which heeds not your empty culture.

Sport smirks: Aye, well, we've got the masses on oor side, pal, eh?

'Fuckin lovin this.' Frannie grins, high-fiving a random passer-by.

Jack sways atop the camel-hump of Dolby's shoulders, pretending to be the tallest man in Manchester. 'So many people!' he squeals, and claps. There's no sticker book in the world can beat this. Dolby is smiling, and I can see how pleased he is at Jack's reaction – his DNA itself is glowing – and a secreted packet of happiness inside me bursts, leaks.

We roam through the city, a many-headed beast, the men knitting the wool of the impending game with the needles of their chat: Kirk Broadfoot in the centre of defence? Lee McCulloch starting or sub? To Boyd or not to Boyd? Rab and Jeff clack-clack-clack the possibilities while Frannie explains for my benefit, 'There's a big hole in the right midfield,' making Bex and Chaz glance at me as though to say, You don't *know* this? The guys we pass appreciate Wee Wife with winks and 'awright, darling' and she curtsies for them until a thunderous look in Cage's eye warns them off and he thuds through their centre. I cling to the edges of the conversation, sometimes scratching out, 'That's who I'd play?' or 'No, not *him*.' Cage turns his planetoid grunt towards me a couple of times and I fade down to mms and reallys.

At one point, Frannie spots a policeman and the quip builds momentum behind his mouth before he stoats up to the bobby and goes, 'It's The Bill!' and tries out an a capella version of the theme tune. Jeff and Rab join in on backing synth, before the three of them are improvising a funky-policeman dance while the policeman looks on, caught between amusement and weariness.

'Very good,' he applauds.

'Bet ye get that aw the time,' Frannie says.

'But you thought you'd do it anyway,' the policeman says, with a shrug.

'Aw a bittay fun, nay harm done,' says Frannie, although I've heard this from him before – always when I was on the wrong end of his mockery in the back-seat of Belinda – and the subtext is: Aw a bittay fun, many years of psychological damage done.

'You boys going to behave yourselves today?' says the policeman, folding his arms.

Frannie feigns reeling backwards as though shot. 'Whoah. We've no even done anythin yet!'

'Yet?'

Cage steps forwards, and there's just a slight tightening of the policeman's gaze as he blocks out the sun. 'Hey, c'mon, pal, that's no fair. We're guests in yer city. It's your country that's had the hooligan problem, no oors.'

The policeman holds up his hands and says, 'That's okay then, gentlemen. We'll get along just fine.'

Cage frowns and turns away, magnetically pulling us up the street with him. 'Nice tay ken we're welcome.'

'But we're not welcome,' I say.

Cage stops and looks at me. Everyone else stops also, as though on his silent command.

'They telt us not tay come unless we had tickets,' I say, then add, 'I mean, it's their city.'

Cage cocks his head, all the better to bore his gaze into me. 'Well, whit are you daein here, then?'

Even Frannie sniggers at that one.

'Least they could show us is some courtesy.' Cage tuts. He looks at me long enough for me to know that what he actually means: it's the least you could show me as well. Then he stomps onwards, swigging from a bottle of Strongbow, and I drift into his general slipstream, as the Imperial Destroyer of him navigates a way through the asteroid field of Rangers fans crashing about the streets.

I find myself just behind Wee Wife, her short, thick-legged walk. Spontaneously, she does a dance, a hop-skip, and I can see her as a lassie, forty years ago, on her way to school. As though aware I'm watching, she turns to me and sings

roll up   roll up for the mystery tour
roll up   roll up for the mystery tour

then lifts her can of Special Brew to me.

'No thanks,' I say, hand cutting the air. 'I don't really drink.'

'Hoo! Whit? Ye don't really drink? Hear that, everybody?' she shouts, and Jeff, Frannie and Bex turn. 'The laddie "doesnay really drink".'

'Oh, he drinks awright,' Frannie chortles, nonchalantly high-fiving another complete stranger. 'I've seen that boy drink a bottle ay whisky and look neither up nor doon.'

Bex holds out a Becks – his nickname makes more sense to me now. 'There ye go, mate, on the hoose. Fire in.'

'No, thank you,' I say.

'"No, thank you",' he repeats, tickled, and does a wee, mocking dance. 'Sortay answer's that?'

I've realised the strategic mistake in not drinking: I'm a target. *Not drinking* suggests *crap in a fight*, which means taking the heaviest bolts of abuse when an electrical storm of banter builds up in a group of men.

'I'm not a drinker,' I explain. 'Bad experiences.'

'Aye, we've aw had bad experiences.' Bex laughs. 'That's the fun! Ye a poof, likes?'

'I'd just rather not.'

'Whit, is it the company?' says Bex, drawing closer to me. 'We no good enough or somethin?'

'Not at all,' I say evenly, and let him work out what I mean by that.

Bodies stream past us through the streets, trailing songs and scarves. We are just one tiny drama among thousands of them here. Bex holds the beer out to me. 'Well, fuckin join in, then.'

Frannie's watching this exchange, and I can tell he's secretly hoping Bex will win it. He doesn't know what Dolby knows and has always been uncomfortable every time I refuse a drink in his company. But he can see that Bex is walking a fine line with me, is actually jiving along it, and I go back a lot longer with him than Bex does.

Things are turning. It was inevitable. We are men.

'C'mon,' says Bex, waving the head of the bottle at me again. 'A Scotsman who disnay take a drink? That says poof tay me, likes.'

'Well,' I say, feeling my teeth clench, 'maybe that's the problem with our country.'

'Poofs?' goes Bex, declaiming to the rest of the group, and there's a smattering of laughter. 'Aye, ye're no wrong there!'

'Look, fuck off, mate.'

Bex's gaze flickers, before he hurls it back at me and says, 'Whit's that?'

'I'm no wantin a drink,' I say, and stare directly at him, and a thousand pissheads from a thousand nights are squaring up to me and here we go: the predictability of it. Adrenalin goes all Formula One in my system.

'Oh,' says Bex, legs becoming sprightly. 'Oh. Ye wantay go, likes?'

'Haw,' says Frannie, his hand on Bex's chest. 'Keep the heid, pal.'

Bex starts dancing on the end of Frannie's hand. 'You'd better tell your mate tay stop fuckin eyeballin me.'

I'm staring at him, faint smile on my lips that he doesn't know is nerves, and folding my arms. In my second year at Stirling Uni I worked behind the bar in the union. First week on the job I phoned Brian the Mann for advice. He'd been serving in Smith's since he was eighteen. I could almost hear the pride crackling on the line – the Chipmunk become one of his very own – and his voice took on that of Bryan Brown talking to Tom Cruise in Cocktail: Oh, my son, my rebellious son. 'Stand yer ground, mate,' he telt me. 'Ye dinnay go for them, but ye dinnay retreat. It confuses them. Be solid and look them in the eye, cos the second ye break eye contact ye've lost.'

'He's still daein it,' says Bex, an arm flapping up and down. 'Don't you fuckin stare at me, ya cunt.'

I'm quivering inside but I won't break eye contact. It's freaking him out. He's making a lot of noise, but he's not advancing. Frannie has his hands on Bex's shoulders, trying to imprint calm into them, while Bex jabs a finger in my direction. 'Tell him tay stop fuckin lookin at me like that!'

Then Wee Wife is somehow placing herself between Frannie and Bex, throwing her words up into his face. 'You leave the laddie alane. Aw he says wis he wasnay wantin a drink and you start on him? Whaur's yer fuckin manners?'

Bex's shoulders relax and he purses his lips, but the adrenalin still makes shapes with his limbs. 'Awright, Chrissie, awright,' he goes, holding up his hands. 'Aw I wis sayin wis on a day like this he should be joinin in the perty, eh?'

'Ye called him a poof,' she says, finger holding him to account. 'The laddie doesnay know ye, and ye called him a poof.'

'Aye, but I was just jokin wi the boy,' he says, and steps forwards hand outstretched. I shake it, but he gives it a squeeze, of course he does. I squeeze back. 'Nothin meant by it, pal, awright?' He squeezes it again, places his other hand atop it.

'Nae problem, mate,' I say, but let him end the handshake.

Cage and Dolby, realising something's happened, have turned and are ambling back towards us. Dolby's frowning, reading the scene, Jack is oblivious, still glancing around warily at the forest of adults, and Cage has the curious eyes of someone who's discovered a card sharp in a casino. 'Whit's goin on here?'

'Put a muzzle on yer boy,' says Wee Wife, pointing towards Bex, whose gaze is lowered, like that of a plaintiff in court. 'He just fuckin started on Frannie's wee pal there for nay reason. Nay reason at aw.'

'Ho, you,' says Cage to Bex. 'Behave yersel.'

Bex's shoulders sink as the full weight of the law descends upon him. 'Listen, Cage, I says sorry, awright?'

'We're doon here for a gemme,' says Cage, with quiet wrath. 'No tay start bother wi other bluenoses.' Cage turns his gaze to me, his neck grinding stonily. 'Even if they are wearin a stupit fuckin Captain America T-shirt.'

Wee Wife cackles and slaps me on the centre of it. 'Aye, he's got ye there, right enough, eh? A fuckin superhero T-shirt! Come on, son, screw the nut.'

Cage turns back round and heads up the street again, and

Dolby's staring quizzically at me as if to say *fuck was all that about?* and I shrug and we all start walking again, the moment unravelling in a dozen different directions in my head.

Wee Wife pats my arm. 'Worked in a bar for twenty years, son,' she says. 'I ken the score.' She mimes a drink problem: the raised jar, the buckled legs. 'If you dinnay wantay take a drink the day, you dinnay take wan.' Then she walks on, sprightly, as though she's on her way to the circus.

Frannie stares at the fat number 8 writhing on her back. 'Alvin, dinnay get involved wi her,' he whispers. 'That's Chrissie.'

'She seems awright.'

'Aye, she is. That's the problem. She's in the Welly drinkin from about one every day since she lost her job. Just sits at the bar tryin tay get folk tae "play" wi her. She's like ivy. Clings tay ye and ye cannay get her aff.'

'Ach, she's harmless. Backed me up there, didn't she?'

'Mate,' Frannie says, arm reaching round my shoulder. I can smell the Stella on his breath. 'Aw them books at that uni and ye still cannay see whit just happened?'

'Enlighten me.'

'Chrissie's the wan who starts laughin at ye for no havin a drink, but Bex is the wan hauled up for it.'

I turn the ignition key of the incident again – me refusing drink – but can't find the biting point of who said what and when, and the memory stalls.

'She can turn—' Frannie clicks his fingers '—like that.' He nods at me and there's a heaviness in his eyes. 'But she's obviously no the only wan, eh? Thought for a second there ye were gonnay deck that cunt.'

'He'd have deserved it.'

Frannie weighs this, sniffs. 'Mibbe so. But that's no the Alvin that I mind fay Falkirk. You wouldnay say boo tay a goose back then.'

'That,' I remind him, looking up at the sky, its pale blue emptiness, 'was a long time ago in a galaxy far, far away.'

'We must not think of the things we could do with, but only of the things that we can't do without.'

George comes out really quite sensible at times. You'd be surprised. I call that downright wisdom, not merely as regards the present case, but with reference to our trip up the river of life generally. How many people, on that voyage, load up the boat till it is in danger of swamping with a store of foolish things which they think essential to the pleasure and comfort of the trip, but which are really only useless lumber?

How they pile the poor craft mast-high with fine clothes and big houses; with useless servants, and a host of swell friends that do not care twopence for them, and that they do not care three ha'pence for; with expensive entertainments that nobody enjoys, with formalities and fashions, with pretence and ostentation, and with – oh, heaviest, maddest lumber of all! – the dread of what will my neighbour think, with luxuries that only cloy, with pleasures that bore, with empty show like that?

Three Men in a Boat by Jerome K. Jerome

The road from Stirling towards the university became smooth lawns and woodland, and Dad's car slipped into the campus like a wary swimmer making that first stroke into open water. Students in their natural habitat. They glanced at the car as we passed, and I feared them leaping into the road to attack us with quotes from the classics.

I'd arrived. I'd really arrived.

'Whit's the name ay the buildin?' Dad said, peering at signs that directed us through the bushes and slopes and, wait – was that an actual golf course? Were those Trudis and Dickys firing shots to the horizon and clinking glasses? Fwa fwa fwa. Steady on, I reminded myself. It's Stirling University, not Oxford-as-depicted-by-Hollywood.

But, still, it felt like a helluva jump from the crush of the school bus and the drill of the bell. It was *their* air I would breathe as soon as I stepped from Dad's car, I realised, and it would be like discovering an entirely new and gorgeous smell. I had no understanding of academia beyond the tweed-suited bookworm who saves the day in children's fantasy novels, no way of knowing what being a student would entail, except for dark mutterings from Brian about 'pen pushers' who are 'up their own arses' and 'no livin in the real world'.

Even then I remember thinking, Who wants to live in the real world?

I took out the letter. 'Um,' I said, 'A. K. Davidson Hall.'

Dad found the sign and turned the wheel, letting the campus swallow us further into its leafy maw. Lecture theatres. The sports centre. Residential blocks. A. K. Davidson Hall. We parked. It was like parking in Valhalla. Through the windscreen, a mere skelf of a boy was buckled beneath a box, carrying his earthly belongings into the next life. Dad turned to me. 'You awright?'

'Aye. Piece of piss.'

'Let's go, then.'

I let the air out of my lungs.

He looked at me and placed his hand on my shoulder. 'Remember you're as good as any ay them, son.'

It felt like the sort of thing Captain America might say to a rookie recruit in The Avengers, after they'd found themselves teleported to an intergalactic arena.

Remember you're as good as any of them, son. Even that ten-foot-tall Lizardman with the harpoon.

But, Cap, I only know how to make sparks with my fingertips. They're not even deadly!

In you go, son, just watch the – ah! Shit. Oh, well. He was a good kid. Him and his funny little sparks.

I was attending an actual university!

For most of the kids who'd stayed on at school in fifth and

sixth year, that'd been expected from birth, the way speech, upright motion and piano-playing were expected from birth. But it wasn't for me. I was from Hallglen. That's not like being from other parts of Falkirk, your Lionthorns or Windsor Drives or Gartcows Roads. Hallglen weans are no more naturally expected to attend university than they are to suddenly, say, disappear off backpacking for a year or restore an old boat. You heard of people doing such things, but they weren't ever you. Hallglen was a hive for labourers, call-centre operators, supermarket staff, offshore workers: they droned from it to work and back obediently each day. TV evenings. Take-aways. Bookies. Concrete.

On account of mine being a one-parent household and Dad being on incapacity benefit, my accommodation was covered by a grant (and, given I'd had to virtually nursemaid him during his breakdown, this was a reward from the universe at last). My student loan gave me five hundred pounds in my bank account for the semester. The most money I'd ever had, up until that point, was twenty quid from Dad to go on a night out in Falkirk, and even then the Lads had been forced to subsidise my drinks, slapping a tenner down with a tut and sending me to the bar ('Scoot, runt!') yet there I was with FIVE HUNDRED POUNDS!!! It hadn't occurred to me that this would be spread over five months, to include everything from feeding and clothing myself, to buying the new U2 album when it came out, which is why, on 10 September, in the Year of Our Lord (Bono) 2001, I found myself living outside Falkirk for the first time, rich beyond my wildest dreams.

Dad opened the car door, my cue to do the same: *Hold steady, men!* The boot disgorged a mouthful of Pink Floyd T-shirts and brick-like Stephen King novels. Dad lifted boxes, while I walked on my tiny nervous pincers into a reception area that chattered with new-term sentience, where people lounged in poses that transmitted low-level *love me I'm terrified* vibes. My senses alert: could I detect intellect in the place, somehow, in the décor, the chatter of accents? What was the benchmark for pretentious here? Newsnight Review was enough for Frannie ('Correct me if I'm wrong but a film's either "gid" or "shite"'). Brian's upper limit was any man who dyed his hair. For Dolby, who really did for a few weeks change his name to 'Uriel', well, let's just say he was coming at things from the other end of the telescope.

Me and Dad humped my stuff upstairs: the graphic novels (smiley face on Watchmen smiling watchfully); my Burtons shirts, jeans, shoes, whole damn Falkirk uniform; kitchen utensils; a lava lamp tinkling with bottled mystery. People came and went through the hallways doing the same, fathers grimacing with labour, their sons and daughters passing shy glances to each other. A text:

`Settled in yet?`

Knew it'd be Dolby first.

We placed the last box down in the centre of the room, huffing and muscle-weary. Then we stood there and took it in. Wardrobe and a sink and a desk and a bed. 'Where do you cook?' Dad said.

'I have to cook?'

The communal kitchen was also empty.

Fridge. Hob. Sink.

'I have to cook?' I said again.

I walked him back down to the entrance, where more handbrakes were being yanked and boxes ejected, and parents, voices thick with worry, kissed farewell to offspring coiled-up with the message to go – Go just GO. Dad jangled his keys at me. He was in full-on-father mode, maybe conscious of the other fathers around him, the historical persona required for This Day. More hands on shoulders. More sighing. This would be the scene they'd select for Dad's Best Dad clip at the Best Dad Awards. 'Now mind, I can pick ye up if you ever needtay come hame. Only twenty miles that way.'

He pointed towards a Falkirk that might or might not've still existed, for all I knew.

'Could come back at the weekend,' I said, mainly to satisfy him.

He mused. 'Make it the weekend eftir.'

'Okay.'

'You and Derek be all right the githerʔ' I said quickly.

Dad's face arranged itself. He nodded. 'Me and him's fine for now.'

'For now?'

'Day at a time. A lot still tay be said. But we're grown-ups.'

'And you'll be fine?' I gave this question a bit of presence.

He nodded again and put his hand on my hair, rubbed it a bit, kissed my head. 'I'm through it, son. Thanks for all yer help.'

This. Oh, this.

'Yer mum would've been proud,' he said, and I felt a cloud become damp inside my mind.

'If she'd been sober,' he added, and I smiled, and it was stemmed.

Sons and fathers.

'Don't be pishin the bed noo.'

'Same goes,' I said, then put my arm around him and patted his back. He sniffed as I pulled away. Then he climbed into the driver's seat, and, with one last salute, drove off. Everything to do with home went with him.

Woodland and scree glowered at me from the hillside. Summer was cooling above the campus, an upturned blue etched with white detail.

The world. The whole world.

Those trees had been there for decades, had overlooked every student who'd ever arrived at this place, their ambition clutched beneath their arm like a teddy-bear. Now there I was, blinking in the cool late-summer sun with mine. I went back up to my new room and plugged in the lava lamp and stereo and, while a red, melting mass oozed and flowed through purple liquid, and Radiohead's Kid A started up eerily, I unpacked. Everything in its right place. The remnants of my old life: a plastic Han Solo figure, a pewter seventeenth-birthday tankard; then I Blu-tacked to the wall photos. Dad. Derek.

Mum.

aye, son?

Me, Brian, Dolby and Frannie sitting on the bonnet of Belinda as though in an album-cover shot. These plucky kids from Falkirk have hit the charts like a bullet with their début effort! Brian, sturdy and dependable, would be on bass; Dolby would be the intense and creative guitarist; Frannie would be prowling the front of the stage, offering his hand to the lassies in the front row. Which left me on drums. Invisible. Just keeping time.

But if Spinal Tap have taught us anything, it's that drummers are replaceable.

Footsteps. From upstairs, voices curling out from beneath doors, the building gradually filling with life.

It was all past. Falkirk was a series of photographs. Something else had started.

I was *becoming*.

I threw on my leather jacket and headed out to buy food, feisty as a mountain man, over the bridge that spanned the loch and the burble of birds, nature and new students. Girls. Boys. Boys. Girls. Hello. Hi. Hiya. I wanted to pick up speed and run right through the campus, glance round and see them all following me, like the kids in Rocky, and I'd race up the steps of the Wallace Monument and we'd all stand on top of it, bouncing up and down, fists in the air, gazing round at the whole of Central Scotland. We are young. We are not ashamed to be clever. And we are free of what has held us back.

It is lumber, man – all lumber! Throw it overboard. It makes the boat so heavy to pull, you nearly faint at the oars. It makes it so cumbersome and dangerous to manage, you never know a moment's rest for dreamy laziness – no time to watch the windy shadows skimming lightly o'er the shallows, or the glittering sunbeams flitting in and out among the ripples, or the great trees by the margin looking down at their own image, or the woods all green and golden, or the lilies white and yellow, or the sombre-waving rushes, or the sedges, or the orchis, or the blue forget-me-nots.

Throw the lumber over, man! Let your boat of life be light, packed with only what you need – a homely home and simple pleasures, one or two friends worth the name, someone to love and someone to love you, a cat, a dog, and a pipe or two, enough to eat and enough to wear, and a little more than enough to drink, for thirst is a dangerous thing.

Three Men in a Boat by Jerome K. Jerome

Soon Frannie is waddling through the streets of Manchester, his face cross-hatched with desperation: 'Seriously, boys, I needtay shake the dragon.' He glances round, spots a side-street, but doesn't get very far before he bumps into a guy he knows – 'Awright, Terry, ya bawbag' – and is swallowed up in a crowd posing for a photo. Their motley arrangements of home kits, away kits, retro kits and chest-hair kits make a manly patchwork. They're grinning and singing and, as Frannie is absorbed into the rank, something switches on in him. He forgets his swollen cow-bladder. Snap! He's into it. They slap his back. 'Mon Rangers,' each says, an ancient, customary greeting. The joy in his face. How pure he looks. How new. How he's already formulating the ways he'll package this for his grandchildren, or for Brian, if we can ever afford to fly to California to visit the bastard. The group cheer and sway, until a policeman approaches and tells them off for something. Can't hear what he's saying, but can read the Morse code of their faces: eyebrow dashes of irritation, open-mouth dots of remorse. Arms are raised like those of defenders appealing a penalty. The policeman seems to let them away with a warning, and they shake his hand, comradely. Soon as he's round the corner? Song flows through them again, and each time a pretty girl passes there are kettle-boiling-over whistles and they go,

Every other Saturday's my half day off,
It's over to the match I go.
Happily we wander down the Paisley Road,
Me and my wee pal Joe-oh-oh-oh,
We love to see the lassies with the blue scarves on,
We love to hear the boys all roar . . .

At this, there's an actual roar at actual lassies with actual blue scarves on, actually lapping up the song. Everyone's eyes are shining.

But I don't have to tell you what's the best of all.
We love to see the Rangers score-oh-oh-oh . . .

Three dozen men have their hands in the air, to clap the chorus, Frannie indistinguishable among them, lost in the soar of it.

Me oh Me oh Me oh My!
Oh how we love to see them try!

Frannie strolls back to us, the sun glinting off his shades, his chin raised and imperious like a rock star at T in the Park. He's even forgotten that he needed a pish. He looks as though he's made of light.

'Yese should've went in, boys.' He smiles. 'The water's lovely.' Bex, Jeff and Chaz accept him back into their ranks, showing him the photos they just took of him on their phones.

Frannie nods at his own image with all the modesty of Cat from Red Dwarf.

The pubs are as thronged as the streets. We peek in to see queues four deep, then go off in search of less populous watering-holes. Soon we reach the canal area, which isn't too bulky with fans, diluted by curious business-people quaffing wine and catching rays. Their glasses: chilled. White shirts: crisp. We shrug at each other and descend the steps to join them. Canal water laps gently. Jack scoots towards it going, 'Ducks!' and Dolby's straight on the case.

'No, son, back from there.'

Dolby and Jack. The mental cord that exists between them: a man so in touch with another human being that it makes you yourself feel utterly disconnected from the world. I know no one at all, do I? Not the way that Dolby can know his son, Jack know his father.

Happy-sad.

Whenever I go back to visit him in Falkirk my own dad and I sit, like Dennis Hopper and Peter Fonda at the end of Easy Rider, eyeing a scoured landscape and thinking,

We blew it.

I take in the sight of Dolby and Frannie together, in their element. For all the women Frannie goes through, it's the solidity of these units of life – pint, mate, pub – that puts him most at ease in his soul. A simple lighting of the hearth. I miss them. I miss the Dolby we knew before he had Jack: every few seconds now he eyes the wee man and twitches, senses alert.

If I were a good man, as the Floyd once sang, I'd understand the spaces between friends.

'Awright,' says Frannie, raising a glass at some office types sitting next to us.

'Hello,' they say professionally.

'Hu-llo,' Frannie replies, dancing faintly. 'We are the Billy Boys.'

'Uh . . .'

'Disnay matter,' Frannie says. 'Just a wee joke.' Jack steps about in the sunshine, watching ducks drift by like elaborate origami. He flaps his own wings and they flick away across the canal, a spray of them; Jack makes a cross face. Me, Dolby and Frannie sink in our seats, summer layering our skin. We grin at each other, for no reason. 'Shell we hev a toast?' Frannie says, and we raise aristocratic glasses. I raise the peach schnapps and lemonade I've allowed myself today. Just the one. Just for the occasion.

Me: 'To still being mates.'

Frannie: 'To the Gers.'

Dolby: 'To Brian.'

Our faces debate, until someone clinks and we just go, 'Aaaaaay.'

Clink. Clink. Clink.

Frannie turns back to the suits. 'Yese gonnay be watchin the fitba the day, boys?'

'Pardon?'

'Are. Youse. Going to be. Watching. The. Football. Today?'

'Oh,' one says. 'Um. Probably not.'

'How no?' he says. 'Manchester no excited about this, likes?'

'It's not that,' another says, tugging the cuffs of his shirt, 'just think it's maybe safer to be off the streets while the game takes place.'

'Safer?' says Frannie. 'C'mon, man, we're aw Brits the gither. Whit do ye think we're gonnay dae tay yer city, likes?'

'Pardon?'

Frannie breathes in, then out. 'What. Are. We. Going. To. Do. To. Your. City?'

'I don't know,' one of the guys says. 'What *are* you going to do to it?'

'Partfay perty?' says Frannie. 'I mean, apart from party?'

'It's the party that we're worried about.'

Frannie turns back to us. 'Gettin this? Fuckin paranoid this lot, eh?'

'Ach,' says Dolby. 'Must be a wee bit scary for them, Fran. I mean, look at the amount ay Rangers fans here.'

Frannie shakes his head. 'They kent we were gonnay come. They hadtay expect this.'

He leans back in his seat, dons shades, and angles his face up towards the sun.

'Frannie,' I say. He turns his head and I see myself in his shades, Manchester rising behind me and my squinting features. 'No city,' I explain, 'can prepare in two weeks for a hundred and fifty thousand people just turning up. When William Wallace did that the English released the *army*.'

Cage looks over at me and does the growl of a storm in the distance. 'Just let them fuckin try.'

Dolby glances at him.

'I didn't mean to scare the ducks, Daddy,' Jack says, clutching Dolby's finger.

'I know, son,' says Dolby, and kisses the top of Jack's head.

Chrissie comes careering over to our table, a wind-up toy. With fangs. She's singing Total Eclipse Of The Heart. She's filled a glass that could double as an astronaut's helmet with white wine and she's parading up and down the canal bank, letting it slosh before she takes an Orca-like gulp and tries to get the two suits next to us to dance. She reaches out her fingertips to them, with the plea of a cabaret performer, and the guys smile faintly – caught between ignoring and obeying – until one of them takes her hand and shakes it with a gentle farewell.

'Aw, c'mon, boys,' she says. 'Wee bittay eighties music, naw?'

One of the guys turns away from her, which is enough to make Chrissie step up her campaign, draping an arm around him and leaning into his face: 'Turn around . . . Bright eyes!'

'Not really my thing,' he mumbles.

'No really your hing? The eighties are everybody's hing. I mean, they're the eighties! Ken whit I mean?'

'That's more my mum and dad's music.'

'Och, whit ye sayin, ya cheeky bisem?' She playfully slaps his chest, but lets her fingers rest there. 'Oh, here, you're solid.'

He smiles reluctantly, but his shoulders are tense and he catches the eye of his friend, who realises that they're completely outnumbered and has a fake grin stuck to his face for Chrissie's benefit. She comes down off the last note of the chorus to see me and Frannie watching her, and rolls the wine around in her glass before raising it. I applaud. She bats her hand as if to say, Och, away you. Frannie hisses at me, 'Dinnay encourage her.'

'Oh, what?' I say. 'Aren't women allowed to get drunk and sing songs as well?'

Cage has his back turned away from Chrissie's antics, watching the canal slip past.

'Boooooys,' Chrissie appeals to us, her voice curling on the word, 'were the eighties or were they not the best decade for music?'

Dolby holds his hands up to let Jack punch them.

'Personally?' I say. 'I prefer the seventies.'

She hoots as though this were a punchline. 'Oh, aye! Abba! T-Rex!'

'I was more meaning the Floyd.'

'Och,' she goes, takes another gigantic sip of her wine, 'they're too far oot there for me. That's music for weirdos.'

Frannie stifles a laugh. 'If the cap fits, Alvin . . .'

'They werenay *excitin* like the Human League and Duran Duran. Cannay make me dance.' Her eyes flash and she is suddenly a short-skirted teen with big permed hair and a Lambrusco glow. 'No for a Setirday night in the Maniqui. Me, Janey Barnes and Helen Miller, we were hot stuff. Oh, and there was that time when me and Helen hit the Buzz Top, looking so *fine* in oor wee skirts, absolutely *caked* in blue eyeshadow, and we had a hip flask ay voddy round the backay the auld picture hoose, whaur Sportsters is noo, and Helen was sick!' Frannie nods, exhales, smiles, inhales, nods, smiles, grits his teeth and looks at me. But I'm liking it. I'm liking her. I'm liking the way she illuminates present-day Falkirk with the synth-colours of the eighties – light blues, pinks, yellows – turning Sportsters back into the old ABC Cinema, changing the signs above shops, re-creating, for as long as her story lasts, a world that no longer exists. I'm liking her face, animated, as the thrill of her youth blooms before us. I'm liking it until she severs it with a neat, 'I'm no borin you, boys, am I?'

'Aye,' says Frannie.

She bares her teeth at him in a silent laugh.

Cage has quit staring into the canal and is focusing his Robocop vision on our surroundings: the vague, jazzy, white-wine feel drifting out through the open doors of the bar, with their wooden blinds and invitation to a certain type of clientele. It's all so at odds with the Rangers support dotted at tables, basking in the sunshine like Second World War soldiers enjoying downtime in some French garrison town. But there are civilians among us. Cage stares at the two guys at the next table, and I follow his gaze to see them the way he sees them.

One is wearing a fedora hat and a tight T-shirt. He is tanned and his skin is clear and healthy. He is picking at a salad and talking animatedly while his friend nods and listens. His friend is in a lilac shirt rolled up at the sleeves and a pair of grey flannel trousers. He muses at something his companion says and goes, 'Yeah, that's how they learn.'

Cage glances about himself one last time and says, to no one in particular, 'Whit's the nameay that street whaur they filmed that programme about the poofs?'

'Queer as Folk,' goes Frannie.

'That wis in Manchester, eh?'

'Canal Street, specifically,' I say.

Chrissie's gaze flicks over at me.

Cage smirks and nods towards the guys next to us. 'We're at a canal, are we no?'

'Ye think this is a gay bar?' Frannie blinks and moves his head round on his neck like a lost explorer, as though gay men are creeping up on him from the darkness beyond the fire.

Before anyone can stop Cage, he's crouching forwards and laying his ham-like forearms on his knees. 'S'cuse me, boys?' he says, and they can barely conceal a sigh as they pause their conversation to say, 'Yes?'

'Is this Canal Street?'

The guy in the fedora chews his salad, then leans back in his seat to look at Cage. 'So what you're basically saying is: are we gay?'

'That's no whit I asked,' says Cage. 'I'll repeat the question. Is this Canal Street?'

Fedora wipes his lips with his napkin. 'What's it to you?'

'Leave it, Victor,' his friend says, then addresses Cage directly. 'Listen, we hope you have a good time and get the result you—'

'We're guests in yer city,' Cage says, ignoring him in favour of Fedora, 'and just wantay ken the name ay this street. *Victor*.'

Dolby and Frannie are watching this unfold – flicking between Cage and Fedora – and even I want to know the answer now. Fedora stands and says to his friend, 'Okay, Peter, let's go. I think the atmosphere is starting to turn.'

Cage grabs at his heart as though they've stabbed him. 'Ho ho, there's nay need for that attitude.'

'Attitude,' says Fedora, gripping his napkin. 'Nice.'

'Simple question! Ye dinnay needtay take the huff.'

The guy in the shirt, Peter, picks up his jacket and shuffles through our chairs, saying, 'Excuse me,' quietly, making eye contact with no one.

Fedora adjusts his stance, takes in Cage from head to foot. 'If you don't mind,' he says, 'could you please leave the city the way you found it?'

'Whit – covered in poofs?' laughs Cage. But no one else does.

Fedora notes this and sniffs, zipping up his jacket. 'Think you lost the crowd there, friend. So at least you're not *all* trolls.' He thrusts his hands into his pockets and does an eyebrow-flash at Cage. 'It's just you.' Then he cuts his way through us and joins Peter, who glances back at us almost apologetically.

'Queer as the driven snow,' says Cage, taking a gulp from his pint, as though his point has just been verified by a team of independent experts.

'There was nay need for that,' says Chrissie, standing up from the table in protest.

'Aye, awright,' says Cage, turning away from her. His eyes are focused on nobody. His fingers slip slowly down the wet body of his glass.

Dolby has his bottom lip pressed against the top one, and I recognise it from nights spent driving round Falkirk in Belinda: it usually prefaced either a rant about his working day in Whirlpools Direct or a nugget of philosophy culled from the Ancient Wisdom of Bruce Lee:

> It is like a finger pointing to the moon. Don't look at the finger! Or you will miss all that heavenly glory . . .

'Can always tell a poof,' says Cage, in the absence of anybody saying anything. 'I can *smell* them.'

'What do they smell like?' I say, setting my peach schnapps down.

Cage repositions himself in his chair and the corners of his mouth lift slightly, as though he is glad that at last someone is taking him on. He just hadn't expected it to be me. He takes two large gulps of Stella, then also sets it down. 'Lavender and spunk.'

He cackles and raises his hand for a high five, which Jeff returns obediently.

'Mate, you ken what that is,' I say, folding my arms. 'That's homophobia.'

'Homophobia?' Cage says, amused, as though the concept itself is standing there on the table, wagging its tiny, politically correct finger at him. 'Listen, I've been tay the doctor's and let him feel ma balls, Alvin. I am definitely not *homic* of any *phobes*. Good luck tay them. Just that . . .' He makes the sort of face you'd use when considering an offer during a haggling exchange.

'Just that whit?' Dolby says, able to enter the conversation now that Chrissie's dancing with Jack to the sound of the Pet Shop Boys' version of Always On My Mind, which is playing from inside the bar, making me wonder if Chrissie herself requested it. Given it's an Elvis cover, it's even managed to get Auld Alfred up boogying, his hips shuffling and his eyes shining to a soundtrack of cheers from Bex, Jeff, Chaz and Rab. I can see him forty years ago, a Teddy Boy out on the razz at the local Palais in some mining town. Chrissie birls round him – whoo! – and Alfred takes her hand and Jack's and they form a festive circle.

Cage leans forwards to scrutinise Dolby and me. 'Right,' he says, as though forced to summarise a lesson we missed cos we were off sick. 'Look at them.' He gestures to two girls in Rangers tops at a nearby table who, to be fair, are absolutely gorgeous. 'Like perfect wee bitsay fruit, aren't they?'

Frannie turns his head and muses, then quotes that bit in Naked Gun when a large-chested woman says, 'Is this some kind of bust!' and Leslie Nielsen says, 'It's very impressive, yes.'

Me and Dolby nod, just to see what Cage's thesis will be.

'Poofs are poofs, I mean.' He rolls his hand, and we see the UVF tattoo on the back of it, 'Live and let live an aw that. But I just dinnay understand how they cannay fancy women. Everybody else does.'

'*Everybody* else?' I say, feeling something click in me, something cold and logical. Something that's the opposite of Cage. I open my mouth, primed to take him down, but just then Frannie enters the fray – 'Well, when ye think about it, gay guys dinnay make sense in evolutionary terms' – forcing me to engage them both. I stare at him and his eyes do a there-you-go, and he's serious. He's fucking serious.

'Put it this wey, Alvin,' Frannie says, while Cage nods solemnly like a co-presenter on a news broadcast, 'I've never met a lassie who didnay get turned on at the thought of snoggin a really hot bird.' He starts to tick the list off on his fingers. 'So, if straight guys fancy women *and* straight women fancy women *and* lesbians fancy women, that must mean the gay guys are at it.'

'Frannie,' I say, clutching my hair, '"at it"? It's no an insurance scam. Why would somebody fake their whole sexuality?'

'You tell me,' he says, levelling his gaze at me, and for a second I expect a writ of accusation.

Cage has been energised by Frannie's Darwinian testimony. 'See aw that camp twirlin about and high-pitched screechin? Does ma heid in. Face uptay it: *yese arenay women!* Tellin me that's no fake?'

'Straight guys ramp up the laddishness when they're oot wi their mates, don't they?' says Dolby.

'Ramp it up?' Frannie says. 'I tone it doon! Youse couldnay handle me ramped up!'

I mock-applaud, which annoys Frannie, and he presses a finger into the table. 'Sayin ye don't fancy lassies, Alvin, is like sayin ye don't like . . .' he glances around himself '. . . sunlight . . . or music . . . or food or somethin. I mean, there's scientific evidence.'

Dolby adjusts his seat and says, 'Oh, this should be good,' as

Frannie and Cage present the data of their exhaustive research.

'Women *look* great,' says Frannie.

'They *smell* great,' says Cage.

'Their voices sound nicer than oors.'

'They dinnay walk up and doon Grahams Road in Fawkurt, battering fuck ootay folk every weekend.'

Cage gestures to Chrissie, sitting on the canal bank, kicking her legs, singing at the ducks. 'No strictly true.'

'They've got tits. They've got legs.'

'Men have got legs,' I point out.

'Aye, but they dinnay have *legs*.' Frannie demonstrates just how long these legs really are. They flow from his shoulders, down past his ankles and all over the floor. Men would cower from the legs of this giant woman.

'Lassies dinnay have hair aw ower their bodies,' says Cage.

'They dinnay fart, then waft it up at ye,' says Frannie.

'Some ay them do,' I say.

'Aye, but no maist ay them.' Frannie raises his hand as though in court. 'Now be fair, Alvin. I'll no stand for any of yer *sexism* about this. *No maist ay them*.'

Cage clears pints from the table so he can lean forwards on it. 'It's just no possible for a man tay fancy nay women at all. Nup. The poofs are AT IT.'

Cage can see how clearly irritated I am and holds up his hands to block my words. He looks at Rab and Chaz for back-up. They murmur, 'Aye, Cage, disgusting.'

'I mean dinnay get me wrang,' says Frannie, 'it's no a moral issue.'

'It is for me!' snorts Cage.

'Gay folk dinnay even needtay dae it in the "privacy ay their ain hames" or anythin like that. I'm no a prude.' Frannie laughs away the very suggestion. 'They can it fire it up whitever hole they like.'

'So whit *is* the issue?' says Dolby.

Frannie exhales the entire argument, presents his conclusion. 'I just dinnay believe that gay guys can like *that* hole mair than the other yin.'

'Exactly,' goes Cage.

My innards are growling. 'Mate,' I say, making a force of the next bit, 'you are talkin pish. Cocks have to be sexy enough to appeal to fifty per cent of the population or else the human race would die oot. Why's it so impossible tay imagine that some guys like them tay?'

Jack drifts back to us, just as I introduce the word 'cock', making Dolby take his hand and lead him down the canal bank for a 'wee walk to see mair ducks', glancing back at me as though to say: Eject, man.

Frannie makes a baffled face. He can understand a cock being described by another guy as 'like a fuckin donkey's' or 'tinier than a snail's shell', but '*sexy*'? What would a 'sexy' cock even look like? What criteria would be applied to such a thing? What kind of colouring, gradient, curvature would be deemed the aesthetic of a 'sexy cock' and under what circumstances would you ever, *ever* tell a guy he has one? 'What about bisexuals?' I continue, pressing home my case. 'They just see attractiveness where they find it, whether it's a man or a woman.'

'Pish,' says Cage, the back of his hand batting bisexuals from the air. 'I dinnay believe in them either. Fence-sitters. And I bet they like the sensation tay.'

I laugh with nerves, which Frannie takes to be approval. 'They're just like Fawkurt supporters,' he announces. 'Too feart tay commit tay wan side ay the Old Firm. Bisexuals are gayer than the fuckin poofs.' He holds his pint victoriously. 'In ma book.'

'Hmm,' I tell him. 'Just as well I'm no *readin* your book.'

Frannie raises the Stella, sups it, then says, 'Ye must've done some Mickey Mouse degree at that uni then.'

mamamama ma ma mamama ma mama mama ma

Cooking pasta in the kitchen, losing myself in the stirring and the smallness, I heard the door open behind me and everything was live. Mother of God, I was going to have to face a fellow student. Fireworks went off in my heart: I was actually about to hold a conversation with a stranger I'd be living with on a day-to-day basis. Keep stirring, keep stirring.

'Hello there.' Male.

I tapped the wooden spoon twice on the side of the pot, before placing it down and turning. He was leaning in the doorway, regarding me with curious eyes. Black ringmaster's jacket, with gold embroidery. Baggy, low-slung, hip-hoppy jeans. His T-shirt said 'The Strokes' on it and had been ripped, deliberately. So had his jeans. Scuffed trainers with a Converse logo. My first thought was: I can see the waistband of his boxer shorts. My second was: I am way out of my depth.

'You just arrived?' he asked, as though we were at a party.

'Aye,' I said, trying to give the word some heaviness and presence.

'Thank God the parents have all gone, eh? Everyone can bloody relax a bit. I mean, chill, Mother, take a gin!'

He was still slouching in the doorway. He looked like he was made to slouch in the doorway, as though doorways, in fact, had been invented for him to slouch in. Then he unfolded his limbs and moved, like a slow, louche insect, towards the table, sat down and stretched, yawning. I watched him, my mind a terrifying vacuum. I was being asked to chit-chat with the cover of one of those magazines – Esquire, GQ – read by MEN, a handsome, sleek thing in non-Falkirk clothes.

'Yeah,' I said eventually. Then: 'Make it a double.'

His eyes widened with pretend-panic, and I knew that if I could come up with something else to say we might be in an actual conversation. But then he took a copy of the Guardian, and I was jolted by an almost exquisite vertigo. He was perusing headlines that were actual sentences and didn't rhyme. My dad referred to the Sun, with no small amount of pride, as the working man's Bible (although he hadn't, at that point, actually been a working man for three years). Looking back, that moment – that first encounter with another student, the shock of someone ripping their T-shirt and jeans deliberately, the casual opening of the Guardian, the knowledge that I was going to be living day to day with this person, as though we were somehow the *same* – was the first infection, the first minuscule, middle-class germ entering my body.

'*Soooo*,' he said, turning pages, 'I'm John.'

Oh, my God, a London accent! A Guardian reader from London! It was like being in the midst of the aristocracy! Focus on the pasta. Stir the fucking pasta and get a grip of yourself, you baby. I wiped my hands with a dishcloth, to prove I had manners, then stepped towards him with my hand outstretched. In the second before he shook it I had a spasm of indecision about whether to go firm or soft. The Lads went firm, but what was expected with a Guardian reader from London? I let him lead.

His was firm. I firmed mine up, but too late, and it felt awkward.

'Awright, mate,' I said, 'I mean, like. All right. Good to meet you. I'm Alvin.'

His lips twitched slightly and he stared as though I'd told him about my vestigial tail. 'Alvin?'

'Aye.'

'That's your real name? Alvin? As in Alvin and the Chipmunks?'

'As in Stardust, actually. Glam rocker fay the seventies? Ma mum wis a big fan. But, aye, I'm aware it's no a very Scottish name.' I was flying now! 'Which kinday makes ye stand out at the school, so I'm really glad I'm no still there, eh.'

He covered his mouth with his hand, smiling.

'Whit?' I said.

'Nothing.' He shrugged it away. 'Just your accent.'

'Whit about it?'

He fought the smile, then sniffed and composed himself. 'It's just taking me a while to get used to the fact that I'm in Scotland.'

I didn't know how to respond to this at all.

'It's a great accent, though,' he said quickly. 'Love it. Love the Scots.'

I didn't know how to respond to this either. Was it a great accent? Whose accent exactly was he measuring mine against? Billy Connolly's? Sean Connery's? Groundskeeper Willy's? The obligatory snarling baddie on EastEnders?

'You love a party, you Scots, don't you?'

'We do like a drink,' I agreed, waiting for my mental programming to produce something intelligent to add to that, something sociologically profound about the Scots' relationship to alcohol. 'Sometimes we like two!'

He grinned, as though I'd told him a secret, and went, 'Yeah yeah yeah. Or ten!'

With a thrilling sense of ambition, I dared entertain him with a comedy mime of a Scot walking home drunk, dropping his keys and looking gormless.

'Yeah yeah yeah!' he laughed, clapping.

I waited for him to say something funny about Londoners but he didn't. He leaned back in his seat and placed his hands behind his head. 'Cool name,' he said, then tried it on, as though it were a garment: 'Alvin. Al-vin.'

'Well, like I say,' I added, going back to my pasta, which I realised I'd left on a high simmer, 'I did get the pish taken out of me at school for it.'

'School?' John snorted the word. 'What do people know at school, eh? No, it's a good name. Unusual.'

I mumbled thanks, picked up the wooden spoon and stirred, and scraped at the pasta stuck to the pot by the heat, and stirred.

ma ma mamamama ma ma mamama ma ma mamama
ma mam ma ma mamamama mama mam a ma mamama ma

Sunlight is hammering Manchester and none of us wants to move. The air purrs around us like a cartoon masseuse . . . *and relaaaax* . . . and we're on that first sip of the first cocktails of British Summertime 2008, tasting sun-kissed months that haven't yet happened. Chrissie is still wandering the tables, singing, '"Club Tropicana drinks are free . . ."'

'Youse brought sun-cream?' I ask, breaking the doze.

'Of course,' Dolby says. 'Need to keep the wee yin covered.'

Jack stirs. 'But Mummy says people look better on X Factor with a tan.'

Dolby tuts. 'Mummy says, Mummy says. Ye'd look better on it with *skin*.'

Then we all drink our cocktails again and smile at each other, in that lads-on-our-holidays way. We're going to be doing more of this, I can feel it. I'm *with* these boys again, my oldest mates, and suddenly my life in Edinburgh – its bookshoppy daytime and sofa nights – feels like a craggy, touristy nothing. I'm back among them.

But then a cloud passes in front of the sun. Frannie's been reading my Word magazine and harrumphing at its 'pseudo-pretentious bollocks'. He chucks it back in my direction. 'It's like the NME with a beard.'

And this irritates me more than it should, since I know what he's actually saying is that *I'm* pseudo-pretentious bollocks. Then, as though in a neat one-two, Cage sneers at a Rangers fan having a piss in the canal, 'I hope you wash your hands, ya Pape,' and I realise that, even during a lovely summery lull like this, it's constantly here: the eternal devil resplendent in green, yellow and white, blowing kisses.

Celtic Football Club.

IRA.

Sinn Fein.

Vatican.

Glasgow City Council.

It's as though, without something to oppose, these men would disappear into the ether, and I think of that Clive Barker story in The Books of Blood, about two remote villages that, every hundred years, lash their own citizens together into the shape of lumbering giants and fight it out across the landscape. That's Rangers and Celtic, twin enormities smashing each other over the Clyde, the pulleys and ropes of their fists hauled by working men in green or blue, motivated only by their hatred of the other. Without these men, the giants do not exist. Without the giants, the men do not exist.

Cage laughs at his own Pope/urine interface joke. Jack looks at Cage. Dolby looks at Jack. Then Dolby looks at Cage. 'C'mere, son,' he says, pulling Jack close. 'Tell me whit song ye're gonnay sing for X Factor.'

Jack muses, sniffs, and I remember f r a n n i e   d a n c i n g r o u n d   t h e   g r a s s   h o l d i n g   u p   a

burning stick

and shaking his hips

Brian smirks

takes a giddy hit from the hip-flask

loch shin on a fishing trip

this the week before I go

to the university of stirling in september of 2001

one   big   fucking   final   celebration

to see me away

veers between carry on lord of the flies and some existential play characterised by silence or the dull poking of a fire

falkirk   faraway

listens to our laughter   our singing   waits

to absorb the four of us back into its giant maw

but we don't want to go back   o sweet belinda   Look at the stars! Look at the moon! Look at the water! We are free!

you must return my sons   falkirk is our home You cannot stay out here among this beauty for too long   even the longing for it is not for you

That morning, at Loch Shin, I'd woken to find the fishing-rods listlessly drinking the water, Brian and Frannie snoring beside me, probably dreaming of Rangers reaching a European final one day. Their bodies lay there, drunk and useless, but their subconscious minds were twinned, singing. Dolby was awake, in his green Barbour jacket, perched by the spent fireside. He was reading Clive Barker's Weaveworld. He glanced over the top of the book as I yawned and blinked in the dawn light, then mumbled, 'The boy Barker.'

'Makes Stephen King look like he's been asleep for ten years,' I said.

'Makes *all* of us look like we've been asleep for ten years.' He sighed. 'Can ye imagine writin somethin as good as this one day, Alvin? Goin intay WH Smith's and there's a book like this wi yer name on the front?'

Our gazes met, thickened.

Dolby raised the novel back over his eyes, muttered, 'Ye'd better enjoy that university,' and the blurb on the back of the book read:

> *Weaveworld* is an epic adventure of the imagination. It begins with a magic carpet into which a world of rapture and enchantment has been woven; a world which comes to life, alerting dark forces and beginning a desperate battle to preserve the last vestiges of beauty which humankind still has access to. hic!

Banter's flowing like splashed beer now – bigtime showtime. I'm relaxed and starting to enjoy myself, mainly cos Frannie's in good form, and that'll always do it, the Franman's unfurling patter, a big roll of blue ticker-tape chucked from a top-storey window. Jack, on Dolby's knee, is listening, rapt, as though Frannie is Roald Dahl himself. We sit there next to the canal, overlooked by luxury apartments, balconies louche with professional couples sunbathing, but down here Frannie is prince, regally leading us into a story with a tantalising, 'Ever tell ye about the time me and Brian went drinkin doon Paisley Road?' Then he proceeds with his audience from imaginary bar to bar, teetering on lunacy, before shutting the tale with a neat, 'So it's the last time I pay good money for that!' The party roars. The way Frannie positions himself inside the story, swaggering, the daft voices – at one point, for some reason, he impersonates a piranha – the pauses, the boom-boom ending to each joke, little studs of showmanship glinting like cufflinks as his hands conjure another tale of ye-had-tay-be-there-ness, and I picture Frannie in twenty years, when he'll be forty-seven, standing at the bar impressing Jack, his own son and his pals, maybe a wee girlfriend in there too. The pals laugh. Even the wee girlfriend laughs. 'Your dad's great,' they'll say to Frannie's future laddie. 'Yeah,' the boy will say.

But the words *shut up, Dad, ye're embarrassin* are gritted in his grin.

Because that's just what happens to us. To men. To women. To humans. We are young, then we are old, and then we die.

My mind starts drifting down the canal, splashing between of the ducks, away towards the fens and lakes of England, but it's brought back when I hear a small chink and turn to see Chrissie placing a pint in front of me. She steps away from the table like a posh waitress and touches the air once. 'One does not believe that one more drink would harm the gentleman.'

I raise it to her appreciatively, and she winks, then asks the people next to us for a light by simply waving her cigarette with purpose in their direction. They comply.

A debate has erupted between the Cage and Frannie about the future legacy of Sir David Murray, the Rangers chairman, and there's much 'ach' and 'och' and crossed arms and headshaking. This is probably quite similar to the way Dolby and I argue about Floyd. He's more of a David Gilmour fan, and while it's easy to be seduced by the beauty of Gilmour's guitar-playing and voice, I think he underestimates the enormity of Roger Waters's lyrical and conceptual contributions to the band. But, hey, all in all it's just another brick in the wall. Neither of us is ever going to rip off our T-shirt and Hulk out about it. When Frannie's talking Rangers, he takes things seriously. There's no 'It's all about the taking part' or 'Winning isn't everything' with him. Whatever your opinion on Rangers is, he's anticipated it and is a step ahead of you. He did a bit of writing for some Rangers fanzines and websites a while back, but let it go.

Tesco.

'How many copies you selt ay yer books?' he said to me, during an afternoon pint in Behind the Wall one time, holding up the copy of Follow, Follow with his name printed in it.

I took that one silently. I'm the one with the university education. I have to take it, otherwise I'm a dick.

'Come on,' says Cage, staring at Frannie and slapping his

own knees, as though daring someone over an assault course. 'Nine league titles in a fuckin row, mate, enday story. Whit's the problem wi David Murray?'

Frannie sniffs and stares back, and I can feel the shotgun of his thought reloading.

The chairmanship of Sir David Murray over the institution that is more beloved to Frannie than anything on earth – more precious than the lips of any girl he has ever kissed, or the handshake of any man he has ever called friend – is a matter just about fused to his bone. Cage presents his case to the gathered jury of the rest of us. Even the ducks are probably taking notes. 'Mo Johnston, Brian Laudrup, Paul Gascoigne? These were major signings, Fran, ma man. Put us on the world stage. We've been winnin everythin in sight for the last twenty years. And here we are in a UEFA Cup Final? Whit ye greetin aboot, ya cunt? Murray's a god!'

'A god?' says Frannie, and I see it happen. His mind – his deepest, truest self – has clicked into position. He is focused. He is poised to propel himself into the moment, into the vast, living conscious composed of arcane stats, team-sheets, formations, trophies won and trophies lost, penalties scored and penalties missed, transfer fees, heroes, histories, conspiracy theories, the vast shifting power game of multinational football, with a depth of analysis that would baffle Noam Chomsky. Israel/Palestine? The war in Iraq? The permanent inequality created by global capitalism? Frannie couldn't give a fuck. But he can construct you an intricate, articulate thesis on the current status of Glasgow Rangers, on their *meaning*, which will draw in strands of economics, sociology, Scots-Anglo-Euro political relations and, inevitably, the Northern Ireland question, with all the confidence of a university lecturer. Even although I usually disagree with almost every one of his conclusions (he has, it's fair to say, a certain bias), an intense pride for him glows within me at such moments. Now that enormous Rangers-only intellect is roaring out of Frannie, the full force of it is turned on Cage. Cage folds his arms against its blast, while me, Dolby, Jeff, Bex and Chaz become Colosseum spectators, Jack loses himself in the sugary blink of his DS game, and Chrissie does the Dirty Dancing dance with Auld Alfred on the canal bank, the two of them infused with summer and white wine.

'The financial state of Rangers, mate?' spits Frannie. 'It's *dire*. There's talk ay Lloyd's fuckin Bank takin control ay the club. And Murray doesnay even defend the reputation ay the supporters.' Frannie draws his bottle neck along the rows of watching faces, their general nodding. 'Many times ye heard that shower in Parkheid tryin tay make oot that Rangers are the sole cause ay sectarianism in this country? Media go along wi it, and whaur's Murray's defence? Naywhaur. He's a businessman, Cage. Doesnay give a fuck aboot the supporters ay this club.'

Cage opens his mouth to speak, and Frannie's face sharpens, darkens. All his fizz is gone, something flinty happening. Cage cuts a hand through the air. 'Listen, if we win this the day then oor finances will steady oot and we'll have another European title tay oor name.'

'And if we dinnay win it?' says Frannie. 'And this is oor wan chance at a final? Whaur's the fuckin money gonnay come fay then? You just watch that cunt Murray fly the nest.'

'Oh, whit?' says Cage, but there's a hesitation about his response. 'Ye dinnay hink we can win the day, mate? Hardly a Rangers mentality. Poor show.'

'Rangers could be fucked in the next few years, mate. We could go tay the wall.'

There's a pause while everyone takes in the enormity of this. Rangers teetering, falling from the cityscape of Glasgow across which it strides, shedding tiny blue bodies as it disintegrates.

'Listen though,' Cage says, patting Frannie's arm and breaking the mood, 'whit about that fuckin Neil Lennon?'

'Aw, aye, he's a dick,' says Frannie, instantly connected to Cage again. 'See, if ye were fightin him and he went doon? Ye wouldnay think, "Right, that's me won." Ye'd clap yer hands and go, "Let's get started."'

The Cage slaps Frannie's back. Frannie nearly flies into the canal. 'Ken whit I'd dae?' Cage says. 'Right. Ken whit I'd dae? I'd get one of his baws and I'd tie it to this lamp-post. Then I'd get another and I'd tie it to that lamp-post. And I'd just be like this. Twang. Twang. Twang.'

The Cage mimes twanging Neil Lennon's scrotum. Mimes Neil Lennon's pain.

'Twang. Twang. Twang.'

Leave him alone! I want to shout, as though to a school-bully. What did he ever do to you!

Frannie slaps his thigh with Tom-Cruise-chat-show laughter, 'Ha ha ha!' he goes, convincingly enough. 'Aye, take *that*.'

The Cage grins, a shark taking a shit. Then he hauls Frannie towards him, wraps an arm round his neck. 'See this yin? This yin's funny. I like him.'

Frannie smiles bravely and attempts breathing through one nostril. The Cage releases him – pfoo! Fran exhales again.

'No too sure aboot you, though.'

Takes me a while to realise Cage is pointing at me.

The whole crew turns to look. Dolby's eyes flick towards Cage.

'Really?' I manage. 'Why, uh, why's that?'

Cage runs a big hand over his big head. 'Ye dinnay really say much, ken?'

I laugh nervously. 'That's cos, uh, I don't really have much to say.'

His eyebrows lift on his meaty forehead like twin cranes. 'Well, that cannay be true. You're the educatit yin. University degree an aw that. Work in a bookshop.'

'He's still a Rangers man,' says Frannie. 'Through and through.'

No, I think, *I'm really not.*

The Cage holds up his hands, the innocent party. 'Listen, no sayin he isnay. Just noticed he didnay dae much singin on the bus, that's aw.'

'Neither did I,' Dolby adds.

'Aye, you were drivin, though,' Cage says. 'Concentratin, ken? And ye've got yer wee laddie there.'

Dolby puts his arm around Jack.

'But I didnay see this yin givin it "Hullo Hullo".'

Frannie places his bottle on a beer-mat. 'Mon, Cage, it's no the boy's thing. He doesnay like aw that.'

'Fuck was he doin on a Rangers bus, then?'

Dolby's face is tight, waiting for Cage to toe / cross the line. Frannie's shifting tensely.

'I'm just here,' I croak, 'for the banter.'

'Think ye're above aw this, wee man?' Cage says. 'Eh? Think we're just bigoted scum?'

'We *are* bigoted scum,' laughs Frannie. 'Ken? No one likes us. We don't care!'

'Me and him's mair kinday . . . armchair supporters,' says Dolby, understating wildly. He's never been to a match in his life, and is an armchair gamer all right, but not the football kind.

Cage isn't interested. Dolby doesn't have a degree or work in – *the horror, the horror* – a bookshop. There is no perceived threat hovering in his words. Cage has decided to engage me in a pre-emptive strike. 'Favourite ever Ranger?'

'Cooper,' I say instantly. Not a lie. Used to love watching Davie Cooper on Brian's old Rangers Greats DVDs – the way he shimmied and feinted through a defence – but I'm exchanging the currency of Cooper's tragic death at a young age and feel a bit grubby for using the man's legacy in this way.

Cage nods. He picks up a pint and drains it. Then he starts stamping his foot to the beat. '"Hu-llo! Hu-llo! We are the Billy Boys."'

There are a few uninspired murmurs around him.

'"Hu-llo! Hu-llo! Ye'll know us by our noise."' Cage stares at me. 'Ken the next line, wee man?'

'Aye.'

'Sing it, then.'

'Um . . .' I begin, testing out just how much time clearing your throat can buy.

Frannie says, 'C'mon, Cage, supposed to be a perty.'

'Aye,' says Cage, 'a perty I'm tryin tay get started! Sing the next line, wee man. "We're uptay our knees in"?'

'"We're uptay our knees in . . ." um . . .'

'In?' he says, leaning forwards. 'Whose blood?'

'"Feen . . ."' I swallow.

He pats Chaz's arm and laughs. 'The boy looks like he's gonnay pass oot! C'mon, pal, ye allergic tay the word?'

'Son?' Dolby says. He is taking in the whole group as though they're turning demonic before him, and even I'm shocked when he stands up and says, 'You needing the toilet, wee man?'

'Uh,' I say. 'No.'

'Not you. *Jack.*'

Jack's gaze climbs all the way up the totem pole of his father. 'Not really.'

'Frannie,' Dolby commands, 'goan take him tay the toilet.'

Cage is contemplating this, just feeling the weight of it, happening before him. Dolby's tall. Dolby has stood. Dolby has requested the removal of his son from the scene.

'Aye,' says Frannie, tugging at the hand of Jack, who is glancing between Dolby and Cage, sensing something, 'C'mon, pal. Let's just make sure ye're no needing.'

'But I'm no needing . . .' Jack's whine trails off as Frannie pulls him into the bar.

'Right,' says Dolby, his face filling with crimson. 'Enough ay this bullshit.'

'Whit bullshit's that?' says Bex. All eyes are on Dolby now. Cage is acting as though a stand-up comedian's stepped onto the stage in front of him.

'This Catholic-Protestant pish. Yese chuck yer lot in wi these daft concepts . . . a fitbaw team, a religion. Blind alleys, mate.'

'No daft tay us,' says Jeff. But they're still listening.

'Yese are fuckin workin class,' says Dolby, sweeping his finger round them. 'Catholics arenay the enemy. The enemy's up there.' Dolby points to an invisible race of gods floating above Manchester.

Cage sniffs and taps the side of his beer bottle.

'Yese hearday this credit crunch?' says Dolby.

'Obviously,' says Chaz. 'We're no monkeys.'

'Nice wee cute phrase, eh?' says Dolby. 'Credit crunch. Sounds like a breakfast cereal, eh?'

Rab snorts and looks to the group to convert this into laughter.

But Dolby isn't giving up the floor so easily. 'Do ye realise whit they've done tay us?' he says, a teacher now, shaming a class into silence. 'Do ye ken whit the implications are gonnay be in the next few years? On yer jobs? On yer mortgages? On yer pensions?'

'You tell us, mate,' says Cage, reining in his defiance.

Dolby places his fists on the table and leans forward onto them. 'They are about tay fuckin shaft us, Cage. And it's got absolutely nothin tay dae wi Ulster, or whether or no a wafer really is the body ay Christ, or even yer precious team winnin the day.' He points at the sky again, and two or three of them actually glance up. 'They're comin tay get us.'

Then, his anger too much to be contained, or realising he's just spoken as though the Nazgul themselves are on our case, he turns from the table and strides towards the steps that lead to the street. I swallow and see them all there, cowed and drinking their confusion, and charge after him, unutterably proud.

'Mate,' I say, grabbing his shoulder and spinning him round. His eyes are alert and alive.

'Phone Frannie. Let's get ootay here,' he seethes, the hippy in him banished. 'I've had enough ay these pricks. That Cage is doing ma heid in.' I wonder if this is for my benefit, cos of the bother I've been getting from Cage.

'I'm fine, man,' I reassure him. 'I'm not sixteen any more, I can look after myself.'

'Alvin,' Dolby says, in the same voice he uses when he comes back from the toilet on a mong night to find I've replaced his iPod in the docking station with mine, 'it's no always about about *you*, pal. I've got the wee man wi me. I'm no wantin him around this any mair. And the worse hings get doon here, the worse that journey's gonnay be on the wey back up the road.'

'We shouldn't have come.'

'Well.' Dolby's head bobs about this issue. 'We're here noo, so let's make the maistay it. If only for the wee man.' His mouth twitches. 'And for Frannie. We cannay let him doon.'

'Can we no?' I mutter.

Dolby narrows his eyes and shakes his head.

'We could always take Frannie and dump the restay them?' I suggest.

'Well, that's whit I'm sayin,' Dolby says. 'Head tay another bar, say we'll get them back at the—'

'No,' I say, staring at him. 'Dump them . . . in Manchester.'

Dolby recoils. 'Ye mean leave withoot them?'

I nod slowly. 'No as if we're ever gonnay see them again.'

'Aye, you live in Edinburgh,' he says. 'Fawkurt's no that wee. I'd get ma fuckin heid kicked in.' I let this tick and turn in his brain, though. He breathes in and then out. 'Only as a last resort,' he says. 'Only if wannay them smacks wannay us or somethin.'

Oh, I almost want them to now! Something bares its teeth inside me. Dolby folds his arms and takes me in, the fullness of me there before him. Half admiration, half suspicion.

'Leavin Fawkurt's really done somethin tay you, man.'

mamamamamamamamamamamamama ma ma ma
mamama ma mamama ma mamamamamama ma ma
mamamama ma mamamama ma ma ma mamamama
mamamama ma ma mamama mama

Sometimes I wonder what my life at Stirling University would've been like had it not been John I'd first encountered in the kitchen that day, had it not been John who'd bounded across, tasted the pasta sauce and said, 'Add pepper,' had it not been John who was the first person ever to tell me that not only was my accent cool, but so was my name, and taken it upon himself to invite me to the Long Bar with the new friends he'd been 'collecting like chloroformed butterflies' that day, had it not been John who'd bought me my first tinkling drink and introduced me to Greg, Malcolm, Gordon, Mark, Robert, Elaine, Lucie, Emma, Liz, Laura, Jen, Anthony, Tony, Graham, Nick, Hannah, Douglas, David, Charlotte, Brett, Joe, Susan, Daragh, William, Andy, Skeeter, Richie, Sara, Lenny, Ursula, Eric, Sudesh, Nora, Karen, Richard the Fish, Orlagh, Louise, Kenny and Amber. The student union seemed five times busier than Rosie's in Falkirk had ever been on a Friday. It preened with youth. And no one had their own pre-set crowd to hang around with yet, so everyone was talking to everyone. *Everyone was talking to everyone!* Such things did not happen at school. All the brainy and alternative kids had just been given the run of the world, not quite knowing what to make of it yet, waiting for the eventual fist or catcall, but the only thing that came for them was more booze. People stepped around each other at first, nodding and umming into drinks, their interests making a hopeful cloud of insect-life between them. Fresh-faced lads fell into sturdy sport chat. Pot-smokers sensed each other's stash. The denizens of the Games Workshop raised their armpits to each other and grunted. We drank. We drank more. We asked each other – routinely, as though on some vast speed date – So where are you from? What are you studying? What hall are you staying in? Where are you from? Whereareyoufrom whatareyoustudyingwhathallareyoustayingingwhereare youfreomwhatareyo

A thousand kids whirling away from the parental influence for the first time ever, who'd all just been given a big load of cash and let loose on a campus with a loch, ducks, rabbits, squirrels, an off-licence, two bars, two nightclubs: out of the way of neds, weapons, surveillance cameras and the police.

To me, the University of Stirling on 10 September 2001 was Utopia itself.

I nodded when people spoke to me, and listened to the bizarre array of accents – Scouse, Weegie, Teuchter, Fifer, Londoner Brummie, Geordie – which I could pick up and sample as though from a box of chocolates, tasting their crunchy, hometown awkwardness and the sweet ambition rolling from their centre. The jukebox rapped out Dr Dre, and we sank pints and pool balls and contemplated Tennessee Williams plays, that new BBC sitcom The Office, and the amazing sound that Kylie Minogue had managed to find on Can't Get You Out Of My Head. Haven't you heard it? It's out next week. Oh, it's amazing. Amazing. It's going to change everything.

John seemed connected to it all, the fulcrum of the evening, neither too showy nor too shy. He sat in the same corner of the union all night, and people moved magically round him, touched his shoulder here, slid a drink before him there. The girls pecked around his clothes – his hat, inevitably, did the rounds – or just listened to him talk about how he was going to be a music journalist. He'd already done a gig review for the NME. The NME! Then it was the dogs he'd left behind in London, Jarvis and Jacko, while girls' faces melted into canine sympathy. 'Jarvis,' he sighed, 'gets really moody, but he's got a good heart. Jacko's just a big show-off. He loves everybody.' A girl said something about how hard it was, how much she was going to miss her hamster, and there was a flick of irritation on John's face, which landed and flew off before she could notice, and he was saying, 'Yeah, it's difficult,' and nodding himself out of the conviction that it wasn't, y'know, remotely the fucking same. As she impersonated her hamster, bucked her teeth and turned an invisible wheel with her 'cute wee paws', he glanced knowingly at me, and I grew annoyed at her because I wanted to hear John talking more about his dogs.

ma ma ma ma

We detach from the rest of the supporters' bus, making the excuse that Frannie's off to meet Stuart Storrie; there's much pointing to phones and handshakes and some comradely, 'Mon, Rangers'. Cage eyes us as we go. 'Aye, youse enjoy yersels, boys, eh?' He blows me a kiss and the rest of them guffaw, and as we go up the stone steps from the canal that leads back onto the street, I feel my skin hiss.

'Just ignore it, Alvin,' says Frannie, as though he's glanced at the thermometer above my head.

'Aye,' I fume. 'Wankstain.'

Jack, being carried up the stairs by Dolby for speed, widens his eyes at me, and damn he's tucked that one away. A BAD WORD. Bloody Cage. Blimming Cage. Nope, doesn't have the same ring as Wankstain. I'm almost proud to introduce it into Jack's vocabulary. 'Are we sharing the bus with those men on the way back up, Daddy?'

'Aye, pal.'

'They're very noisy.'

Frannie tuts and mutters, 'It's a fitbaw match, of course it's noisy.'

We've just made it up onto the street, into the blazing sunshine, when we hear a doof-doof-doof of jogging feet and then, 'Boys! Boys!' and all of us turn to see Chrissie puffing her way to the top step. 'Wonder if I might come wi yese?' she says, hand flapping in the direction of the canal bar. 'That lot are daein ma heid in. Prefer the company ay younger men onywey.' She winks at me.

'Right,' says Frannie, the day seeming to freeze around him. 'Well.'

Chrissie skips in front of us, glances over her shoulder to see if we're coming, then punches her fists, one by one, into the air rhythmically. '"Follow, follow . . . We will follow Rangers!"'

Frannie huffily stuffs his hands into his pockets. 'You'd better feed her and water her, Alvin, and take her oot for walks.'

'Don't be so sexist,' I mutter, watching Chrissie stop random strangers for a boogie. They leave her waltzing embrace each time with chuckling shoulders, sometimes even photos on their phones.

'Jesus Christ,' Frannie says, watching her. 'That's somebody's mother.'

'Leave her alone,' Dolby growls. I wonder if Leanne's on his mind.

We all troop away in silence for a bit, as we hear huge drums beat from somewhere in the city.

The sun has reached the topmost point of the sky, lording it like Ra with his arms folded. We walk through the streets, which are full with bodies now, making Jack into a tiny, intrepid fairytale character among the forest of them. As we round a corner, we discover a film crew who've set up camp, interviewing a thick-necked bald guy. Frannie removes his shades and raises a hand for us to stop, eyes flicking from the camera to the presenter to the singing fans providing a lairy backdrop.

'This is Manchester,' the bald guy's saying, mock-steel in his voice. 'Glasgow Rangers are playing Zenit St Petersburg from Russia in the UEFA Cup Final. For most Rangers fans this will be the biggest day of their footballing lives.'

He works the air as though he's showing the audience at home how to prepare a cake.

'But there have been rumours the day will be infiltrated by *thug* groups hell bent on causing . . .'

He pauses, and it's not hard to imagine the camera zooming in on his wide, toad-like face.

'. . . CHAOS.'

Chrissie calmly walks across and stands between him and the camera. 'I just wantay say, on behalf of the Rangers support, that there will be no trouble here today. This is sensationalist journalism from an ex-England hooligan.' She turns to point towards the presenter, who has thrown up his hands as though this is the tenth time today. 'This is a celebration of football and youse should be ashamed of yourselves. So there.'

Having said her piece, she trots back to us and makes a simple nod for us to stroll on.

'Like yer style, Chrissie,' Frannie says.

She gives him a cheeky smile. 'So did halfay Fawkurt at wan time, son.'

Randomly, we've found ourselves in the city's northern quarter, a warren of indie bars, record shops and gig venues, which instantly bewitches us. We stand transfixed for at least a minute staring at a giant mural on the side of a building, Manchester music legends: Morrissey, Shaun Ryder, Liam Gallagher, Ian Curtis. The mystical significance of this. Our heads are bowed, as they bestow momentary cool upon us. Chrissie plays with a stray dog, teaching it how to eat Maltesers: 'Now crunch . . .'

'Ah, Manchester,' Frannie says. 'It's just rock 'n' roll.'

Our hands chop from our heads in salute. Jack does the same, then says, 'Who are we saluting?'

'Authority,' said Frannie, staring into the big blue eyes of Liam Gallagher. 'The man just had *authority*.'

We walk into a bar, which my Edinburgh-honed senses can

immediately tell is hipster: they're playing Talking Heads and the woman serving behind the bar is dressed like a 1950s film star, with bright red lipstick and an elaborate Marilyn Monroe coiffure. Night and Day, it's called. Chrissie goes strolling into the centre of it, turns round once and points at the barmaid.

'You look brilliant, hen,' she says, giving a thumbs-up, which makes Marilyn smile as she pulls a pint.

Frannie mutters and checks out the skinny-jeaned patrons, their winklepickers and Mad Men-parted hair, as though it's all just farted right under his nose. Chrissie goes to the glowing jukebox, tugging Jack after her, 'Mon, pal, help me choose a song,' and Jack sprints towards it as though it's the mothership from Close Encounters of the Third Kind. I head up to the bar – order a Stella for Frannie; another white wine ('large, please') for Chrissie, which I'm hoping she won't notice is actually a small; orange juices for Dolby and Jack, and for me—

'Yes,' the barmaid says, her hands already pouring these drinks.

I intend to say Diet Coke but what comes out is, 'And a white wine for me, please. Large.'

'Okay,' she says, as though I'd simply asked for a drink and not broken a vow, made on the sofa last week watching The Wire, when I realised that the glass, which was just about to touch my lips, was my ninth of the week.

It was Tuesday.

I check over my shoulder: Dolby and Frannie are deep in conversation about Cage. The phrases 'mental health' and 'anger issues' and 'bet he's in denial about actually being a Catholic' are lobbed back and forth. Neither of them notices what I've done. When the wine arrives I take two gulps – it burns wonderfully, fresh and sharp – and Marilyn sees this. 'You don't do things by halves, you lot, do you?'

'If you were stuck inside all of this,' I say, batting a hand towards the epic scale of it outside, 'what would you do?'

'Sugar,' she says, handing me Frannie's pint, 'I *am* stuck inside it. Some of us live in this city, you know.'

I carry the tray of drinks back to the table, as the first pleasant calm from the wine just stretches in my mind, and set it down. 'Put it this wey,' Dolby's telling Frannie, 'I just think yer pal Cage is a wee bit, eh, intense.'

'Hey,' I point out, 'did you not hear yourself doing the whole Che Guevara bit?'

Dolby holds up his fist and poses for history's photo.

'Lightweights,' Frannie grumbles. 'That's just a supporters'-bus cerry-on. I dinnay like it, but ye just learn tay ignore it.'

'C'mon, man,' says Dolby. 'No really wantin Jack exposed tay that kinday bigotry.'

'Well, whit the fuck did ye bring him for?' Frannie tuts, with the expression of a man who has just accidentally filled his car with diesel.

'Ho,' Dolby says. 'Easy, tiger.'

Frannie directs his eye around the bar for something with less irritant value, succeeds: two girls sitting further down, early twenties, their bright parakeet laughter. His whole face changes, clicking with intent, and he stands, tugging my jacket.

I look to Dolby for silent advice; he opens his hands as though to say, *be my guest*, and almost automatically I am rising and following Frannie on wingman duty.

Wingman duty terrifies me. The infinity of ways it can go. Frannie loves to play with the possibilities, can stretch his fingertips into them, shape them, roll his personality up in them, and the role of the wingman is crucial in supplying laughs after a gag, or supporting a story with a smirk and a poised, 'Oh, this is a good one,' but, really, no one wanted to be Goose in Top Gun. They wanted to be Maverick. And Frannie has flown a thousand successful missions over enemy lines. For the last ten years he's had his pick of Tesco's yearly intake of school leavers, choosing his moment when the tills are slowest, and tedium has softened her defences, beep beep beep beep beep

sixtypoundsninetyplease beep beep

beep beepbeep beephundredandfivepoundsplease beep

see you hen?

beep beep beep

beepbeep beep beepbeepbeep *see me whit?*

fortytwopoundsthreepenceplease

beep beep beepbeepbeep beep

beep beep

ever tied a guy up? *Em . . .*

He's twenty-seven, old enough to have that experienced man thing happening for a teenage lassie, not old enough to totally creep them out. Plenty of disposable income, which goes on Mod clothes, his car, gigs, and now, of course, that Tag Heuer.

It's like skywriting to them. Frannie gets to live out his Fredo-from-The-Godfather-bangin-checkout-girls-like-they're-cocktail-waitresses dreams; she gets to go into work on the Monday and slag him off. Everyone moves on, changes partners, a dance, a new recruitment intake, another staff leaving do. It repeats itself. The Circle of Life. Let's face it, he's trapped in it. All of us are, our version of it anyway, getting on with our day, breathing the deodorant cloud of our own egos and just trying not to fuck ourselves up more and more each year.

We join them and the girls appraise us: Rangers top, Captain America T-shirt. They project nothingness at us, and I sense immediately the uphill struggle. 'Hi,' I say, trying to make the word one of infinite fascination.

'Hi,' they say.

I haven't arsed anything up yet, though. This is good.

One of them is a blonde wearing what looks like a man's suit; the other has a nose ring and dyed red hair. Frannie couldn't have chosen more poorly, I know this immediately, but according to him there is no such thing as the wrong target, only the wrong arrow. 'There's nay use blamin them for your lame patter, ya shower ay desperate fucks.'

Which I thought was pretty decent of him, actually.

He appraises the girls and opens his routine, grinning, limbs relaxed. 'Hello there, ladies, I'm Frannie, this is ma mate, Alvin.' He holds up a hand commandingly. 'Please, no chipmunk jokes. It upsets him.'

'Ha ha ha.' I laugh on cue.

Nose Ring cocks her head. 'Were you named after the chipmunk?'

'Naw,' I say. 'Em. My mum was a big Alvin Stardust fan when she was wee.'

'Who's Alvin Stardust?'

'Aw, he'll be able tay tell ye that.' Frannie bats my arm with the back of his hand. 'Alvin's the brainy wan. Got a degree and everythin, despite the fact that he has about as much common sense as a—'

'What was your degree in?' the blonde girl interrupts him to ask me, and it feels like a brief touch of the accelerator.

'The bin by now, probably,' Frannie says, and I shoot him a look. He shoots one back: Keep yer end up, mate, we can win this.

'English literature.'

The girls nod eagerly and Nose Ring says, 'Hey, that's what we're studying. Up at the Met.'

'Sorry,' Frannie cuts in, 'whit did youse girls say yer names were?'

'Oh,' says the blonde. 'I'm Terri and this is George.'

'Right,' Frannie says. 'Both boys' names.' I can see his eyes working this up into a quip but Terri turns to me before he can unleash it.

'So, Alvin.' She's actually smiling now, patting the top of the table just in front of me, 'Random English graduate chat. What did you do your dissertation on?'

'Uh . . .' I say, worried about telling them the truth (Clive Barker). 'It was a comparison between . . . Lord Byron and Robert Burns.'

'No way,' George says. 'I'm doing a module on Romantic Poetry right now.'

Frannie is watching this conversation unfold, and although he's nodding and going, 'Mm,' he's also swallowing more than usual.

A conversation catches light between me and the two girls about our favourite Romantic poems, and George smiles and goes, 'Yeah yeah yeah. I mean, some of that stuff had real revolutionary potential, y'know? It's not all hearts and flowers and shit.'

'Oh, totally,' I agree. 'I mean, the French revolution really galvanised the English poets at that time.'

'We could be doing with some more of that now,' George adds.

'So inspiring,' I say, while Frannie coughs.

'But!' Terri says. 'What a *scoundrel* that Lord Byron was.'

'I know.' George growls and drops her voice. 'I would've definitely given him one.'

'Oh, me too,' I add and she smiles, her gaze solidifying on mine for a second.

'Whit?' says Frannie, head swivelling.

The way that all three of them are looking at me forces me to expel the word, 'Kidding'.

'I wis gonnay say, likes!' Frannie laughs and touches the girl's wrist reassuringly. 'It's awright, he's no wannay them.'

'One of them?' she says, and moves her eyes, calculatedly, down towards his hand.

'He's no a poof. He just acts like it sometimes.'

They both blink at him, before turning back to me, synchronised. One of them leans forwards and pats my arm. 'We hope you guys have a good day, but we've, uh . . . we've got to go.'

'So soon?' says Frannie. 'But I didnay get the chance tay propose!'

They push themselves up from the table and make medium-strength goodbyes.

'Sure thing,' he intones, watching them go.

'Love the Captain America T-shirt,' Terri tells me.

'It loves you,' I manage, and it sparks a smile, and then they're out the door and Frannie is going Cujo on me. 'For fucksakes, Alvin!'

'What?' I say, as we rise and cross back to the table, dragging our bloody carcases.

When we sit down, Dolby and Chrissie demand a match report. 'That didnay go too well,' she says, amused.

'Ye're shocked?' Dolby asks her. 'You never had a night oot in the Martell wi them.'

Frannie covers his eyes with a latticework of fingers. 'They must've thought I was like you!'

I fold my arms and examine the various angles and contours of this. 'What do you mean, *like me*?'

'I mean a rock 'n' roll party animal who sooks jelly-beans from nuns' fannies, Alvin. Is it no obvious? Fuck is aw that "I fancy Lord Bunton" business about?'

'Lord Byron.'

'Think they wanted tay be the fillin in a gay sandwich?' He

looks at me despairingly, then pauses. 'Actually, I'm quite hungry. Is it too late tay order lunch?'

'Em, aye, man,' says Dolby. 'It's half three.'

Chrissie chortles and Frannie runs his hands through his hair. 'Somethin funny, hen?'

'You're jealous ay him, aren't ye?'

'Whit?' he goes. 'Of Little Lord Fauntleroy there?'

'Why don't you shut your mouth?' I snap at him, and Dolby is widening his eyes at the two of us and commanding, 'Lads,' and pointing at Jack. 'It's not the time or place for it.'

But Chrissie has found Frannie's exposed underbelly and is prodding it with a sharp stick. 'Wee Alvin done better than you just then and ye cannay take it.'

'Hey,' Frannie says, deflecting this, 'I've got tay let him win once in a while, eh? Just so he can mind he's still got a dick.'

Jack looks up at his daddy to gauge his reaction to this word. 'Frannie,' says Dolby, 'I'm no gonnay ask ye again. Mind yer language.'

'What's a dick, Daddy?'

'I'm looking at one, son,' Dolby growls, his eyes demolishing Frannie.

Jack does some mental origami. 'Uncle Frannie's a dick?'

Chrissie's giggling and clapping. 'Ooh!' she goes. 'Got it in one, pal.'

Frannie raises his bottle with a Hollywood cockiness, and opens his arms to the whole bar, shouting, 'I'm a dick! I'm a fuckin dick, everybody!' – and instantly I see his future. He has threads of silver in his feather-cut hair and he's ducking and diving around Tesco, still evangelising about Mod to the school leavers, and this, ultimately, is his fate, my fate, Dolby, Brian and Cage's fates, the fate of every single man on this earth:

Old Bastard.

The lines won't come with as much confidence, the girls won't smile as readily, but Old Bastard will try anyway. He'll try even if they don't want him to. He'll patronise them. Then he'll grow angry when they reject him. Old Bastard goes home to children who won't be able to imagine that he was ever a beautiful boy-child with dreams cascading about him. All Old Bastards were once Young Men burning with a sense of their own significance. Born to rule the earth. *We are drifting*, I want to tell Frannie, clinging to him on a life-raft in the middle of the sea. *We are losing ourselves. Our worst natures are winning.*

But men speak of no such things.

'Come on,' I protest. 'I was talkin tay them on their level. I was tryin to show them that Rangers supporters arenay aw bigots.'

Dolby laughs. 'Since when were *you* a Rangers supporter?'

'Ho!' say Frannie and Chrissie, both at once. 'Bigots!'

'For the club,' I protest. 'For the club's self-image.'

'Listen,' says Frannie, 'ye really think it's gid for the club's self-image that oor fans present themselves tay the world as poofs?'

'Look,' I say, something emerging from its torpor to take him on, 'this is Night and Day. One of Manchester's coolest bars. That kinday talk goes doon well in here.'

'Get yerself backtay Canal Street.' Frannie flaps a dismissive hand. 'Goan make us some cash.'

'Dinnay push it,' I grunt at him.

Chrissie's watching this, rapt, as though we're cockerels she's thrown into a ring together. Dolby sighs like Joe in Reservoir Dogs, seeing Mr Blonde and Nice Guy Eddie wrestle around his office. 'Awright, boys, come on, quit it, eh?'

Frannie looks about, impervious to the indie spell of the place. 'Prefer the Scotia anyway.'

'The Scotia?' I scoff. 'Well, I prefer my kidneys where they are.'

'Problem wi the Scotia?' he says. 'Oh, is it too *Fawkurt* for you these days, Alvin?'

'Whit's that supposed tay mean?'

'The Scotia's a good boozer.'

'Exactly,' I say. 'It's a boozer. Ken. For *boozers*?'

'Fuck off, ya pretentious prick.' Frannie folds his arms. 'Whit happened tay you, man?'

'Wooft,' Chrissie says, raising her eyebrows. 'Whaur's that come fay? You boys dae it *properly* when ye faw oot, eh?'

'Stirling University,' says Frannie. 'That's whaur it comes fay.'

'Mate,' says Dolby, 'easy. Ye're outtay line there, Franman.'

Frannie pulls back his seat, which clatters to the floor, and heads to the toilet, a cowboy quitting a poker game. He eyes a couple of skinny guys at the bar, supping lattes in their drainpipe jeans and T-shirts for bands none of us will have heard of, as though they're actually eating oysters, reading the

Telegraph and discussing how they can rid themselves of the proletarian scum.

'Christ, man, whit's his problem?'

Dolby lets the argument go. 'Just ignore it, ye ken whit he's like. Ye insult his favourite pub, it's like insultin him. The Scotia serves his blood on draught.'

'I'm no puttin up wi that, man.'

Dolby's grinning.

'Whit?'

'Ye not noticed?'

'Noticed whit?'

'Soon as Frannie challenged ye, yer accent went Fawkurt.'

'Did it?'

'Aye,' says Chrissie, glittering with this, as though my true accent is a pearl she's just found in a clam on the beach. 'Can ye no hear it?'

'Naw. I mean. No. I mean.' I cover my face. 'Och, I dinnay ken.'

Chrissie screws up her eyes and looks along a finger at me. 'Like it or no, boy, you are still one ay us. That's whit yer real problem is wi yer pal Frannie there.'

'Whit do you mean?'

'I bet he's no changed any. I bet he's still the same guy he always wis?'

'Unfortunately,' I say. 'So whit?'

'But you're no. Ye just dinnay want tay face whaur ye came fay. Aw he's doin is remindin ye, so ye should lay aff him.'

Her face settles into a so-there, and I open my mouth to

reply to this but nothing comes out.

Just then a barman shouts, 'Hoy!' and we all turn to see him dash past and start hammering on the window, at the other side of which stands a Rangers fan freely pishing. 'You can't do that here!' the barman barks, but the fan swings a big cow gaze up to peer through the steam and decipher the barman's facial expression. His penis is fat and wrinkled, in full view of the bar, the gush leaving a yellow fan on the glass. Dolby turns Jack away from it with an 'Oh, Jesus Christ.'

Chrissie's straight up at the window, banging on it like a Fury who's been locked up for a thousand years. 'Ho, you, ya dirty bastard! We've got weans in here. You should be ashamed of yersel!'

The man opens his mouth and lets his tongue unroll from it, starts flicking it up and down at Chrissie. In an instant, she's making for the door – 'Oh, you fuckin cheeky—' and we watch her through the glass, muted, remonstrating with the guy, arms flailing, while he casually tucks his penis away and trots off.

Frannie comes back from the toilet, looking at his phone. His gait is loose, his bad mood dispelled as though it were a mere programme glitch. 'Another text fay Brian,' he says, holding up his phone and smiling.

'Another yin?' says Dolby. 'No got work tay dae in that bar ay his?'

'Askin how the day's shapin up.' Frannie starts texting chirpily.

'Whit ye tellin him?'

'To stop botherin us when we're in a brothel.'

Jack finishes scribbling and glances up. 'What's a brothel, Daddy?'

Dolby clenches before he fires a hot look at Frannie. 'It's, uh, a place where ladies of the night live, son.'

'Ladies of the night,' says Jack. 'Like . . . vampires?'

Frannie laughs. 'Mind whit Brian telt us about his mate in Amsterdam? Guy says she put an alarm clock nextay the bed. Soon as it went aff, so did she. Like a microwave. Says he wis *that* close.'

One of the bar staff approaches our table, lifts our drinks.

'Hey,' I say. 'Wisnay finished that.'

'That's whit Brian's mate said!' Frannie adds, with d-doom tsh!

'Sorry, guys,' says the barman, retrieving drinks with obvious relish, 'You'll have to go, we're shutting the place.'

'At half four?'

'Police orders,' the guy says. 'Sorry.'

Frannie hmmmms, hides his drink as though it's a party game. 'Police?' he says. 'Orders?'

Dolby shoots me a glance as if to say: Jack.

'In which case, gents' – Frannie lifts his nose snootishly – 'we'll take our custom elsewhere.'

'You'll struggle,' the barman says. 'All of the bars are shutting.'

'*All* of them?' says Dolby. 'Every bar in Manchester?'

'That's right. Pubs are packed out. Police think things are getting a bit rowdy.'

'Ken why that is?' says Frannie.

'Why?'

'Cos yese don't sell Irn Bru.' The dude gives him a wiseguy look, then turns for the bar, indifferent to our plight.

I glance out of the window grimly. Chrissie has lit up a fag and is sucking on it, arms tucked into her body, and her face seems vague, troubled, watching the street fill up around her.

'Suppose we should just headtay the fan zone?' Dolby suggests.

'Aye,' says Frannie. 'Sun's shinin. Buy a cerry-oot. Let the red, white and blue intay oor hearts.'

The crowd marching its way to the game. Raised cans. Clapping hands. Mouths stretched with song. Someone slams against the window; a thudding blue ricochet. *Ho, ya fanny!* His mate turns him round, throws him back into the mass.

'Sure it's safe?' I say.

Chrissie is patrolling in front of the window, fag jutted, vigilant for pissers.

'Course it is,' Frannie says. 'We've got her.'

'Are we goin out into all them men, Daddy?'

'We are, son, aye. That's the only way we can see the game.'

A Zenit fan drifts past, a lost ghost. He sees Jack through the window, smiles and waves. Jack waves back. Then the man shifts between the bodies of Rangers fans and out of sight. Jack cranes his neck to look for him, but he is gone.

ma

ma ma

ma ma

The mist shivered on the water's surface and John proclaimed himself to the campus, to the heavens, like a lost god, while all of us laughed, eyes twinkling and bewildered with drink. Stirling University answered us back: Yes. You belong here. Back at A. K. Davidson Hall, though, the booze and the tiredness overtook everyone and they pinballed to bed, realising that Fresher's Week had another five nights of this left in store. John watched them all go, personally affronted – 'Come on, my room doesn't even smell of anything yet!' – but apologies were batted away with weary hands and he was turning to me and offering a hopeful shrug.

'I'll stay up with you,' I said, with all the might and presence of a child reading the news.

'Good.' He winked, before running down his corridor with an insane shout and bounding into his room.

By the time I caught up with him, he'd lifted himself onto the study desk and crossed his legs. I could see the brand label on his boxer shorts where his baggy jeans fell down past it. He fished in a drawer to retrieve what looked like a pipe and a bag of grass (I'd seen this paraphernalia at school parties, mythical and strange). Humming what sounded like The Simpsons theme-tune, John filled the bowl, while I nodded sagely as though demonstrating how totally cool with this I was.

Parties drifted and trilled across the campus, spectral revelries. Everything was still alive out there. John's room had art prints on the walls – that one with someone screaming, and that other one with sunflowers, I can't remember what they're called – and beneath them keyboards and electronics were lined up like artificial intelligences. While he prepared the weed, I pressed a wee Casio with leads plugged into a bizarre machine. It was mute.

'Do you want it on?' John said. 'Can you play?'

'No,' I said. 'Well, apart fay the Jaws theme.'

'A whole two notes?'

'Aye, but whit a two notes!'

John smiled and lit the pipe. He was still wearing his hat and it bent low over one of his eyes. I could see the sparse chest hairs peeking out from the ripped neck of his T-shirt. I wanted to ask him why he'd ripped his T-shirt, but knew what the answer would've been: Cos it looks cool as fuck, mate. I was wondering what the Lads would make of him. Up his own arse or a good geezer? What would he be like on a stag night? Would he bond with Brian over 'fit birds', Frannie over fitba, and Dolby over films? Would we roll, leery and pished, towards a lap-dancing bar, toasting the blessed union of Scotland and England? Or would they want to punch fuck out of him? The impossibility of knowing this made him exciting.

John blew out some smoke, and it touched the air with soft fingers of illegality. He held out the pipe and lighter and I took them from him.

It wasn't as though this hadn't happened to me before. I mean, you couldn't be a Pink Floyd fan without someone offering you a cheeky toke while Dark Side of the Moon tolled its stoner approval. I'd always refused, prim and polite, but for some reason my left hand was turning the business end of the pipe towards me as my right clicked the lighter, long before I could even formulate the thought: *Remember what happened to Syd Barrett.*

None of the clichés took place. I didn't cough all over John's room. Instead, I was aware of a gentle burn at the back of my throat, then a phantom-like presence in my lungs. When they released, I was thrilled to see a dragon-cloud, which had actually been inside me, rise into the air. I was a criminal Bilbo.

'Woah,' John said, flapping a hand at the smoke. 'A heavy hitter.'

I gave him the pipe back as though it was no big deal. John gestured to it and said, 'Need to see where I can pick up a regular supply in this town. You know anyone?'

'Whit's that?' I said, and couldn't help it: a cough finally stepped out of my lungs like a weak deer.

'Do you know anyone I could buy some weed from?' He thought about it. 'And maybe some E.'

The question scrunched in my brain for a second. 'Whit makes ye think I'd ken anyone who could get ye drugs?'

'Um, well,' he said, 'your accent. Sorry, I just presumed . . .'

You're simply the best!

Manchester roars Tina Turner, Hunly, and Jack glances up. As we turn out from Oldham Street onto the busy thoroughfare of Market Street, men in identical blue football shirts appear from out of lanes, bars, supermarkets, jigging with their drinks and dreams of winning, the cheery, dancing columns of them filling streets, a churning river heading, directed by some divine sense, towards the centre of the city, the Gathering, the Mecca promised to them for millennia, where they will meet, as a vast parliament.

Aye, it's pretty fucking busy all right.

An auld guy in a Rangers scarf and hat combo comes up beside us, does a wizened turn on the spot and pretends to play the flute.

'Gon yersel, pal,' says Chrissie, clapping his bony shoulders. 'Ye havin a gid yin?'

The man rolls his head and tries to speak, his face glowing under the brief heat-lamp of Chrissie's attention, then says something like, 'Sorta ffffff kinda um wis wunnern.' He falters and pats Frannie's back instead. 'Ye know the score, mate.'

'How can I know the score?' Frannie laughs. 'The game's no started yet!'

Then with the utmost clarity the old guy raises a finger to Chrissie and goes, 'You are a beautiful wummin.'

'Aw,' she says, giving him a hug and beaming at us as though he's just supplied evidence in a case she's been trying to crack for years. 'And you are a gentleman.'

He nods and smiles, humbled by this comment. 'Thanks, hen. Have a good day, lads. MON, THE RANGERS.' Then he stumbles off and collides with a building.

Jack, pulled to and fro, and with no other children to stimulate him, has started to whine. He's turning about on the end of Dolby's arm and saying, 'When are we going home, Dad?' in a twisty voice, and Dolby very patiently replies, 'You'll enjoy it when the game starts, pal,' but his eyes look as heavy as Jack's dragged heels.

We pass a supermarket, its sliding doors like a gag reflex disgorging blue bodies. 'Right,' says Frannie. 'Booze. We'll overlook the fact that it's Sainsbury's an no Tesco. We need tay stock the fuck up.'

'I'm oan it!' Chrissie says, her voice smart as an army general's. 'Alvin, will you demonstrate yer good breedin and help a lady oot?'

'Um,' I say. 'Me? But I'm not even drinkin.'

Dolby now has Jack teetering on his shoulders in an attempt to keep him entertained. Frannie, I can see, has no intention of going anywhere with Chrissie that he doesn't really have to.

Chrissie looks up at me hopefully from beneath her fringe. 'Please, son,' she says. 'I'll no be able tay cerry oot the cerry-oot without ye. I thought you were a man wi manners.'

It's as though Sainsbury's last board meeting was infiltrated by a militant Protestant outfit, who'd forced exclusive trading-rights for themselves only. The queue is a shifting blue serpent that writhes right through the Snakes and Ladders board of the store. We are jostled, hustled, bustled, wrestled; we clamber through to the alcohol shelves barely intact. That's where the real fight begins. All along the aisle, hands grasp for cans and bottles: Strongbow, Tennants, Jacob's Creek, Gordon's,

Smirnoff, fucking *Cinzano*. For a second, me and Chrissie are stunned by the raptor-fastness of it, before realising we might lose out completely. We start unloading twelve-packs, waddling with them towards the queue. If you can call it a queue. It's more a sort of double-helix shape.

'Going to take us an age to get served,' I groan.

'Fuck that,' says Chrissie, loaded with as many six-packs as she can muster. 'Let's just take it.'

'I'm not going to steal drink, Chrissie.'

'Why no?' she says, her gaze sharp. 'Ye give a shit about the profits ay Sainsbury?'

'That's not the point.'

Her face drops. Her shoulders slacken. 'Listen, son, I have just lost ma job. Did ye ken that? I just wantay enjoy masel the day.'

'What's that got to do with me stealing you drink?'

'It's no just for me. It's for yer mate Frannie.' She throws a stare at me. 'And you. You want some tay, don't ye?'

'I'm not drinking today,' I say emphatically. 'Well. Not drinking any *more* anyway . . .'

She softens her voice. 'Please.'

So much like a conversation with Mum. 'No.'

'Thoosands ay folk in here!' she hisses. 'Look at them. They're totally overrun. Think they'll even notice us leavin? Whit they gonnay tell the polis? "He wis wearin a blue top." Aye, that'll narrow it doon.'

'But—'

'Partfay anythin else, there's a hunner and fifty thoosand

folk oot there, pal. The polis have got bigger things tay worry about.'

I bite my bottom lip and look up the queue to the sweaty, harassed, barely coping staff. They're struggling to push buttons and talk at the same time, utterly staggered by the tide of people swarming towards the tills, let alone remain vigilant for thieves. The queue does not move forwards, but sideways, with elbows and attitude and 'fuck you'.

'Ken whit you need, Alvin, ma boy,' says Chrissie, her eyes tipped with something narcotic. 'You need tay let the animal oot a wee bit mair.'

that's whit he's afraid ay, hen

Then she disappears like a supernatural sprite, and I glance through the crowd to see her hauling the stash, bow-legged, towards the exit. The words 'Oh, bloody hell' are barely out of my mouth by the time my legs have started waddling after her. We are outlaw penguins. We don't look back. We head right through the supermarket door, which beeps, causing the Richter-scale in my heart to leap. 'Move, move, move!' she commands, as though we're in a heist caper, and I increase waddling speed, waiting for a big hand to halt my progress. But nothing happens. We are out into the street. Everyone goes about their Rangers-related business.

I stare at the carry-out in my hands: unpaid for. I am a thief. For the first time in my life I have stolen something more expensive than a Creme Egg (and then I was only six). I am breathing, alive. Anarchy in the UK! Chrissie is grinning. 'Ye see?' she says. 'Feels gid, doesn't it?'

'Yeah.' I smile. 'It does, actually.'

The crowd roams around me, as I heave my stolen goods away, somehow feeling lighter and more powerful. Sainsbury's lose. The People win. I glance back at the shop to see a few more such victories waddle out from the front door, bearing loot.

We make our way towards the camp with the spoils of the hunt, the occasional snort and self-congratulation leaving our lips, while the city moves around us, suddenly insolid and malleable. The guilt and shame of looting is overlaid by a powerful feeling of . . . justice . . . of taking something back from the vast supermarket chains that have thudded their way into towns all over the UK and claimed them. God, this must be how Dolby feels *all the time*. I crack open a can of Tennants and toast Chrissie.

'To letting the animal out to play,' she says, and narrows her gaze at me.

'Indeed!' I grin. I feel young and, looking at the faces of everyone who passes, watching the way they run, shout, greet each other as brothers, I see the attraction of this, can understand Frannie's need for it. There is no system around us when we are part of this mass. There is no structure. No law, no responsibilities as a son, a father, an employee, a citizen, an upstanding member of society with the correct values intact. There is only the law of the crowd, of its restless, unpredictable will.

My heart is beating like fuck.

Chrissie goes, 'Hmph!' and rests the stash on a low wall, where she sits to catch her breath. 'Geez a minute, son,' she says, hand pressed against her chest. 'No as fit as I usedtay be.'

'None of us are,' I say, glancing at a policeman further down the street and, yep, there it is: I'm aware of the system again.

'So, Mr Stardust,' Chrissie says, with a mischievous look in her eyes, 'ye're writing a book?'

'Um. Aye. As it happens.'

'And whit makes ye hink ye've got anythin tay say, likes?' She reaches into the carry-out and checks the cans, as though there's a qualitative difference between them. She chooses a McEwan's Export, the red can with the wee drunken Jacobean dude on the front.

'Well,' I say, searching my new-found confidence for the answer, 'I just like the idea of communicating with people I've never met.'

'Don't geez that.' She tuts, and bursts open the McEwan's. 'Ye can communicate wi people ye've never met online.'

I'm being careful with my words now, apportioning them with more care, given how closely Chrissie's inspecting them. 'I like the idea that one day I might go into a bookshop and pick up something that has my name on the front.'

'Oh, we're closer tay it noo,' she says. 'Here – open wannay them cans for me, wid ye?'

'Closer to what?'

'It's about ego.'

'Ego?' I say, thinking she must have me confused with Frannie. 'Well. No. I disagree. I don't really have an ego.'

She takes a long gulp, while her eyes do incredulity over the lip of the can. Her heels patter against the wall like a wee lassie's. She descends from the swig with an answer. 'Ye don't have an ego, but ye're expectin somebody who's never met ye to spend eight or nine oors ay their life readin Words Wot You Have Wrote, and pay for the privilege? You think that what you have tay say is *that* important?' She raises the can and makes it dance in front of her face with glee. 'Oh, you boys, you boys and yer divine right tay have yer say. Yese don't even know yese are doing it.'

I fold my arms and summon my thoughts. 'Listen,' I say, 'I'm not that kind of guy.'

'Oh,' she chortles, 'let me guess: you're wannay the so-called "nice guys".'

'Chrissie, it has often seemed that a man's attractiveness to women is in inverse proportion to his respect for them.'

'Eh. Whit? Talk English.'

'But things like manners, politeness, punctuality and being a good listener have never stopped feeling important to me.'

'Well, aye,' she says, just about finding something to agree with in this. 'Fine.'

The drink is flexing its muscles in me now. I swig from the can, feeling good about what I'm saying, almost regal about the right to defend 'nice guys' from the negative smear campaign they have undergone throughout history by dirty bastards who can't keep it in their pants. 'I can book a table at a reputable restaurant and order a decent wine. I can talk books, music, films and politics. *Passionately*,' I add, 'if the mood takes me. But I do *not* have an ego.'

She slurps from her can, smile twitching.

'I'm really not what Frannie thinks I am. I'm as scared about my future as everyone else.'

'Ah . . .' she says, rolling a finger for me to continue, and it comes flying out of me, taking even me off guard.

'I mean,' I explain, 'I don't know what class I am any more, Chrissie. I don't know if I have a glittering life working in a bookshop. I mean, there's a recession coming. The nation won't exactly be crying out as one: "Where the hell are the English literature graduates? Can we get them to the front, please!"'

'Aw, boo-hoo,' she murmurs, closing her eyes and drinking.

'I don't know if my mum's alive, I don't know if she's dead. I don't know if I fancy men or wom—'

I stop. The sentence rears behind my teeth and I swallow it.

'Whit's that?' she says, eyes open with a new curiosity.

'I'm lost,' I say quietly. 'I don't know who I am or what I stand for.'

She sniffs and sets her can down on the wall. 'C'mon, Alvin,' she says, draping herself around me. 'Let's dance, pal, eh?'

Her arm around my neck, her fingers in my hair. I laugh, despite myself. The drink in my system relaxes.

Chrissie sings The Young Ones by Cliff Richard, then presses her cheek against mine. Then she places her head on my shoulder and I find myself, cautiously at first, and then with certainty, touching her hair.

'Why does he no love me any mair?' she says, her face pressed into my chest.

'Who?'

'Him. Richard Burton.'

'Richard . . . Burton?' I say, thinking: Oh, God, she's losing it.

She steps back and holds my hands. Her eyes are damp and her mascara is starting to streak. 'He doesnay ken howtay love, Alvin,' she says, a teary smile creasing her face, 'and I hadtay dae aw this . . . stupit stuff . . . just tay get his attention.' She shakes her head and blows some hair away from her face. 'Ma mascara runnin?'

'Aye.'

She hiccups a laugh and dabs at her eyes.

'I think you're beautiful,' I tell her, and it feels like the most honest thing I've ever said to anyone.

She gives a little snort. Her fag juts between her fingers and smoke trails the air. 'Naw, Alvin son, I'm no beautiful.' Her tongue touches the back of her teeth and she rolls her gaze towards mine. 'I'm *cunning*.'

For a brief second I'm chilled, but then she shakes her head in disagreement with herself. 'But I just want tay be a good person. I dae.'

'You *want* to think of yourself as cunning,' I say, as our souls step invisibly from our bodies and meet. 'You need to think of yourself like that. To protect yourself.'

She nods weakly. 'Yes,' she says, then hiccups again. 'So none of yese can hurt me.'

'Who?' I say.

'Men!' she hisses, flashing her mascara-scarred face at me.

I shake my head. 'You don't needtay change a thing about yersel, Wee Wife. I mean, uh . . .'

'Sorry?' she says, freezing. A stick-insect brittleness enters her limbs. 'What did you call me?'

'Chrissie.'

She coughs and straightens her stance and the alcohol seems to leave her system immediately. 'Listen, pal. I'm no Wee. And I'm naybody's Wifie. Awright?'

'No, of course not,' I say. 'I didn't mean that.'

She takes her fag from her mouth with one hand then lifts her McEwan's with the other, burps. 'See, youse men and yer fuckin . . .' She drums her nails against the can. They make a metallic drik-drik sound. 'Maist lassies, right, leave school and just want tay get a gid job, a nice hoose, some braw weans and a husband who's no gonnay thump them, and mibbe, as a wee bonus, we might still wantay jump each other's bones eftir thirty years. Men? Naw, they've got tae be *worshipped.*'

'I never said I need to be worsh—'

'Aw, but ye want yer name aw ower yer books so ye'll, em, *live on eftir yer death* or whitever?' She barks bitter laughter at me, a finger of each hand pointing into my face. 'Ye're gonnay fuckin die, pal! Once ye're in the ground it disnay mettir two hoots if naybody minds who ye were, or if they start namin streets eftir ye. Ye're gone. Ye ken nothin about it. Move on. Somebody else's turn, ya fuckin—'

'But—' I say, wondering how this has happened, but remembering Frannie's warning to me: *She can turn* (click) *like that.*

'Wee man,' she says, eyeballing me, 'ye're just no that

important. Look around ye. Look at aw these thoosands ay folk. Every wan ay them. They get up, they go tay work, they come hame. And that's their life.'

A pipe has burst in her – it's pissing out now all over the place. She's hopped off the wall and is hurling words at me like throwing stars.

'See, when I was your age, Alvin, I was gorgeous. I was really gorgeous. I looked like fuckin Liz Taylor.' She gives a laugh. 'Every guy wanted tay fuck me. It was *easy*. Men felt like the maist natural hing in the world tay me. I could rip the pish out them and they'd still come back for mair.'

Chrissie takes a draw of her fag, smokes about ten years in two seconds.

'Gonnay answer me somethin, Alvin. How is that noo I can sit in bars in Fawkurt toon centre aw day and not one guy wants tay talk tay me?'

She takes a deep breath, and when she lets it back out her eyes are wet. She tugs a bit of hair away from her face.

'I wantay talk tay ye, Chrissie.'

She dabs at her eyes again and tries to smile. 'Alvin, ken whit? I like you, pal. I wish ma laddies wis mair like you.'

'I'm sure they're trying their best,' I say.

'Are ye gay?'

I regard her evenly. Her forehead lifts. 'No,' I add quickly.

Her smile lengthens. 'It's awright if ye are. I mean, I'm no like them. I dinnay give a fuck.'

I stare at her and she twirls a fingernail at me.

'You have shagged a guy. And if you havenay, ye've wanted tay.'

Her gaze intensifies on mine and something feral, which I remember deep in my bones, happens. We stare at each other and when she leans forwards to me her voice is low and sugar-coated. 'Tell ye whit, pal, gie me another can oot that bag. Then I want ye tay tell me some ay the dirty things ye've done wi men.'

ma

ma

ma

The campus outside John's window was glistening with frost and starlight, as the smoke created a layer of calm between us. We swapped chat about what we thought of the people we'd met so far. John was perceptive but not cruel, as though merely observing the markings on animals, but his lip wrinkled with dissatisfaction at what he considered over-generosity on my part. According to him, I liked people too easily. What could I say? I was just happy to be there at an *actual* university where people received *actual* degrees. But, the sleepiest of adventurers, I'd only moved twenty miles north from home. John, for his part, was living and studying in some alien little town – not even a city! – in another nation, and I was detecting a sense that *we* would have to prove ourselves to *him* rather than the other way round.

'But then,' he said, tapping the ash from the bowl, 'I

thought, Where is Stirling? What do I know about Stirling? Nothing, except that it's in the middle of fucking Scotland, y'know?' He laughed ribaldly at something. 'And I thought, Let's just make it into a big adventure, yeah?' He filled the pipe back up. 'Let's, like, *subvert*.'

'Subvert whit?'

He hummed and refilled the pipe, and I had to spin an answer out of pure conjecture. After a while my silence became awkward and, panicking, some words flew out of the fire exit of my mouth. 'I can't believe you've moved all the way from London to Stirling. I only came twenty miles.'

John looked at me quizzically. 'You didn't want to go further?'

'It's far enough.' I gestured to the window and a campus that was a thicket of possibility.

He shook his head, medium-amused, like someone acknowledging the punchline to a bad joke. 'Listen,' he said, 'you're cool, Alvin. Great name, great accent. But we're gonna have to find ways of making you more intrepid.'

I felt the world in my head move slightly. Lift. He must've noticed my eyes change, because he edged closer to me, let a smirk out to play.

'Feeling it?'

'I think so, aye.'

As though someone had turned up a dimmer switch in my mind, everything came into focus around me: the sharpness of the colours in his posters for Fight Club and Moulin Rouge; the density of the night sky outside; the echoing ghostchatter from further along the hall. The inside of my head suddenly felt larger, more atmospheric, lunar.

'Whoah,' I said.

John's hat tipped over his eyes as he took another hit from the pipe, and I looked at the sparse chest hair below his clavicle, the ease of his limbs, the firmness of his jawline.

When he rose and crossed the room to sit at the keyboard, I had to banish that episode of Friends in which Ross shows off his music in Central Perk, adding robotic vocals that go 'infinite tiiiiiime' and 'eeeeelectrifying'. By the time he started playing I'd managed to control the giggles, which was just as well since instead of the expected bloops and wheeps a rich piano concerto flowed from his fingertips. I was silent. John leaned into the keys and his face went blank and his neck muscles undulated as the music rose.

I nodded along foggily and picked up a random book, The Outsider by Albert Camus, remembered that they'd made it into a film in the eighties, with Tom Cruise, Emilio Estevez and Patrick Swayze in leather jackets and greased hair. They'd taken liberties with the adaptation, though, given the blurb on the book said,

> Meursault will not pretend. After the death of his mother, everyone is shocked when he shows no sign of sadness.

Arsehole.

John noticed me reading, and stopped playing, and I placed the book down quickly, but the annoyance was passing through his frame and, just for a second, I liked it, how he was on the back foot. 'All right, all right,' he said, quitting the keyboard. 'I'll put a record on, then.'

'A record?' I scrunched up my face and indulged the idea that at least in *one* respect I might be cooler than John. 'Whit century are you livin in, man?' I sniggered stonily. 'Who buys vinyl instead of CDs? In 2001!'

He ignored this so completely it was as though I'd mocked the human habit of shoe-wearing. Then he drew out a random LP that said Belle and Sebastian on the sleeve, 'This lot are one of yours actually,' and he inspected the black sheen of the record for a few seconds, the glinting Saturn's rings of its grooves. 'Just think vinyl sounds warmer, y'know?' he said. 'Like you're in a different time period.'

I stumbled towards the record box on the floor, my fingers flicking a litany of strange names. Not for him the staple diet of the Eagles, Oasis, Queen, Meat Loaf, Eminem and Guns N' Roses we'd survived on as we'd roved around Falkirk in Belinda. We sat in his room with an endless supply of fresh smoke and, with one leg crossed across the other, listened – without talking – to Miles Davis's A Kind of Blue, a slow, flowing spell of a thing, a liquid architecture that I became lost in, became tiny inside, curling through the notes, letting myself dissolve into them, while John stared at the mothership of a moon above the campus and vague, tipsy bodies drifted across the lawns.

The needle crackled as the LP reached the end. The sounds of parties died like guttering fires. The campus was dark and empty. I placed my chin in my hand and looked at John, the flawless contours of his skin.

'Gorgeous,' I mumbled, my gaze heavy and the whole world pulsing softly. 'I mean, I don't even ken whit *species* of music that wis.'

'Mm,' he said, then dipped his gaze towards me. 'Do you want to see my cock?'

'Um,' I found myself saying. 'Aye. Sure.'

John started to unzip himself, while my mind adjusted to this turn of events. I could see the pressure in his jeans. He pulled them down to his thighs, hooked his thumb into his pants and lifted them over.

There it was. A cock.

'Do you like it?'

'It's quite hard,' I said.

'Yeah,' he laughed, 'that's what happens.'

I smiled.

'Touch it.'

Even the word 'touch' sounded faintly delicious. I was aware of my own breathing. John opened a drawer and brought out a light blue feather. 'Touch it with this.'

I held the feather. He brought himself closer to me, as I reached out with the tip of it and drew it down the length of him. It whispered against his skin and he moaned. I let the soft edge of the feather part against his hard-on, which twitched obediently. I liked making it do that, being able to control its responses like that.

'That feels good,' he said, under his breath.

It did feel good.

In the same natural way I'd taken the pipe from him, I found my fingertips stretching to land gently on John's cock. It was warm and smooth. I closed my hand around it and moved his foreskin up and down over the head. He growled. I was enjoying making the skin slip back and forth. I was enjoying the thickness of him in my hand, how full he was. I stroked it until he started to gasp and tighten, and his cock fattened, and warm come was splashing down my hand. Then I slowed my rhythm and looked up to see his eyes staring into mine fiercely. 'Take your cock out,' he instructed, 'I want you to come too,' and as I reached down into my pants he took my face in his hands, lifted my mouth to his and kissed me, and the moonlight from the window seemed to fall on us like snow

mama mama mama mama mamama ma

ma ma ma ma

ma

ma ma

ma ma ma ma

ma ma ma ma

ma ma ma ma ma

later, as we were lying there on the pillow, staring up at the ceiling, covered in a thin layer of sweat, my mouth was open and I was talking and there, in the half-light, the campus trees leaning across the window-pane, it tumbled from me, and I wept. How I'd come home one day to find the house simply empty, how Mum had just vanished, how me, my father and my brother had grown around the gap but never over it. I spoke of these things while John murmured, 'Oh, how awful,' and 'Yes, of course,' and, 'You poor thing'. The trees outside breathed, keeping the world alive.

'Ma mum,' I told John, 'is almost certainly dead.' I looked at him and his eyes were with me, bringing it from me. 'Or else . . . why would she never have come back?'

A night which I would never see again – a single turning of the Earth – would soon be completed and tomorrow a new one would take its place. John hugged me and I went limp. What is a hug? How had this strange method of human communication evolved?

'I've got you,' he said.

– the story is severed as a boy who must be all of sixteen teeters up to me and Chrissie, reeling from side to side and says, 'Scuse me, sorry tay interrupt, folks.' His hand touches my chest, lightly pushing me away to lean in towards her, 'Just wondering if ye've got a light, sweetheart?'

'For a fine figure of a man like you?' Chrissie mumbles, rolling her eyes and bringing out her lighter. He's topless, too drunk to notice that he's sunburned, Union Jack draped across his back, swaying while Chrissie lights his fag, before he takes a strong pull on it and blows a huge cloud of smoke into the air. Then his dazed eyes focus and he bats his hand against my T-shirt. 'Whit's this?'

'Captain America,' I reply flatly.

He laughs and his limbs roll. 'Ye're no American, though, pal,' he says, holding up the Union Jack in his fist. 'Ye're a Protestant.' His face squeezes itself with silent hilarity. Then he wanders back into the stream, heading towards the fan zone, clapping his hands high in the air and a song unfurling in the fag smoke.

'So you're gay?' Chrissie says.

I shrug and feel the weight of this asssertion. 'I still have absolutely no idea.'

'Come on . . .' she says, tapping the air once with her cigarette. 'Who dae ye like better, men or wummin?'

I watch Sunburn merge back with his gang and jump on the shoulders of one and go, 'Aaaaaaaaaagh,' while his pal carts him round like a horse and Sunburn pretends to whip him. 'Aaaaaagh.'

'I'm just as afraid of men,' I say, 'as I am of women.'

'Ye're afraid ay people.'

I nod. What would be the point of denying it?

Her gaze holds mine, before she lets it drop. 'Me tay,' she says quietly, smoking while we listen to the distant noise of the pre-match build-up painting itself onto the air.

'Listen,' she says, chucking me another can, which I've caught and opened before she can even start the next sentence. 'We aw have things that happen tay us that we cannay explain.' Something in her eyes, held back, gathering force, and then she opens her mouth. 'Me and ma former husband, Mr Richard Burton, went tay Rome on oor honeymoon right. Never went before. Wanted tay go. So we went.' She sniffs. She's not looking at me now, scratching at her chin, as the endless parade of fans clap their way past us. Her voice curls around a sentence I wasn't expecting: 'Ended up in the Vatican.'

Here we go . . .

'And there's the nuns and the priests.' She glances at me with a half-smile, then does a mock-shiver. 'And the rosary beads. But the place itself, man.' She gazes up at the buildings, the sky beyond it, the universe beyond that. 'Huge. Incredible. Beautiful. And there wis this shaft ay sunlight. This enormous beam that comes streamin in. And I stood there in it. The warmth on ma face. It felt pure. It felt . . . true.'

She sips from her can and lets this settle inside her.

'And when he came to find me, I wis cryin.' She shakes her head at the memory. 'Unbelievable.' Then she points her fag at me. 'Noo, I fuckin hate thay Celtic bastards, Alvin. But I stood there in that light in the Vatican and I felt that. So how dae ye explain it?'

'I can't.'

'Exactly,' she says. 'I'm no scared tay admit it, pal. I felt peace up here.' She taps the side of her head slowly. 'And I'm no usedtay feelin that.'

She takes a last draw of her fag, before throwing it to the ground and grinding it with her toe. 'So you,' she says, 'shouldnay be worryin about who or whit ye are. Ye're alive. Enjoy it.'

'Yes . . .' I mumble, as the sun peeks over the horizon of her conclusion.

'Noo,' she says, picking up the rest of the booze, 'havin loved ye, wee Alvin, I'm gonnay leave ye.'

'Where are you going?'

'I'm going to join ma man.'

'He's here? In Manchester?'

'Sure is. He's a Rangers man. Whaur else would he be?'

She reaches up with her free hand and touches my face, then draws me towards her and kisses me. It's soft, slow, tender, and

Yes.

'Ye know, wannay these days?' she whispers into my ear. 'You will wank yourself silly thinkin about me.'

My breath is held. My cock twitches and starts to harden.

Then she pinches my cheek, almost tugs at it, and says, 'Noo go backtay yer wee pals, son. I've got business tay attend tay.'

I stare at her, any understanding of the world dissolving. 'Chrissie, have I—'

'Gon,' she says, pointing off up the street as though I'm a dog she's trying to shoo away, 'Beat it. Get tay fuck.'

By the time I've made my way through the streets to the fan zone at Piccadilly Gardens – arms loaded down with drink, cock tingling with Chrissie, head floaty and real – I'm still smiling. My mind is churning with dreams. I'm standing with Chrissie in a giant sunbeam in the Vatican. Guys collide against me and rebound – 'Sorry, pal' – the litter-bedecked streets, the offices and supermarkets and brand-name clothes stores and the cornucopia of shitfaced faces are insubstantial around me.

When they see me coming towards them through the crowds, Frannie raises his wrist and taps his watch with all the authority of a schoolmaster welcoming a sleepy pupil. 'Whaur the fuck have you been?'

I raise the carry-out as proof.

'Have you been drinkin?' says Dolby, and I roll my head around on my neck like the Tin Man after he's been oiled. I'm still smiling.

Jack stares at me with a private detective's curiosity. 'Uncle Alvin, where's Chrissie?'

'She wandered away, pal.'

'And ye let her?' Dolby yelps. 'Ye see the state she's in?'

'She'll be fine,' says Frannie, breaking into the twelve-pack for a can. 'Believe me, mate. She'll be fine. Whit do I owe ye, Alvin?'

'A sworn alibi.' I laugh, and dump the twelve-pack on the ground. Jack eyes it warily: he knows what this stuff does.

'Ye nicked it?' Frannie says, his expression staggering backwards.

'I did, aye.' Jack covers his mouth with his hand, as though a teacher has just fallen onto the floor.

'Fucksakes, mate. Lootin shops?'

'Frannie,' I say, 'it's only a crate of beer. I think Sainsbury's can afford it.'

'Lord Sainsbury's one of the richest men in Britain,' Dolby confirms. 'He owns about half of Scotland.'

'Doesnay matter,' Frannie huffs. 'It's folk like you, Alvin, that'll give us a bad name doon here.'

'Rather than the rampant bigotry?'

'I'll bigotry you.'

'Go on, then,' I reply, feeling the need to do a sprite-like dance. 'Bigotry me.'

Frannie scowls.

Piccadilly Gardens is huge and raw and rippling, a sea of heads, arms, flags. Fans clamber atop monuments, trees, lamp-posts, bus shelters, fountains. The police try to haul them down, but as soon as they do, others replace them. The statues become so crowded with bodies that people fall, taking others with them. And the *sound.* Blistering waves of *sound.* The number of men who'd fit comfortably into a stadium are crammed into a city square. It is terrifying. It is epic. It's a scene from fucking Tolstoy.

'Man,' says Dolby, craning his neck to see over everyone's heads, 'look at it all.'

I stand on the twelve-pack and gaze round at the thousands upon thousands of them. 'Amazin,' Jack says, then waves his arm, trying to see himself on the screen. 'I wish I could see something, Daddy. Daddy, why can't I see something?'

'You're no big enough, son.'

I don't say the thought that's on my mind: Fuck's he doing here, then?

At the other end of the square, the screens show pre-match footage of the teams' progress to the Final. People half cheer Rangers goals. Then Jack squeals, 'Look, Daddy,' and we feel a disturbance in the crowd off to our right: a lumpen shape heading tank-like towards us. The crowd moves from its mass.

'They have a cave troll,' Dolby groans.

'Gents,' says the Cage. 'See yese found yerselves a good spot.'

'Aye,' Dolby says.

'Alvin.'

'Hello.'

'Heeeeey.' Frannie alone maintains the illusion that we're pleased to see Cage. 'Whaur's the rest ay them, man?'

'Got split up,' says Cage, with a glum weight. 'Cannay find them. Em, can I have some ay yer cerry-oot? They fucked off wi mine, likes.'

Before we can be thankful that he even *asked*, he's torn into it. 'Stella,' he gasps, then roars, 'STELLAAAAA!' He drinks and gulps, throat bobbing wetly, before looking round at the crowd. Nods. Sniffs. Satisfied. And though we're expecting Cage to launch into something barbed with 'Fenians' immediately, he just happily takes in everything around him. And more Stella.

'Whaur's Chrissie?' he says, glancing round as though expecting to see her pixie-face peeking out from between the forest of legs.

'Took off on her ain,' I say (tutting at myself for saying 'ain' instead of 'own').

'Whaur tay?'

'Lookin for her boyfriend.'

'Boyfriend?' says Cage, the word injected with surprise, before he sighs and shakes his head. 'Aw, see that woman . . .'

'Aye,' I say, perhaps too meaningfully, and he glances at me.

Then he revolves around fully and lets his belly face us. 'You boys havin a gid day?'

'Aye,' I say. Cautious. 'Why?'

'Whit about you, buddy?' he asks Jack, swaying up there on Dolby's shoulders. 'Whit's the best thing that's happened tay you the day?'

Jack eyes him warily, then decides to say, 'Daddy said he's going to teach me how to cook when we get home.'

'Is he?' says Cage. 'And whit ye gonnay cook?'

'Pizza.'

'Pizza? I *love* pizza.'

'Do you?'

'Yeah. You can't beat a nice piece-a pizza.'

'Ha ha,' says Jack. 'That rhymes. Did you hear that, Daddy? The man said, "You can't beat a nice piece-a pizza."'

'I heard him, son.'

'You're funny,' says Jack. 'What's your name?'

'Gordon,' says Cage, offering a handshake, which Jack returns with a dainty little hand. 'But you can call me Fun Gordon.'

'Like Spongebob? That nearly rhymes.'

Cage winks at Dolby. 'He's a wee cracker.'

'He is that.'

'Got wan masel,' he nods, swigging, 'lassie. Fourteen. Ex has custody, likes.'

He and Dolby exchange weighty looks, as though remembering days of ration books and bomb-shelters.

'I loved that woman tay,' sighs Cage, 'really fuckin loved her. And noo this.'

Dolby sniffs. 'I kicked mine oot,' he says mournfully.

'But noo ye want her back?' goes Cage.

Dolby casts his eyes up towards Jack, and Cage nods an understanding, and I immediately sense my role in this disclosure episode, which is to take Jack – 'C'mere, you' – and throw him up and down and make him laugh, then lay him horizontally in my arms and spin him round and make him go, 'Aaaaaaaaaah,' as though he's in a centrifugal machine, and beyond the whirl of it I hear Cage push the full weight of himself into Dolby's life.

'Listen, mate,' he says, in the voice of a football manager coaxing a rookie, 'ye've kicked her oot awready, so ye've punished her. That's it done wi. Take it fay me, if ye keep punishin them, it doesnay work.'

'Whoah!' goes Jack, then does loop-the-loops with his voice as I birl him. 'Whoooah, whooah, whooah.'

'Let her stey wi this Neil bastard. If he's the cunt ye say he is then he'll show his true colours eventually, and she'll start pinin for you. In the meantime, you be nice as pie tay her. Ye gie her everyhin she wants. Aw the money, aw the time wi the wean. Ye fight her on *nothin.* That's the only wey she'll ever come back tay ye. The *only* wey.'

Jack is giggling, 'Uncle Alvin, turn me upside-down, turn me upside-down, aaaaaaah.'

'Then when she comes back,' Cage adds, 'ye treat her like a princess, mate. A fuckin princess. Life's better wi them than withoot them, believe me.'

To buy them more time, I tickle Jack, feel him collapse underneath it, his eyes vanished inside two gleeful slits.

'Don't,' Dolby says, hand on my shoulder. 'Ye'll make him pee himself.'

I give Jack back to him, missing the feel of him in my arms as soon as he's gone. He clings to his father like a baby monkey, pressing his face against Dolby's chest, and I can see the red rings round Dolby's eyes.

Cage turns away, his work done, and lifts the bottle to his mouth. Swallows. He's breathing deeply, and staring at his shoes. Two brown shoes. The sort of shoes you'd be given if you went into a shop and asked for 'a pair of brown shoes'. They are not the shoes, in other words, of a happy, confident, outgoing person. It's weird how different Cage seems without a busload of disciples to boast towards. Here he is, brother-in-arms with Dolby and trying to impress Jack, but there's a new ponderousness, as if something neglected inside him has turned towards Jack's light. He's surrounded by thousands of his people – clapping, stamping – and as he makes faces at Jack, as Jack chuckles, Cage's hulking frame seems as though it's being operated from inside by tiny men.

'Fuckin hot now, int it?' he grunts at the sun. For a second I think he's going to reach up and turn it down. Then he really shocks me when he pats my arm and says, 'Listen, wee man, I didnay mean tay have a go at ye back there.'

'Oh,' I say. 'Uh, that's okay.'

'Aw this business wi the missus. Just got me a bit wound up. Sure ye ken the score.'

'Aye, the score's, like. It's like . . . a draw, int it?'

Frannie winces, but Cage thankfully ignores it. 'Ye got a bird yersel?'

'Um. Not exactly.'

'Not . . . exactly?' Amusement jigs on his face. 'Aw, I see. Wannay *them* kinday arrangements.'

'Wannay what kinday arrangements?' I say, the cold starting to flood my veins. I remember how it began that night in the bar at Bridge of Allan, when Stirling University Rugby Club took over the place, thumping a tattoo on the table with their drinking songs, as John and I shouted to each other to make ourselves heard, and they noticed us. Oh, they noticed us, all right.

'Wannay them on-off kinday things? See each other when yese want?'

'Em, aye,' I say. 'One of them.'

He touches my shoulder with his beer can. 'Nice. Tellin ye, son, keep it like that. Cos see men and women? See, unless they're actually on the job and shaggin there and then? They just dinnay work the gether.'

'Funnily enough,' I laugh, 'a gay friend of mine once said the same thing.'

He laughs too, instinctively, then pauses. I drink from the can, swallow, instantly regretting the joke. But it buzzes past him and he grins. 'Gay friend, ha ha. Gid yin. Listen, I cannay work it oot, though, wee man. Ye're obviously no that big on the Rangers. Why are ye here, exactly?'

Funnily enough, I want to reply, I've been wondering that myself. I want to point to Frannie and say: Him. I want to point to everyone here and say: Them. *I want to know what being a working-class Scotsman truly means cos I haven't a fucking clue any more*. But there you go: despite (or maybe – haud the horses! – because of) a degree in English, it's impossible for me to articulate it without just sounding like a pretentious dick. So instead I say, 'Thought it'd be a gid day oot wi the Lads, ken?'

He nods, recognising the correct response, but waiting for the rest.

'And I wantay see Rangers get a result,' I add, and he nods more heavily this time.

'So you were a student, aye?'

Here we go. 'Aye.'

'Some debt ye've ended up wi.' His face betrays no sarcasm.

'Yes,' I say, 'it is.'

'I'm wantin ma wee lassie to gotay uni, eh? Cos she's a clever wee hing, ma lassie. Lot cleverer than her auld man here, eh?'

I don't know whether he wants me to agree with him or not. I hedge my bets. 'You must've done well bringing her up, if she's going to uni.'

He winces a little, as though it were in doubt. 'Aye, well. Dinnay wantin her turnin oot like her faither eh? I mean, I wis a fuckin bampot when I was younger, ken?'

'That right?' I say, feigning astonishment.

'Aye, no noo I'm a faither likes. I mean, I've calmed doon. But I minds this wan time – I was mibbe about nineteen? I was runnin wi a gang fay Langlees, and we were chasin this boy fay Camelon who'd done wannay ours. I'm fuckin bombin it like this.' He mimes the thrill of the chase, working his meaty arms up and down. 'And he turns intay this lane that's got a fence at the end and he's like: Aw, naw. And we're thinkin: Right, we've got ye! Boy tries to climb the fence.' Cage's hands claw at an invisible fence. 'And I'm carryin this hatchet.'

'Hatchet!'

'Aye, like a wee axe hing?' he says, then carries on as though he'd merely said: Aye, like how water becomes ice at freezing temperature? 'Onywey, I chucks it at him like that—'

Cage throws the hatchet in slow motion, his eyes trailing its progress as it whirls and chops through the air.

'And soon as it left ma hauns I minds hinkin: Please, God, don't let it hit that boy.'

He scratches the back of his neck and contemplates the target, and he's silent for so long I have to say, 'Did it?'

'Naw,' he sighs, 'it didnay. But the lads loved that I'd thrown it. Thought it was cool as fuck.' He shakes his head. 'So it was eftir that I joined the Church.'

This small still word almost cavorts in front of me. 'Church!' I splutter.

He cocks his big head, amazed that I'm not still with him on this. 'I dinnay mean *heavily*, like. I mean, I'm no a Bible thumper. Just talkin about a wee bittay neighbourliness, Alvin, eh. Wee bittay love in oor hearts, that's whit we aw need.'

'Right,' I say, doing a Google Images search in my mind for LOVE and finding that, just as I suspected, it looks nothing like Cage.

But he's on a roll now, as the stacked pile of chips of his ego diminishes. 'Like wance a month at the church on a Sunday, they'll have Who Let the Dads Out, when we aw come in and watch the weans. Ken? It's gid. It's a gid feelin aw comin the gether like that. The sortay hing whit's missin fay the world.'

'Okay,' I say, still not able to believe the strange, conversational avenue we've ended up walking down.

'That's why aw this –' Cage lifts his can and sweeps it round 180 degrees '– *community* means so much tay a man.'

The crowd stamps and claps, tens of thousands of voices blending into one.

We are Rangers,
SUPER RANGERS!
No one likes us,
We don't care,
We hate Celtic,
Fenian bastards!
We will chase them,
Everywhere.

'Yeah,' I say, '*so* much.'

A can goes flying above our heads, spilling beer on our sunburned skin. There's a rumble of discontent around us and dark looks thrown over shoulders. 'Fucksake, eh!' goes Cage, wiping the beer from his bald head. Someone next to us goes careering, clown-like, into a stranger, who pushes back. Faces turn sour, stances are squared, threats are spat out, and I can see Dolby tensing, as Jack teeters on his shoulders, eyes roaming round the crowd. Then he's pointing off towards the distance. 'Daddy, look there. Look at all the *police*.'

We crane our heads to see the van doors open at the edge of the enclosure, figures in black with helmets and riot-shields emerging, forming a line. Staring at the crowd.

LET'S ALL DO THE BOUNCY BOUNCY!
LET'S ALL DO THE BOUNCY BOUNCY!

Without announcement, arms are linked all around us and everyone is pogoing. The mesh grows larger and veers towards

Dolby, who is still balancing Jack on his shoulders. He tries to take a couple of steps backwards but finds his way blocked by a flow of fans who've come into the square behind us. Frannie and Cage have arms round each other's shoulders, bouncing on the spot. Cage looks like the fucking Marshmallow Man from Ghostbusters, with his big, happy grin.

Jack is staring at the screens at the other end of the square now – they have been crackling and cutting out periodically for the last ten minutes. There are vague howls from the crowd each time this happens, which abate once the screen flickers back to life. 'Daddy,' Jack says, 'when are they gonnay fix the big tellies?'

'I dunno,' says Dolby, 'but they'd better do it before the game.'

'Aye,' says Frannie, who has stopped bouncing long enough to appreciate this point. 'I don't think the crowd would like it if they didn't, eh no, Fun Gordon?'

'Naw,' says Cage.

We glance at the crowd, dense enough that we need to keep an eye on the burst-open carry-out. People are jockeying for a good view, there are collisions and frequent 'Fuck off's as the heat and the booze and the packed-in mass and the flickering screens start to act – like high, whining strings – on the swarm around us. We all look at each other and think the same thing.

What if they don't fix the screens?

'Ach,' I say, 'I'm sure it'll be fine. The last thing they're gonnay let happen is a techy failure. I mean.' I laugh. 'There'd be a riot otherwise.'

Nobody replies.

Eventually the Cage nods and says, 'Here we fuckin go.'

The fizzing screens burst on, to show the Rangers team taking the field. The crowd launches thousands of vocal flares.

'Heddy-haw!' Frannie shouts, clapping his hands so hard it must be sore. The Union Jacks, the Red Hands of Ulsters, the Monarchy, the British Empire, the red, white and blue swimming in my vision, I realise I'm in the thick of men addicted to tradition. The glow of power from it all. The whole city united in ceremonial worship. How can something so ugly be so strangely beautiful?

Cage has folded his arms, staring at the screen. Everyone is placing hands on the shoulders of someone in front to try and see. It's as though everyone, a whole army of us, is engaged in a psychic effort of will, a mass telepathy forcing its way to the minds of players only three miles from here. 'C'mon, Rangers,' Frannie mutters, mantra-like. 'C'mon, Rangers. C'mon, Rangers.'

'C'mon, Rangers!' yells the Cage.

'C'mon, Rangers!' squeaks Jack, clapping atop Dolby's shoulders like a Sesame Street puppet.

Two players head for the centre circle. The crowd now is hushed, a huge cat fixed upon a tiny bird. Heat layers the city square, drips on our skins. Dolby looks at me, face tight. Even he and I are feeling it, the pulled-taut nerves all around us. My heart is thudding a military tattoo. A text from Brian arrives: COME ON, RANGERS! Frannie has his arm round me, muscles working my neck. 'We're gonnay dae it,' he's saying. 'We're gonnay dae it. We're gonnay dae it. COME ON, RANGERS.'

The whistle goes.

The crowd roars.

Ferguson to Darcheville.

The screen dies.

The roars become howls.

The screen crackles.

Hands atop heads.

The screen crackles.

'Aw, c'montay—'

The screen dies.

The screen crackles.

The screen reads,

SORRY WE ARE WORKING TO
CORRECT THIS TECHNICAL FAULT

Everyone boos and jeers. The screen is impassive before them.

'Whit's the fuckin score here?' goes Cage, his arms like fortress walls.

'This is pish,' tuts Frannie. '*Pish.*'

'Daddy,' says Jack, 'why aren't the screens working?'

'I'm sure they'll fix them soon, pal,' says Dolby, and glances at me. There's trouble in that glance.

'Fucksake,' grunts Cage.

The jeering is some kind of vast bird-sound from a colony on a remote island. Restless. Sharp in pitch. A chant goes up to the tune of 'Here We Go': *Fix the screens, fix the screens, fix the screens . . .* Ladders are erected at the back of the giant tellies, wee Mario-men in overalls clambering up. It's *that* bad? It's not even a matter of a button that hasn't been pressed in the control-room? There are *actual* men with *actual* toolboxes having to *actually* fix the screens before us? LIVE?

'A hunner and fifty thousand guys travel three hunner miles,' Frannie snarls, 'and *this* is the best they can dae?'

The riot police at the side of the square bend their ears towards walkie-talkies.

The screen goes black. It flickers again. Everyone is still, hands over mouths, then

SORRY WE ARE WORKING TO
CORRECT THIS TECHNICAL FAULT

After a few weeks, university started to settle into a gentle rhythm: cooking, reading, coursework, drinking, essays, napping (mmmm), wanking (mmmm), showering, and a dinner-time routine that found our tiny kitchen filled with three people all trying to cook meals, while another seven waited for a gap at the hob, a communal octopus of arms, wooden spoons and gossip writhing through the room, before we all cleared our plates and the remains of our banter, then disappeared online in twelve different directions. There was a four-year-long intellectual assault course ahead of us and sometimes it was too much. In Week Four, me and John skipped a lecture on post-modernism to escape into town to the Bartnon Bar and Bistro to enjoy the piquant, studenty feel of truant drinking. I was halfway through my fourth cheap whisky when John suggested I come along to an LGBT meeting. My head was buzzing and disarranged and I had to focus on what he was saying, his still, blue eyes holding me up. 'Is that legal?' I said, head lolling.

'You're practically one of us now,' he said, scrawling shapes on the air with his cigarette smoke.

'One ay who? Whit's the BFG?'

'LGBT,' he said. 'Listen. I know what you're feeling. I've been there. But you're just not one of *them*.'

'One ay *who*?'

He stubbed out his fag and presented his case. 'Nothing against your Falkirk friends. I know they're important to you. But, y'know, you're kind of above them.'

Brian and Frannie had been up to visit the previous week, garlanding the campus with their judgement. John and I had tour-guided them round the stretched silver of the loch, the bustling accommodation blocks, the students' union. 'Aye,' Brian had said, like a dignitary visiting Narnia, as freshers hurried past with folders pressed to their chests. 'Ye've got it good here, Alvino.'

'Really enjoyin the course, an a,' I said, with a professional tone.

'Aye,' Brian said, then nudged Frannie and pointed out two stunners heading towards them with an otherworldly poise and grace. 'Whit about them, man? Wid ye?'

Frannie brought down the gavel: 'Aye. Ridheid. Stunner.'

'Nah,' Brian continued, 'ridheids are overrated. They just remind ye that ye're Scottish. Ye ken whaur ye are wi a nice blonde, or even a wee black lassie. Feels mair like bein on holiday.'

'Not too many of them in Fawkurt.' Frannie sighed.

'Why the fuck d'ye think I'm wantin tay go tay California?'

John waited patiently for them to get it all out; Frannie and Brian waited patiently for John to join in. When he didn't, Brian battered on: 'Alvin, even *you* must be able tay score here. Tell me ye're gettin yer hole.'

I opened my mouth and there was a pause in which I almost swallowed myself, before John cut in with, 'Actually, y'know, girls are *smart* here, and valued for their intelligence.'

A weary expression broke across Brian's face, as though he was being nagged by a secretary for missing a meeting. 'That means you've no shagged any of them either, mate.'

So I could see why, there in the Barnton Bar and Bistro a week later, John had decided to show me the error of Falkirk's ways. 'I'm sorry, but the way they talk about women and gay men is disgusting.'

'John,' I said, ripping a bar mat, 'the way *you* talk about women and gay men is disgusting.'

'It's a bit different,' he said. 'I actually like them. It's like criticising your own family.'

'Where I'm from,' I said, draining the whisky and feeling its liquid prickliness in my gullet, 'there is such a thing as loyalty. Ye dinnay dump yer mates just cos ye don't happen to agree wi their political stance.'

'But what do you get from them?' He seemed genuinely confused.

'I get home from them,' I said, rocking my empty glass on the table, wondering myself what I meant by that.

He made a despairing face. 'Can't you feel yourself changing? All that place did was make you unhappy – you've said it yourself. You were desperate to get out of there.'

'Not *that* desperate,' I spluttered.

'Here,' he said, his voice softening as he leaned forwards and took my hand, 'you can be who you really want to be. You don't need them any more.'

ma ma ma mamamama
ma

ma ma ma mamamamama

The Lesbian, Gay, Bisexual and Transsexual Society had their meetings in an actual meeting room. I'd somehow expected a strobe light, a techno soundtrack and a coterie of oiled bodies. Instead there were breeze-block white walls, plain furniture and a coffee machine, the same functional room where the Stirling University Student Association decided whether or not there was appropriate lighting on the walk to Alexander Court, or if entry to the union for non-members should be three pounds or three pounds fifty. There was a long table, around which sat about fifteen people. I came in behind John, who bounded across the room like an animated cat, reflecting back the warmth that came his way. 'Evening, everybody,' he said. 'How are we going to make rock 'n' roll history tonight, then?'

A girl with a short auburn bob tugged his T-shirt as he passed. 'Hoy.' He stopped, remembering himself, and bent to give her a kiss. They exchanged the word 'darling' precisely, like a masonic greeting. 'That depends,' she said. 'We've got a lot to get through.' Another London accent. These exotic English people, everywhere all of a sudden.

'A lot of what, exactly, Sara?'

'Things, things, important things, sir!' she trilled, and raised her eyebrows at me as though to say: *You* know what it's like, don't you?

I totally didn't.

'Are we still organising the trip to Brighton? That's all I want to know.'

'Look at the agenda.'

'Agenda?' John tutted at yet another outrageous demand of the regime. 'Do you think I was born to look at agendas? I have, as I think many of you will know, my own agenda.'

Sara called the meeting to order. John drummed his fingers on the table with either excitement or impatience, I couldn't tell. I looked at the faces that lined the table and there seemed to be a strange, disorienting assortment of piercings, sloganed T-shirts, tattoos, overgrooming and undergrooming, and in one or two cases it wasn't easy for me to tell whether or not they were male or female. I had the heady sensation that I was among a race of fantasy creatures in a Clive Barker novel: the Nightbreed or Seerkind or Imajicans, with their golden eyes, tails, elongated limbs or other beautiful deformities, facing off against the corrupt, conservative order of humanity. But then the agenda began, and I realised they were just students. 'Okay,' Sara announced, 'Item One. We're looking for volunteers to staff the hotline. Carol and William shouldered most of the burden last semester, but both have dissertation deadlines and I think it's only fair that we start taking it in turns. We need sensitive people who are good listeners. So that rules you out, John.'

John nodded proudly, as volunteers stuck up their hands and Sara ticked them off.

'Item Two. Newcomers to the group. Do you want to tell us your name?'

I glanced up to find everyone staring at me, and I desperately tried to think of what the hero of a Clive Barker novel *actually* does when the creatures turn their attention to him.

'Uh,' I said, 'I'm Alvin,' then added, 'Hey!' for good measure.

'After the chipmunk?' said a girl with a T-shirt that read 'Sisters Are Doing It For Themselves'.

'After Stardust?' a muscular blond boy said.

'The second wan,' I said, 'Mum wis a big fan.' No one said anything, so I pressed on: 'I should think myself lucky. She could've been into Randy Newman.'

Everyone laughed, and sugar threaded through my veins. Wow. This was the moment when the hero became accepted by the Nightbreed/Seerkind/Imajicans!

'So,' Sara was smiling, 'do you want to tell us a bit about yourself?'

'Yeah,' I said. 'Uh. I'm fay Falkirk. First year. Studyin

English. I write Horror novels.' I grinned, just to show them I wasn't a psycho.

They blinked at me.

'So, uh,' I said, 'what exactly dae ye dae here? Just sit around and talk about . . . bein gay?'

There was a ripple of amusement and Sara smirked, stirring her coffee. 'Well,' she said, 'for a start not everyone here is gay. What I can tell you is that this is mainly a social group nowadays. We organise events around Stirling, Edinburgh, Glasgow. Nine times out of ten we end up in bars or clubs and, like many other LGBT people up and down the country, we do party a lot.' There was a smattering of hoorays around the table, like muted champagne corks being popped. 'I do run liberation campaigns as well, but that's more in my role as LGBT officer for the students' union.'

'Bo-ring,' John said, and feigned a yawn. Sara's eyes indulged him for a second before she continued.

'The society is about socialising and making new friends in an environment comfortable for people to explore their sexuality in.'

'Did you read that off a sheet?' said John.

'Okay,' I said, and could think of absolutely no way in which I could explore my sexuality in this institutional room.

'So how would you describe your orientation?' Sara asked.

'Um . . . What does that mean?'

'Are you gay or bisexual?'

'I quite like lassies,' I said, 'tay tell ye the truth.'

'*But*,' Sara said, letting the word dip in the air meaningfully, 'you're starting to feel you might not be entirely . . . straight?'

'Oh, believe me,' interrupted John, 'he isn't straight.'

'Hey,' I said, 'I might be straight.'

'Alvin,' John replied firmly.

'John,' said Sara, 'it's up to Alvin to articulate his own sense of self.'

'Sense of self?' John cackled. 'C'mon, this isn't Oprah. Brighton trip, Brighton trip . . .'

'Speak your own words, Alvin.'

'Well,' I said, shifting in my seat a little, 'I dunno if there's a word ye can apply tay it. I mainly fancy women, but sometimes . . . I like men.'

'So you're bisexual?' she said.

'I dunno.' I shrugged, but then remembered the night last week when John had crept into my room while I was in bed and kissed the back of my neck and told me that all he wanted to do was 'spoon' and I'd let him. 'Mibbe. Does it matter?'

'To many,' said Sara, with a homely nod, 'it does. People can get very defensive about these terms because of how other people perceive them.'

'Like supportin a fitbaw team?'

'Sort of,' she said, with a twitch of a smile. 'But if it doesn't matter to you, then it doesn't matter, I guess. As long as you're not feeling an internal conflict.'

THE THROB! It came from outer space! A smooth alien thing from a sexy, sci-fi film starring a beautiful heroine, in a tight silver Lycra jumpsuit, yeah, and the handsome male lead with all his broadness and silent rage and this alien thing takes them over. THE THROB must be dealt with before it defeats the entire human race!

Yes, says the heroine, but look at it. It's ready to explode! As though leaping on a live grenade, John takes the alien in his mouth, sucks on it, and the Throb attacks him and—

'I suppose I'm finding it difficult tay come tay terms with,' I said, then added quickly, so they wouldn't think I was weak, 'but, hey, I suppose that's part ay the adventure, eh?'

She held my gaze and, beneath it, I sensed her interest bloom and realised that this was probably the best possible answer I could've given. 'Well, we have all kinds here. Everyone's at a different place on the spectrum.'

'*Oh*, yes,' said John, meaningfully, and Sara glanced at him with a dimmed-down mischievousness.

'You can be whatever you like here, Alvin,' she said, looking at me in a way that made my skin redden slightly and something unexpected happen in my pants. 'It's all down to you.'

I swallowed and nodded and felt the world around me expand in a thousand different directions.

'Okay,' Sara said, lifting the sheet in front of her. 'Item Three. Who's responsible for the noticeboard in the union?'

SORRY, WE ARE WORKING
TO CORRECT THIS TECHNICAL FAULT

The first bottle – twirling gracefully out of the crowd – smashes against the screen. Another whirs overhead and lands somewhere in front of us, like a flare erupting, then hissing into the sea, before the eerie sound of jeering rises from Manchester. Frannie and Cage stare at the screen, faces locked closed. Dolby blows out air and looks at me with a what-the-fuck face. Wee Jack is huddling in close, saying, 'What's the matter, Daddy? Why can't we see the game?'

'Screen's no workin, son,' Dolby intones, patting him. 'I'm sure they'll fix it soon.'

'They'd better,' Frannie says, nostrils flaring. 'Biggest gemme ay ma Rangers supportin life and I wantay fuckin see it.'

Cage is silent, anger pulsing in his big frame, distending his chest against the wall of his folded arms. Fans are turning to each other, rapping out questions – 'Screens havenay worked all day?'; 'Fuck did they let us intay the square for?'; 'Wantay find a pub?' – looking for a spark in someone's face, a word, a clue that will let them know what the hell's going on. *Who's in charge here?* People are glancing at their phones as though the gods of modern technology will provide answers. The huge screen goes blank again and a jolt travels through everyone. Eyes widen as hope swells –

THERE ARE ANOTHER
2 BIG SCREENS IN THE
VELODROME

– then curdles into spite. Faces darken and snarl. Bottles twirl from random sections of the crowd. The techies retreat from the ladders, propped against the screen, at the sight of the whirling arsenal. The whole square is ringing now with anger. 'Fucksakes!' and 'Sort it oot!' stab from mouths everywhere, like thrown spears.

'This is pointless,' says Frannie, looking at his TAG. 'Gemme's under way.'

'Better get it sorted,' grunts Cage, face set rhinoceros-like. 'This is gettin on ma copious tits.'

'Where's the Vel-o-drome?' says Jack, peering, at least able to turn this into a fun spelling game.

'I have no idea,' Dolby mutters, but then, as though in response, the screen changes its display to

GO TO THE END OF THE ROAD
TURN LEFT
10 MINUTES WALK

This pacifies the square even less, as it's clear that the screen has no intention of giving up the game to us, jealously hoarding it as revenge for this invasion. Cans bounce off its black face. The crowd barks and hands chop the air. Dolby swallows and there are tremors around his mouth as Jack is pulled in tight. Frannie seems ready to blow plumes of steam from his nose. Cage has his hands on top of his head as though pressing balm into his baldness. I am the very definition of innocent bystander, remembering all the reasons why I don't really like football, or crowds, for that matter (unless they're singing along at a U2 gig, preferably to something from The Joshua Tree). 'What do we do now?' I say.

'Fuck it,' says Frannie. 'Let's go.'

'No steyin?' says Dolby.

'Nae point,' Frannie says, finger jabbing at the source of the malaise. 'The techie guys cannay work cosay all the bottles. But if they dinnay get the screen fixed, every cunt's gonnay keep throwin them. So let's heddy.'

'Where we gonnay see the game?' I almost whine, amazing myself that I'm disappointed.

'See if we can find this Velodrome?' Dolby suggests.

Frannie ducks as a bottle pirouettes past, smashes off a lamp-post. 'Well, I'm no fuckin steyin here!'

'Okay,' says Cage, and we crane necks, scanning above the crowd for the best exit.

Dolby mumbles the words on the screen as though it's a sight test: 'At the end of the road turn left.'

'It's a fuckin square.' Frannie sighs. 'There are four roads tay turn left at! So which wan?'

Dolby shrugs. 'Let's just go the wey we came in,' and both Cage and Frannie shrug along with him, so the decision is made to push through the thick, dense scrum of Rangers shirts. It's the first time today I've been glad Cage was here, as he elbow-pushes our way out of the square towards Oldham Street. Everyone else has had the same idea. Some are staying in the hope of the screen being fixed, some are defiantly venting their anger, but the rest of us are grumbling towards the exits. Progress isn't easy, and I can feel tempers being reined in and held all around us, blue-clad bodies shuffling their exasperation inch by inch, and no one's in the mood to start letting others past. But Dolby lifts Jack up in front of him, and as soon as they see a wean they part. Cage becomes a solid snowplough behind Dolby and the raised beacon of Jack, allowing Frannie and me to snuggle into his wake and move our feet through the rubbish slush of cans, crisps packets, pizza boxes. My hands are on his shoulders, willing him forwards, the massed noise of threatened dreams twisting through the air.

As the gates near, a bottleneck starts, and we feel the trash-compactor crush of bodies from either side. Jack's eyes widen, terrified. Dolby has to shout, 'Ho! I've got a fuckin wean here!' before people make slight room either side of us.

'Daddy,' says Jack, screwing his eyes shut, 'I don't like this.'

'Fine, son, let's get you back to the bus.'

'Headin, man?' Frannie says.

'Aye, he's gettin scared. I mean, we cannay see the gemme anywey.'

'We could try Albert Square?' says Frannie. 'The other fan zone?'

'That's in the opposite direction,' Cage says, 'but good shout. Better than tryin to find this fuckin Velodrome.'

'Right,' says Dolby. 'Youse dae that. I'll get the wee man ontay the bus.' Jack's face shows a tiny, scrunched-in relief. Frannie nods once and we change direction, through the human outflow. There are tuts and 'montay fuck's as we try to swim against the tide, but nothing stops Cage motoring through. I look to see Dolby push towards Oldham Street, Jack giving me a wave as he disappears, swallowed like a morsel by the crowd.

After what seems like fifteen years of manoeuvring through everyone, disoriented, pissed-off and thronging towards exits, we reach the other side of the square and go out into a street, to be greeted by the sight of riot police, visors down, fully kitted out in body armour, truncheons and shields. They are impassive, watching us, and I hope Dolby doesn't encounter them at the Oldham Street exit, cos up close they'll be kinda scary to Jack. Fans stride past, but one or two stop in front of the riot cops, staring almost curiously. One goes forwards to ask directions to Albert Square, but the cop draws his truncheon and the fan backs away. Another stands in front of the cop and raises his arms, making his Rangers top into a chest of defiance, and sings: 'King Billy's on the wall! King Billy's on the—'

The cop cracks his truncheon against the guy's leg and he crumples like a doll.

'Holy fuck,' Frannie gasps. 'Ho, mate, there's nay need for that!'

The cop looks in Frannie's direction and I tug him away, back into the thud of Cage's progress towards Albert Square. His shoulders are boxed and determined. Frannie's face is quizzled – he keeps checking back to the boy on the ground, who's holding his leg and screaming obscenities at the cop.

'King Billy's off the wall,' I attempt, but no one laughs, and my face burns with embarrassment.

'Never thought I'd say this,' Frannie mutters, eyes on the

litter-strewn road, the city starting to disintegrate around us, 'but soon as possible, let's get the *fuck* back tay Fawkurt.'

falkirk
a drinker's guide

VOODOO LOUNGE – Stroll down the charming Dickensian cobbled lanes behind the Steeple (at one time in the Guinness Book of Records as Britain's shortest street) and check out this classy new addition to the Falkirk scene. Formerly The Lane, The Canteen and Café Noir (or 'Caf Naf', as it was also known), the offbeat Scarface chic of this place has much to offer. The five gigantic mirrors above the bar, adventurous lighting scheme and cow-print chairs give Falkirk a glinting touch of Miami. On Thursdays, you can ride the giant WKD bottle and compete for the title of Mr Boxer Shorts.

Football Screens: YES
Sample Music: Funky house at weekends from DJ Pez
Drinks promos: Single vodka and any dash for £2

LA BANCA – A new, ambitious player, this large tapas bar has become a home-from-home for the more sophisticated Falkirk punter. With its authentic Spanish décor and its Unique Selling Point – the combination of fine dining and a relaxed bar feel – it's ideal for that romantic night out with a classy partner.

Football Screens: YES
Sample Music: Flamenco

FULL STOP – Formerly 'Comma' . . . until it reached the end of its sentence! A mainstay of the Falkirk scene, having been the driving force behind the continental 'coffee culture' brought to the town around the turn of the millennium. A sprightly, metropolitan décor and friendly bar staff, as well as booths for more intimate socialising, make this a must for any weekend.

Football Screens: YES

Sample Music: Chart/dance

THE GOOSE – Formerly the Newmarket Bar, this hardy perennial rebranded itself to take on Wetherspoon's directly. With its competitive pricing (check out Grill Wednesday – any meat and a pint for £5.99) and cast of colourful local characters, this is an endearing venue for the afternoon drinker.

Football Screens: YES

Sample Music: No music

Drinks promos: Wine from 99p and cocktails from £2.49 on Fridays

ORCHARD HOTEL – Indie kid behind the bar. Check. Friendly staff. Check. Photographs of rock icons (and useful map of Falkirk) on the walls. Check. This is a cracking individual, eschewing generic drinking-den clichés, for those hoping to give their big night on the town out a wee twist.

Football Screens: YES

Sample Music: Eclectic, to say the least. Lunchtime diners are as likely to hear the Pixies or Pulp as Elvis Presley or Take That.

TROPIX – This compact cocktail bar is traditionally Falkirk's only over-25s venue, giving it enormous historical recognition in the town. During the day Tropix is mainly peopled by Falkirk Herald staff, off-duty policemen and teachers who've popped into the town for a quick one after work, such is the fine class of their patron. The disco-ball and mini-chandeliers add a touch of chi-chi, and the barman knows how to mix a mean Black Russian.

Football Screens: YES

Sample Music: Dirty Dancing soundtrack.

We follow the river of Rangers fans past shuttered shops. The few still open, mainly newsagents, have signs saying, 'No beer, no food,' in the window. Rubbish is piled in mounds around the bins, its multicoloured vomit seeming to accuse us: *Look what you've done!* We know we're nearing the fan zone when we hear the roar, and Cage's stolid back picks up pace, shoulder blades rolling beneath the number 9 and the name CAGE, and turn a corner to see another vast gathering, a cathedral rising at one side of the square, and way, way in the distance is, yes, an operational screen! Tiny blue figures knock a ball about on it, to the sound of cheers and clapping and Hullo Hullos ringing round the city. 'Thank fuck,' Frannie says, and we're about to head into it when we notice metal barriers cordoning it all off. Black vans, TACTICAL SUPPORT GROUP, are parked before us like metallic panthers and, as though previously rehearsed, a yellow high-vis jacket is stepping towards us.

'Go back the way you came,' says the helmet.

'Screens have failed in the other square, mate,' Frannie

appeals. 'Just wantay see the gemme, eh.'

'We're not letting anyone in,' the visor says tonelessly. 'Turn round and go back the way you came.'

'But there's nothin happenin back up there!'

The riot cop draws his stick and Frannie flinches.

'Aw, c'mon, mate, play fair,' I say, but he takes a step towards me and I flinch too.

But Cage does not. Cage is peering at the screen. 'It's still nil–nil,' he says, with a faint edge of hope to it. The riot cop moves towards him but Cage does not budge, rooted to the game. Not even his eyes move. 'Back the way you came,' the cop says.

Cage doesn't acknowledge him, the way people don't acknowledge a wasp if they don't want it to sting them. It doesn't work.

'I'm fucking warning you!' the cop says, and Cage turns his head towards him, looks at the visor.

'Ssh,' he says.

Frannie pats Cage's shoulder and says, 'Mon, man, we'll find a shop winday or somethin. Comet or a Curry's.'

'Pal,' says Cage, 'nay offence, but I didnay come two hundred miles tay watch this gemme in a fuckin shop winday.'

Just as I think the cop's about to raise his shield and barge Cage, there's a disturbance further up the fence. Rangers fans are trying to wriggle under the cordon, or clamber over, assisted by those already inside the square. Their success has encouraged others: the crowd that has thronged from Piccadilly Square senses their own strength and surges forwards, tearing into the metal mesh, stamping and streaming through the gap. The cops peel away from us and towards the mêlée, batons raised and coming down on backs, on arms. Fans drop and cower; the barriers collapse and there's a pouring of limbs and truncheons and shouts, which makes us back away instinctively. 'Jesus fucking Christ,' Frannie's saying. Other fans have phones out, videoing this, but Frannie and Cage have realised that this is the last good place to watch the game, and it has failed them; they have already turned and started down a side-street. I'm walking at pace after them, flinching at every small motion around me.

Above us, a helicopter roams, like a giant dragonfly.

I love the smell of napalm in the morning.

Me and Frannie glance at each other, two notches below frightened, cheeks puffed and blooming. 'It might aw kick aff,' he says, and Cage turns to him and nods solemnly, and we stride through the city centre, through the streams of fans searching out somewhere, *anywhere*, to watch the game.

Cage takes out his phone, reads a message, and breathes in. 'Right, Chrissie's back at the Canal Bar.'

'Whit's she uptay?' I say, fearing the worst.

He snorts and shakes his head, a ghost of smile on his face, at something in the message – or the universe – he doesn't want to share. 'I have nay fuckin idea, mate. She is a law unto herself.'

Something about his tone suggests that it's the very reason she was on the bus in the first place.

*

Since the bar is tucked away down a stone staircase leading from the bridge, the police must've missed it when they were ordering the shutdown earlier. Either that, or the venue has realised the police just have bigger things to worry about now, and has become aware of the takings it'll get from a captive audience. It's no longer a wine bar. It's Mordor. The bar 'queue' is a seven-deep scrum, prickly with elbows and sharp glances towards the TV, which is just as well since nobody in here needs any more

hic

drink. There are intricate layers of swearing, encouragement, disdain weaving themselves sonically into the air above everyone's heads – the whole bar roars at once on a phantom shot at goal – as we push our way to the back of the room, peering at the screen. Chrissie spots Cage's domed cranium, the solid fact of him, raises a pint and shouts, 'Oh, it's my boys!' before excusing herself from the company, dipping her forehead, and charging forwards like a totsy wee version of the Juggernaut in the X-Men comics, clearing bluenoses from her path. Cage folds his arms and smirks, poised to meet the force of her arrival, while Frannie shudders as though taken over by an instantly debilitating illness.

'Oh, shit,' he mutters, which is what's probably squirting into his pants right now, as she breaks free of the crowd and flings herself at me.

'Ma Alvin,' she says, smothering me with kisses, while Cage looks on, his jaw clicking, before ignoring her and returning to the screen. 'Are ye awright?' she says, checking me for bruises,

'Did ye get caught up in aw that trouble? I hope you boys have been lookin' after this wee yin!'

'Hey, I can look after myself.' I tut.

'Course ye can.' She nods deeply. 'Aye, I can see ye've got that dangerous look about ye. I mean, Gordon there's been shittin himself aw day fay ye, hasn't ye?'

Cage's head moves up and down on its bull-like neck. 'I'm feart tay be alone wi him. Case he rapes me.'

Chrissie covers her mouth at this largesse, pinching my arm. 'Oh, I think you'd quite like that, Alvin, eh?'

I widen my eyes at her in silent alarm and Frannie frowns. 'So whit's the score?' I say vaguely.

Rangers, halfway through this first half, have most of possession. Even though the screen's too far away to see the finer details, every kick of the ball is accompanied by a change in pitch from the crowd: oohs and aahs and cries of 'Hit the fuckin thing!' slide up and down the scale from hope to despair. Then Darcheville picks up the ball and lifts it over the defence to Barry Ferguson, who slams his shot against the post. The crowd rises as one and then falls, hands on heads, to cries of 'Unbe-fuckin-lievable'. Frannie bites at the air. Cage has settled into his focused silence, and only turns to us every so often to acknowledge a neat/shit bit of play. Chrissie sways her hands in the air, from side to side, trying and failing to start songs. Heads shift this way and that to see beyond heads shifting this way and that. There are stamps and shouts and even I start feeling it, irresistibly, clapping along, and Chrissie tickles me under my chin at one point and says, 'That's it, boy, let it oot,' and Frannie's arm wrings my neck and he's, like, 'We're gonnay dae it, Alvin!'

'C'mon, Rangers!' I say, and the words don't even feel strange in my mouth. King Billy's on the wall. King Billy's on the fucking wall.

The half-time whistle blows and everyone cheers the team leaving the field, satisfied, and breaks out into excited chatter. A guy near the bar starts playing the flute, which brings another flutter of applause. Frannie and Cage have spilled into conversation with a guy next to them: a Manc. I'd forgotten there were real Mancunians in Manchester.

'Tellin yer,' he says, 'I'm a Man City supporter, right, and a Fenian at that, but these fookin Plastic Paddies that bang on about the fookin moother-land when their family have been fookin livin in this coontry for three fookin generations? Yehse are fookin British, right. Deal wid it.'

Cage nods his cannonball head with satisfaction. 'Exactly,' he grunts. 'Posers.'

'Thing I like about you coonts is yer fookin proud to be British, right? The fookin Union, eh?'

The guy raises his pint to Cage and Frannie. They raise imaginary pints to him, bringing Scotland and England into fraternity against the false prophets of the Republic of Ireland. I burp, feeling the alcohol from earlier start to stretch its legs in my blood, reaching my head, lolling around in there, splashing its

hic

liquid limbs and saying stuff

like saying such *stuff*

'Hey, whaur's yer pal Dolby?' says Chrissie, her face suddenly in my vision and I blink and focus on her and say, 'Uh, back at the bus.' Something makes me take my phone out to check on him, but there are no bars of signal. Getting back out from the crowd packed into the bar at this point, back up the stairs to the main road, would require Artful Dodger-like feats of stealth, so I stuff it away and just try to take in the game.

I'm drunk. Am I drunk? I wanna be dru

The fixed point of the TV screen.

For a moment they show an aerial shot of Manchester and for the first time I see the scale of it outside, the thousands and thousands crammed into the city centre, and I think of every crowd scene that people talk about in tones of awe – Live Aid, Oasis at Knebworth, the Iraq War protests, the Make Poverty History march – and I realise: This is it. *This is ours.* The camera pans across the writhing multitudes filling the city and for those few seconds I am enormous. I am part of a vast, living consciousness. A human chain of being.

Even the commentators – memories of World Cups trailing behind them – are staggered. 'This is the largest ever transit of people from one country in the United Kingdom to another,' says Richard Keyes. 'Officially.'

There's cheering in the bar at that one.

'But,' he continues, his face clouding slightly, 'there have been reports of scuffles between police and fans in the centre of Manchester, which, I'm sure you'll agree, Andy, is not such good news.'

'That's not good news at all.' Andy Gray sighs, shaking his head. 'Let's hope that gets sorted and doesn't overshadow what's supposed to be a celebration of football.'

I check my phone again to see if there are messages from Dolby, but there are still no bars of reception, and he's silent out there among it all.

Onscreen, flash images of the discord in Piccadilly Square: the thrown bottles, the bashed fences, the police thumping truncheons against shields

ma

ma

ma

ma

Edinburgh. So much to answer for.

When you're from anywhere in Scotland that isn't Edinburgh, and then you move to Edinburgh, you presume you've made it. Home of the Enlightenment. Home of the Festival. Home of the Parliament. And you've just left Stirling University with a 2:1 in English, a head full of books and poetry and theory, with a beautiful, huge final night with John and Sara – who are both heading back to London – that you are never likely to forget for as long as you live still tingling in your mind and your cock. The parameters of your self feel infinite. You are young and a graduate and constantly reminding yourself that you are in the top ten per cent of intellects in the country, and so the capital city of Scotland calls you, blowing on its ancient, heraldic horn, and you answer. 'Sorry, Falkirk, Stirling, but my life with you both is over. I am a graduate and Edinburgh is courting me. I'm sure you understand.' Thus runs your inner monologue, even although you have absolutely no idea what you might usefully be employed as.

You have £5000 of student loans to pay off, right off the bat, so you wait tables for months at the Fruitmarket Gallery (just to get by for now) before realising that it isn't getting you anywhere, then sign up for a temping agency (just to get by for now), which also yields fuck-all. What you don't realise is that temping agencies need more temps than there are jobs. Your

CV soon amounts to two weeks' data entry at a factor's office, typing numbers and updating files on a computer (highpoint: two cats having a fight outside) and three months' work in the marketing office for the National Trust, with its dingy, underground-fortress levels of security, opening envelopes that have been sent in as competition entries to find out whether or not they've ticked 'Yes, send me more info!' Most heartbreaking are the ones covered with stickers that say, 'Pick Me!' or 'You've chosen a winner!' and old people's shaky handwriting. You spend two weeks volunteering at the Lyceum Youth Theatre, mostly herding kids, who tut at the unfashionable state of your jeans, then one month – one single, thrilling month – as an usher at the Edinburgh Film Festival's Horror strand.

That ends, and thereafter commences the nightly Bartenders' Waltz, courtesy of the Edinburgh outlet of an Irish chain of pubs. Sometimes it's a graceful dance, and you just flow in and out of each other, pouring drinks, your personalities and your focus merging into those of your fellow bartenders; sometimes it's a clumsy clop, with smashed glasses and egos. You hear of a guy, Vinny, in the London branch who can multiple-serve up to twelve people at the same time. 'He's just the best,' your manager tells you. 'Put the hours in, Alvin, and that could be you.' His legend glows across the whole country.

The way people tell you rounds, you are surprised to discover, is important: someone who orders a Guinness last needs a pitchfork through the head. So does someone who says, 'Oh, no, I think *they're* next,' cos it makes you look bad. On the three to five p.m. break during a double weekend shift, you run downstairs to get as much sausage and mash down your neck as possible, then it's straight to the pub next door, where you slam a double vodka and Red Bull and come back for the second half of your break half pished. Then on your fifteen-minute break about half eight, you nip round and down another two double vodka and Red Bulls, so that by the time you finish at one a.m. your system is fizzing with caffeine and all you need is a couple of pints to knock up your booze levels and you're away. You stay out all night with the people you work with, then it's back to someone's flat – everyone still in their uniforms – and get just enough sleep into you before you start your next shift and it begins all over again. You live inside it. Contained. It feels a long way from Falkirk or Stirling University. The Breakfast of Champions: Greggs's Steak Bake and a bottle of Irn Bru. If you do two double-shifts in a row Friday/Saturday, then by the time you reach six p.m. on Sunday you want to go out and get absolutely blitzed again. You know it's been a good staff drinking session when the cleaners arrive in the bar in the morning and you realise you're about to start a double shift, and the whole time you're thinking:

Wasn't I supposed to be middle class by now?

You decide the drinking must stop. You decide the drinking must stop the night you punch a customer for swearing at you under his breath. The rest of the bar staff cover for you against the boss, and say the guy went for you, but you can see they are wary around you, as though sensing a bomb in you about to go off, and during this whole period you don't write a single word of fiction, and so, yes, you stop drinking. Or you try, anyway.

Aye, awright, don't be smug about it

But to stop drinking means to stop working in a bar. Which means your entire friendship group and social life go with it.

Bing! You are in Waterstone's on Princes Street, where you will be employed for the next three years, but you are at least closer to the book trade and given Sci-Fi, Fantasy and Horror to manage. You like making neat pyramids of the paperbacks on the table, and recommending new authors from your extensive knowledge of the genres, and this is why you are assigned to manage the Clive Barker event when he comes to promote the second Abarat book in Edinburgh, and this is why you get back in touch with Dolby out of the blue and end up having a minute-and-a-half chat with

CLIVE! FUCKING! BARKER!

that you will play and replay for ever, and this is how the mong nights begin between the two of you, and you get to know Jack, and this is why, obviously, Dolby decides to text you when he suspects his wife is having an affair, because you never truly lost each other, you and him. It just took that minute and a half of scratching out questions to a slightly bored Horror LEGEND for you to remember each other, the delight of each other. But underlying everything is the vague feeling of disappointment – that as much as you like working in a bookshop, you are not yet *something* – which is compounded by having a degree. You come to realise the only thing it really equips you to do is say, *I have a degree*, and that most companies aren't that interested in how diligently you pored over those books on post-structuralism and semiotics and modernism. By 2008 your landlord is sighing,

'Credit crunch,' at you down the phone, as though these solitary words should make you the most sympathetic man in the world to the news that your rent will be taking a hike. 'I have to protect my investments, you understand.'

'Of course,' you say. 'We all have, uh, investments to protect.'

Rent is expensive in Edinburgh, and this is why people share big ramshackle flats of about five or six folk. You live in Thirlestane Avenue, Marchmont. It's a studenty area, but many of the flats are rented by people who are also still trying to work out what to do with their lives, mainly shambling foreign students, hippies and musos. You are two minutes from the Bruntsfield Links, where the underagers drink, which reminds you of fine nights of your own at that age with the Lads tearing about Falkirk.

Falkirk.

You are also two minutes away from Alphabet Video, which organises its title by Actor, Actress and Director, meaning you can, if you want, find the entire filmography of Bruce Willis arranged together. Across the road the local shop is Margiotta's, an Italian deli turned corner shop. Croissants and morning rolls and reading Catcher in the Rye conspicuously, in the hope that a small, cool, intellectual American foreign-exchange student will comment on it and strike up a conversation with you. One of them does, in the Elephant House on George IV Bridge, one sunny afternoon, but the conversation founders when you ask her if she's seen Candyman, and when she says no, you screw up your face, as though looking in a mirror, and say, '*Candyman Candyman Candyman Candyman*,' in an evil voice.

She doesn't get it.

'You're not supposed to look in the mirror and say it five times,' you explain, rolling your hand with an affable, mock-weariness, 'or he appears. Slashes you. Agh!'

You mime your own throat being slashed.

'I'll, uh, not do that, then,' she says, with a weak smile.

You go, once, to a gay bar at the top of Leith Walk in the early evening. On your own. You order an orange juice. You conspicuously read Goodbye to Berlin by Christopher Isherwood. Nobody talks to you. Nobody even sees you. At one point you get up and ask two men standing at the bar where the toilets are. 'Over there,' they say, then go back to their conversation. You go into the toilet, look at yourself in the mirror, see a short, bespectacled, utterly ordinary young man with dark hair and an Empire Strikes Back T-shirt, who is simultaneously the most dull and the most extraordinary thing you've ever seen. How can this be? Who is this man?

You leave the toilet, pick up your book and say, ''Bye!' to the barman, as though you've known him for years. He mumbles a response and continues to wipe some glasses. And that is your first and last gay bar experience in Edinburgh.

During this time, since you have nothing better to do, you try to learn the guitar and briefly join a punk band, who sing about the military-industrial complex, global capitalism and Gramsci's The Formation of the Intellectuals. You realise it isn't going to work after a choppy slash through Death Camp and Tarantulas of Finance (the titular arachnid a symbol for either the web of global capital or perhaps a more subjective depression, it's really up to the listener), finishing off with a song about racism: Black Purity. 'Guys,' you shout, over the squall of the feedback, 'can we not try to sound a bit more like U2?'

So Vulture Party doesn't work out. And you're *still* thinking: Wasn't I supposed to be middle class by now?

So you start taking your laptop to sit in Costa or Starbucks, in the hope that someone will say, 'Excuse me, are you a writer?'

'Yeah,' you'll say.

'Me too!' they'll say.

'Look at us here!' you'll say. 'Writing!'

'Yes! Doing something in public that we could easily do at home!'

'Just so everyone will know we're writers!'

'Fucking saddos!' you'll both say, then stare down at your half-eaten toasties.

This is when you begin your first novel, How Softly Sail the Ships, about a boy who has come to believe he was born on an alien world, the book ending with his realisation that this is why he has never fitted in with his peers. Will he be accepted back on his home planet, now that he is so contagious with human emotions? There is a love interest: a surge of memories from Zulda, his childhood sweetheart on his home planet, suggests that she has re-opened psychic contact with him, and you convince yourself that this is what you are writing as you sit there in Costa, but mainly you're on Facebook, and this is how your contact with your dad, with your brother, with Dolby and Brian and Frannie, becomes conducted – a white screen collaged with pictures of this otherlife that your family and friends have adopted since you've been gone. Your dad has become a health freak, grinning in rain-lashed running gear. Your brother Derek is balding now, and enjoying Christmas on the Prudential works night out, letting off a party popper. Frannie is in his DJ box at Austin's, with a Jack Nicholson grin and two random girls on each arm, one of them laughing at whatever Frannie has just said, the other looking faintly embarrassed. Brian is behind the bar in California with a deep auburn tan and a pint of smugness in his hand.

Dolby is holding Jack in the hospital.

Facebook becomes how you and your dad and your brother contact each other every year on Mum's birthday. Phone calls are too awkward these days. As people, no one from Falkirk is tangible to you any longer. Static eyes on a glowing screen, like a strange race in a futuristic film. Oh, my God, you begin to think, as you stare at Facebook, the world is becoming sci-fi. Neuromancer. That point in the evolution of the species when face to face contact becomes redundant and all human interaction takes place in the matrix and you start to feel a cold, dull emptiness in your heart where something used to be, and you don't know what it is, but this is why you reply when Frannie pops up in your chatbox.

ello mate!

Awright

wot u up 2

wankin fuck off

:-D

like uv even got a cock 2 wank!

Em . . . u really havin a wank?

Naw!

good!

You think i d have replied if I was?

dunno – ye might like that ya wee poof

heard from brian?

aye enjoyin the life but says he s just working all the time in the bar nay time aff

tell me about it ☹

still though least he s got that fuckin thing in the sky over there – wots it called

??

that fuckin thing they get in california that yellow thing

em

the sun! that s it

ha ha

so he should shut his greetin mooth!

aye good point!

U hear about dolby and leanne

Aye bad news ☹

Never liked her 2 be honest

I didn't really get to know her too well.

Yere no missin much
Messed wi his heid

Bet he d love 2 batter fuck out that neil

Dunno mate he s not really the vengeful type
Think he wants to set a good example for Jack

Id b going round 2 his hoose wi a chair a rope
As a starter

I don't even want to know what the main course is!

Be the fuckin dessert I d look forward 2

crowbar

cunt

Lol

Still though

dolby shouldve screwed the nut earlier and sorted things oot
we could all see it wasnay workin

I've not really been round them enough to say

naw suppose uve no

how are you anyway mate?

I ll tell ye

as ye might ken Rangers are into the UEFA Cup Final

aye I saw that! Congratulations

☺
Finals getting played in manchester
And I am gon fuckin DOON there!!!

Should be good aye

Be well good m8

One 2 to tell the grandkids about 4 sure

oh aye

but on the other hand . . .

yeah ?

last night had a dream about being in tesco when its shut and theres no cunt in and I just walk thru the place wi a shotgun blastin fuck out everythin

Milk frozen chickens shampoo dvds tellies

blam
blam
blam
reload

washin powder
cosmetics
hello magazine
microwave meals

blam blam blam blam

fuck ye

so that s how im doing m8

urself?

and this is why you end up on a Rangers supporters' bus going to Manchester, on the morning of 14th May 2008: because men you once called your best friends are telling you that they're in pain.

A barman is pounding at a slab of ice in a canvas bag with a rolling pin, a jagged tempo beneath the cheering and shouting and the soar of voices as the ball onscreen sails just over the bar. Frannie snaps his fingers and winces. Cage says occasionally, 'Gonnay be fine, they're gonnay fuckin dae it.'

Chrissie is *still* trying to get me to join in an eighties singalong with her. 'Come on, Alvin, you're no really interested in that gemme. Sing wi me, honey.' She spreads her arms, and moves her torso from side to side, doing a permed-Top-of-the-Pops-singer's contorted face. Then she plays a pretend synthesiser, hand pressed to invisible headphones. 'Na-na-na-na-nineteen. Nineteen. Na-na-na-na-nineteen.'

'Gon wheesht,' tuts Cage to her. 'Trying tay watch the fuckin gemme, Chrissie.'

I glance up at him, wondering exactly what harm she's doing (and wondering, more to the point: what harm the *game's* doing?) and she sticks out her tongue at him and makes a fart sound.

He folds his arms, tuts and sighs, ignores her.

Chrissie taps my hand and points at him and I roll my eyes. She giggles silently as though she's just passed me a note in class.

The second half gets under way with shouts of encouragement from the bar, which is now even more densely packed as word spreads about it and refugees from Piccadilly Square push their way in. We concentrate again. We make fists and jab like touchline coaches with each promising kick of the ball. We are one. We are Rangers.

Chrissie has her arm round my neck, and at crucial moments of the game – even just a really good pass into space – she hugs me in close and yelps, 'Mon, the Gers!'

Cage notices this, and eyes me a couple of times. I don't cut my gaze from his. Why should I? Then he smiles as though he knows something I don't and shakes his head and lifts the weight of his stare back up to the screen.

Zenit take control of the second half, and all our hopes start to contract as trepidation snakes its way through the room. Sure enough, twenty minutes from the end, Zenit knock one in and bitter sighs unfurl. 'Fuck,' Frannie says, gripping an imaginary bottle neck. I half expect him to take a neat swig of air. When Cage exhales his frustration the ground almost shakes. Frannie's eyes become lidded but he manages to say, 'It's only one–nil. Be fine.'

We will the team on again. Songs burst sporadically but peter out; shouts are of angst rather than encouragement.

Chrissie, somehow, has managed to find herself another drink (even though she hasn't gone to the bar). She's holding on to a concrete pillar in the middle of the floor, rotating herself round it, singing, 'We are Rangers. Super Rangers!' But when she lifts her fist, the glass goes flying from it, and smashes, and men step back as though it's a nail bomb and 'whoahs' are raised like dainty skirts and there's some sarcastic applause. 'Thank you, thank you,' she announces. 'And for my next trick!'

She picks up another glass and pretends she's going to throw it. The jeerers duck. She cackles and points at them. 'Dicks.'

Cage growls, 'Settle there, Chrissie.'

She waves her hand dismissively at him. 'Jist a wee joke, Gordon.'

Then she grins at me, arm gripping my neck, and pulls me in nose-to-nose. I'm not really sure what my role is here, so I rub my nose against hers, as though I'm a puppy.

'Got yerself a wee boyfriend there?' Cage says, turning himself round fully to take this in, the way someone might turn to a waiter who has given him cheek, and oh no

instantly I understand who her Richard Burton is

and now the Scottish schemie version of Who's Afraid of Virginia Woolf? is about to be enacted before me.

Chrissie ruffles my hair and considers my place in this drama, smiling mischievously, and I can't help it – nervous laughter breaks out from between my lips. Cage grunts and steps towards me. 'Somethin funny, wee man?'

Frannie is still watching the game, completely oblivious.

Butterflies burst from cocoons and flap about in my stomach.

'Frannie, pal!' says Chrissie, as though making sure no actor goes unrehearsed in this play. 'Gon be a gentleman and go tay the bar and get me a drink?' She lifts her empty glass and shakes it. 'Toodle-pip, sir!'

'I think mibbe ye've had enough, Chrissie,' he says distractedly.

'Ho,' says Cage, swinging round to Frannie, 'don't be fuckin talkin to her like that.'

Frannie stands back with his hands raised, then Cage mutters his general displeasure with everyone in the vicinity, shoots Chrissie a look made of clapshot and turns back to the game.

'Hey!' Chrissie shouts, enraged, pushing her finger into him. 'You will not turn your back on me!'

Cage's shoulders slacken and he turns all the way back round again to face Chrissie. He looks tired, as though he's played this scene out a thousand times before, which, I've only just realised, he probably has.

'Why? So I can stand here and watch you flirt wi other guys? Like ye always done.'

She steps right up to him and presses her finger into his chest. 'No,' she says, emphatically. 'No no no! I never done the things you said I done, Gordon. I ken whit they aw *insinuated* about me and that guy, but I never done nuthin wi him.' Some of the punters have decided this spectacle is more interesting than the football and are spectating. Chrissie, perhaps sensing this, lets fly with the next bit: 'I fuckin wanted tay. I wanted tay ride him stupit! But I did *not*, cos I was in a relationship wi you and I loved ye.'

Cage hears this and sniffs. He glances round at the audience, who are pretending not to be waiting for his reaction. Frannie's on tenterhooks: given Rangers are down one–nil, there's at least a grim, viewed-between-the-fingers fascination to be had in seeing the Russian dolls of Cage's bravado become smaller and smaller. 'Aye, well, and what about this cunt?' Cage says, gesturing to me. 'Ye've been aw ower him aw day.'

'HE'S FUCKIN GAY!' Chrissie shrieks, her hand flying in my direction.

Cage looks over at me, considers this, and a smile dawns across his face. 'Is that right?'

'No,' I say. 'Uh.'

'He telt me earlier. He likes bum love. So don't you be sayin I'm flirtin wi guys in frontay you, Gordon Cage. Don't you fuckin dare.'

Frannie is staring at me, stunned. There are titters of laughter from some of the crowd and their eyes on me are piercing like arrows. Oh God, oh God.

Cage has started laughing now, the dark laughter of the arsehole in the back row of the cinema who won't shut up. 'Of course he is! Fuck am I thinkin about?'

'I'm no gay,' I say weakly.

'Ye've had a guy's cock in yer mooth,' goes Wee Wife, turning to me, with her hands on her hips.

Frannie looks as though the map of the world he was taught when he was growing up was fraudulent: Earth is actually an octagon.

I splutter a retort: 'Just cos ye've had a guy's cock in yer mooth doesnay mean ye're gay!'

At that moment, an enormous, embattled sigh descends on the bar as Zenit fire another one home. The crowd deflates, and during the second when Cage, Frannie and Chrissie's eyes flick towards the screen, I charge to the exit, past bodies who jostle elbows and go, 'Watch yerself, fucksakes!' but I'm hammering through and I'm out the door and I'm running towards the stone steps, taking them two, three at a time. Then I reach the top and I'm back into the city of Manchester and there's a police helicopter droning overhead and I don't know which way to go, then a hand is on my shoulder and I'm being turned round and Frannie's staring into my eyes and he's saying, 'Alvin, just tell me the truth.'

'No!' I say, as though cattle-prodded.

'Bullshit, ye're lying.'

'I dunno, man,' I whine. 'Don't put me in this situation. She shouldn't have said that, I never said—'

'Just tell me, mate,' he's imploring, the whole *decade* of him I've known in my life is imploring.

Nerves are threading through my speech, tripping up my words as they try to reach my mouth. 'I mean, like, whit about that whole business earlier? It's unnatural! I mean, fucksakes, man, how can I? How am I supposed to be able to talk to you about it? I mean—'

'I never said it wis unnatural, I said it was against evolution.'

'Same thing!' Even I'm amazed to find myself shrieking and jabbing my finger at Frannie. 'Youse have never understood me!'

That's when he folds his arms and breathes through his nose. 'Aw, I see.' He does a sarcastic head-dance. '*You're* the wan we're no payin enough attention tay? The wan wi the degree and the flat in Edinburgh. The neglected yin.'

'Aye, well, cheers, mate. That's about as much as I can expect from you, then, eh?'

Frannie takes a step towards me, and I flinch. 'I'm no gonnay fuckin hit ye, mate, awright,' he tuts. 'I can be a dick, but I'm no a complete dick. Ye just needtay listen to me for now, though, eh.'

I blow upwards and try to calm myself and nod at him, while continuing to feel like I'm made of marshmallows or something.

'Thank you,' he says, then closes his eyes, thinks something over, opens his eyes again and says, 'You have got a fuckin degree in yer back pocket ye're no gettin off yer *arse* tay use, Alvin. Yer life's awready twice as good as me and Dolby's right there.'

'But—' I say.

He raises his hand and I shut my mouth.

'Now, ye've been away for eight year, and we see ye on the odd birthday, aye. Maybe get a text about how Pink fuckin Floyd are the best band OF ALL TIME every so often. Then ye turn back up for a – let's be honest – glory-hunt on the backay the Rangers the day and have the TEMERITY tay act like a hunner and fifty thousand ordinary Scottish punters, who are celebratin the biggest day of their lives together, are just pigshit thick bigots.' Then he grabs my arm and grits his teeth. 'Ordinary punters who get up the mornin and go tay their work and come hame and love their faimly, who've just came oot tay play here for wan day in Manchester, and dinnay have the ARROGANCE to presume they're special and above it aw.' He's actually shaking my arm now and I'm trying to pull it away from him, but his grip is a vice made tight by time. 'We're whit you came fay, mate. We're your fuckin people mair than these pretentions wanks ye hit it aff wi at university. Whaur are they noo, eh? Fuckin naewhaur. And here ye are back wi yer Fawkurt boys cos ye're on yer ain again. And we've accepted ye back in, even though ye *dumped* us seven year ago. So dinnay be whinin about no bein fuckin *understood*, Alvin, awright?'

With a final sharp tug, I release myself from his grip and stagger backwards a couple of paces, as confused by the world in this moment as I've ever been. Frannie exhales, watching me clutch my arm as though stunned momentarily by the ferocity of his own speech. I take another couple of steps back from him, and he swallows and his tone softens a little. 'I've got nothin against you bein a poof, mate. Honest.'

I breathe and stare at him. 'I never said I was a poof.'

A smirk flashes across his face. 'Naw, ye've just had a guy's cock in yer mooth.'

'That doesn't necessarily make me a poof.'

He actually laughs at that, and then I lower my gaze to conceal a faint smile.

'Listen, mate,' he says, pressing his case more gently now, 'you're away. Brian's away. Dolby's a faither so he's as well bein away. Why dae ye hink I'm always chasin these burds? I'd be on ma fuckin jack jones every night otherwise. So that "understandin" goes baith weys, eh?'

I run my hands through my hair, while adrenalin heaves my lungs up and down.

'Mate,' says Frannie. 'Ye left tay go tay university, fair play. We were aw proud ay ye. But ever since ye've acted like we're some kinday burden.' He points at himself. 'I'm no a burden tay nay cunt. My friendship and respect are a privilege, mate, no a burden.' He's not even angry now, cool and still. 'So you need tay start decidin who ye are, Alvin. Cos if you don't want me in yer life, fine. I'm fuckin gone. Just say the word.'

'I do,' I say.

He nods and lets this settle between us. 'Hope that doesnay make us merried.'

'Till death us do part.'

He offers me his hand and I shake it and he goes, 'Och, c'mere,' and pulls me in for the hug, and it's that moment in films and we let it happen, and he pats my back once, twice, then we're out of it.

'Right,' he says, with the sprightly voice of a man who's just about to rearrange his tool cupboard. Takes out his phone, punches buttons. Voicemail. 'Let's find oot whit's happenin wi this daft fucker Dolby.'

Sirens sound in the distance. There are guys coming from the direction we're going, their strides as urgent as those of Olympic walkers. One of them is touching a cut on his head while his mate barks, 'Ye can get them charged, pal, that's an offence, ye can get them fuckin charged,' and the guy glances up and says, 'I'd get ootay here if I wis youse, boys.'

Something occurs to me. Frowning, I take out my phone to find the bars full with reception, and three texts from Dolby arrive: beep beep beep.

20.21 They're no lettin us through to the bus!

20.40 Chaos. Police bein bastards hammerin fuck oot folk.
Let me ken if youse are all right.

21.12 Me and Jack in lobby of Europa Hotel on Market Street.
Carnage outside. One of youse cunts phone me!!

Frannie hangs up the phone. His bottom lip juts and he stares at the ground. 'It's aw kicked aff.'

'Looks like it.'

'Right. Market Street. Let's get movin.' We thrust our hands in our pockets and bunch our shoulders, as another four guys jog the other way, like spooked impala. Frannie has the same expression on his face he gets when describing a particularly nasty tackle at the five-a-sides. He's shaking his head and muttering, 'Shambles. Absolute fuckin shambles. Totally unprepared for us,' and now seems the last time to point out to him: Em, they didn't actually want us here.

The day has disintegrated. Rangers have lost, and all that colossal potential energy of an anticipated win has become sharp-edged and kinetic. Sirens and helicopters and outraged Scottish accents cut the air as bodies clatter past, clutching their wounds. We've stepped up the pace, gladiatorially. I quicken, tingling, as we turn into Market Street, into the battle zone.

'Fuckin hell,' Frannie intones.

A line of police dominates the centre of the street, batons and shields raised, and fans stalk back and forth through the litter, eyeing them, shouting, singing. One guy throws a bottle – watches as it hovers, smashes – while another videos the action on his phone, grinning. Somerfield. Boots. Halifax. Debenhams. There's a strange, animal tension between the fans and the police, as though each side is waiting to see if the other will advance.

The United Kingdom.

'There's the hotel.' Frannie nods at a sign further down the road, beyond the police barricade. 'Mon.' He is striding towards the riot cops, one of whom watches his approach cautiously behind his visor, as though some eternal conflict between man and beast is about to be re-enacted. I follow him, hoping that when the police see my smallness (and perhaps my Captain America T-shirt), they'll realise we can't possibly be a threat to them. Frannie is on the phone to Dolby, telling him, 'Right, we're in Market Street. Come tay the police line and we'll see if they'll pass ye ootay there.'

But when we reach them, Frannie doesn't make it as easy as that. 'Ho, mate,' he says, gesturing to the entrance of the Europa Hotel. 'We needtay get through there.'

'This street is blocked,' the cop says, in a formal, precise voice. I try to peer through his visor, and can see, behind the dark screen, a pair of eyes, narrow and suspicious.

'Aye,' says Frannie, 'heard it. Oor mate's stuck in that hotel wi his wee boy. We want to get him and head the fuck ootay this city.'

'Don't swear at me,' the cop warns, and Frannie takes a deep breath, teeth clenched.

About fifty yards away, Dolby and Jack emerge from the hotel lobby and talk to one of the riot cops. The cop points with his truncheon back into the lobby and Dolby remonstrates with him, clearly referring to Jack then to our presence further down the street. The policeman looks our way.

'Turn around,' the riot cop tells us. 'No way through here.'

'For fucksakes!' says Frannie. 'Stop being a dick!'

The cop butts Frannie's face with his shield and Frannie staggers backwards, dazed, as though the world has just disappeared then reappeared in front of him. When he touches his face he feels the redness that has bloomed from his nose. I look at the cop, who is poised, waiting for our response, and without even thinking I have picked up a bottle and am shouting, 'That's ma fuckin MATE!' feeling the weight of it in my hand, but then a truncheon comes down hard on my wrist and I buckle and the bottle is smashing to the ground and Dolby is shouting and I glance up to see Frannie grab the cop by the helmet and wrestle with him and the other cop is charging towards us and Dolby is holding Jack and watching helplessly and one of the cops is swinging at Frannie and I'm jumping on his back and pulling at the cop's helmet while Frannie kicks at him and Rangers fans pour, roaring, from all over Market Street to help us and the police ranks thin around us as they run down the street and the guy me and Frannie are fighting manages to wrench himself away from us and tear after the rest of the police and we're charging after him and a battle-cry is escaping my lungs as we close the gap and he glances back terrified and drops his shield and baton to gain some speed and we pick up pace and grab him and he falls and we're all barking and kicking and my foot is coming down again and again on his visor and I'm spitting out, 'Fucking bastard! Motherfucking bastard!' and someone's pulling me away and I turn and it's Frannie and he's shouting 'NO, ALVIN,' and I scream

John crawled across the bed towards me. 'You cool with this, mate?'

'Yes,' I said.

Sara's room was festooned with red velvet drapes and the light, easy cannabis smell still hung in the air between us. Kneeling behind him, topless, Sara removed John's T-shirt and laid her hands flat on his chest while he stared down at me, taut and hungry. 'Oh, I think we're all fine with it,' she whispered in his ear.

'Go ahead,' I said, as the smoke relaxed into my blood and I felt all the sudden pleasure of the world enter the room, human beings mentally attuned with each other

and my mind is eating them ma mamamama ma ma ma mamamama and

John turned and kissed Sara, and they ran their hands over each other and Sara gasped, 'Yes,' as I stroked myself watching the two of them, and Sara unzipped John's jeans and freed his hard-on and squeezed it in her fist and, yes, 'That's it,' I said, 'yes,' and soon her fingers were flashing against her clit, her neck flushed red, her other hand flicking over her nipples, and she looked more beautiful than any woman I had ever seen, and John's big hand tugged at his cock, his eyes intense and staring at Sara's pussy, exposed before him. She looked into my eyes, and I bent down and kissed her. Yes. My hand reached up to touch John's cock as she kissed me back, working it, his full balls and his stiff shaft. He moaned and let me feel him, play with him, and then Sara was doing the same.

We both leaned in and kissed his cock, sucked on it, passing it between each other with fond smiles. While her head bobbed up and down, and his hand roamed through her hair, I felt her breasts, teasing the nipples. She made a soft, ecstatic sound while she sucked him. Then I moved down her body, stroking it with my fingertips, tracing my way down her skin. My fingers parted her wetness and I touched her clit, making her shudder, and rubbed at it a couple of times before easing my finger inside her. John's cock was standing straight up, rigid and full, and I wanted it and

ma ma ma ma
ma ma ma ma
ma ma ma ma ma

the bed shook, Sara's body shuddering as John lapped between her legs. She held her breasts and said, 'God, that's good, God, that's good.' John was bent over the edge of the bed while he licked her and my hands roamed over the strong cubes of his ass, moving down to feel his hard-on, his balls, tight close to his body, and then I opened his cheeks and spat on my cock, before nudging the head of it against his hole and pushing, feeling it slip inside, tingling, while Sara opened her eyes and stared at me and her eyes said, You can be anything you want to be, and I said, 'Yes,' and my soul locked with John's and Sara's and John was moaning as my cock started to fill him and I was grunting, 'Yes fuck yes,' and Sara's face started to dissolve with pleasure and she closed her eyes and said, 'Yes Yes I'm coming I'm COMING I'M

and Mum s screamin   Thump on the flair fay upstairs   Dad swearin at the toppay his voice then a different kinday thump   Derek turned the telly up says stay here Alvin before chargin up the stair   Mum screeches   Some day i m gonnay walk away fay all of yese and ye ll never hear fay me again! Ye ll never ken whit happened! i ll just be like that   *gone*   and yese ll be wonderin yer whole fuckin lives whit yese did tay me i ll be a fuckin ghost
ma   ma ma ma ma ma   ma   mamama   ma   mamamam ma ma ma ma
ma   ma ma ma   ma ma ma   ma   ma ma ma   ma mamama ma   mama
   ma   ma ma ma   ma ma ma   ma   ma ma ma mamamama   ma   mama
polisman comes up tay the hoose   interviews Dad Derek me tell them about how I got infay school and she wisnay there and Dad tells them whit Mum had said tay him about threatenin tay run away   polisman narrows his eyes at Dad when he says this   Derek tells him about times he's had tay go oot lookin for her   how he d found her collapsed in the

Callendar Woods before hand still cradlin a vodka bottle or aboot that time when he found her in the swing park some weans had put dogshit on her dinnay really want tay be listenin tay this Dad touches ma shoulder Alvin son ye look tired Gon uptay yer bed We re nearly finished here now But then the polisman says Actually would it be possible for me to have a word with your younger son alone ? Dad looks at Derek then says tay the polisman Em whit for? the polisman says If you don't mind sir? Dad nods at Derek they baith get up head through tay the kitchen polisman brings his chair ower sits in front ay me Im just starin up at him hands between ma legs he says

Hi

I says Hi

Alvin is it ?

Aye

How s things wi you wee man?

Fine

He reaches for his notebook licks his pencil

Okay Alvin got a difficult question for ye now but need ye tay answer it honestly Can ye do that for me? Are you an honest person?

I try to be

Good lad he says and leans forwards a wee bit Can smell the coffee on his breath Now tell me honestly son Yer daddy doesn t need to know Did yer daddy ever hit yer mummy? Did he? Cos maybe that s what might ve made her run away did yer daddy ever hit yer mummy ?

did he ?

falkirk frannie dolby john sara
ma ma ma ma
stirling dad derek edinburgh it wis aw a
ghost story
ma ma ma ma ma ma ma mamama ma
mamamam ma ma ma ma

ma ma ma ma ma ma ma ma ma ma ma ma ma ma
mamama ma mama
ma ma ma ma ma ma ma ma ma ma ma
mamamama ma ma

i am nothing i am no one

Ye re ma son Ye ll always be ma
wee boy
but you no longer exist no one who listens to me now

I m listening I m here wi ye
always

ma ma ma ma ma ma ma mama ma mamamam
ma ma ma ma

ma ma ma ma ma ma ma ma ma ma ma ma ma
mamama ma mama
ma ma ma ma ma ma ma ma ma ma ma
mamamama ma ma

let it out son

just let it out

my foot is coming down again and again on the cop's visor, which breaks and I'm roaring, 'Fucking bastard! Motherfucking bastard!' and someone's pulling me away and I turn and it's Frannie and he's shouting, 'NO, ALVIN' and I scream

ma ma ma ma
mamamamamama
mama mama m
amamamamamam
mama mama
mamama mam
am am amam
mama a mama

Make her live inside you scooped out hollow a human-shaped machine vacuuming gathered together from spare organic parts ~~gases distended in her~~ When she reached out to touch an object kettle flowerpot slippers it was like some hologram placed photo-realistically across space [once occupied] by her body moving synthetically pre-programmed with futuristic hum She said hello to people neighbours but the emotion behind the utterance had vanished irrelevant data stray bits of binary not the code her mind needed to carry out such tasks ~~such~~ as fill washing-machine answer phone pick up toys go to supermarket register sunlight on skin recognise scents shapes voices of her
   dearlybelovedfamily how to interact she is she s

Dad came into the kitchen, face red and blowing great big puffs of air, as his morning jog slowed to a halt. He looked at me for a second, surprised to see me already there perched at the kitchen table, tapping at the laptop, like the toy bird Homer Simpson leaves to run the nuclear power-station when he's away. He was in his Nike running vest and shorts, and his skin was ruddy-pink from the jog, as though he'd just washed it in a Highland stream for an advert.

'Oh,' he said, doing his warm-down stretches, 'wisnay expecting you up so early.'

'Stuff to do,' I mumbled, closing the screen that had my writing on it. 'Going down to Dolby's later to talk through the Manchester trip with him and Frannie.'

'Watch yourselves,' he said. 'Lottay bodies headin doon there. Could be rowdy.'

Rowdy, I thought, is exactly what I need right now. But

instead I said vaguely, 'Och, it'll be fine,' glancing round at what he'd done with the kitchen. White. Minimalist. Full bowl of fruit and juicer machine. The new Dad. He'd painted the place himself, even bought magazines on interior décor to do it, and periodically throughout my final year at uni, I'd hear all about it in texts that were clearly high on paint fumes:

About to start the kitchen . . . with relish. Though it would look funny painted with relish! Lol

Oh I feel like Rolf Harris. Can you guess what it is yet? Lol

Noooo. Dont want to see any more white paint! Think I'm going snowblind!!! Lol

'Ye goin doon on a Rangers' supporters bus?'

'Yup,' I said, cracking the knuckles of my right hand.

'Do they ken ye don't even support Rangers?'

'Nope,' I said, cracking the knuckles of my left hand.

'Ooooo-kay,' he said, crossing the room to the fridge. 'You want some breakfast?' He brought out the bacon, ripping open the plastic and pulling out the grill with all the precise, focused motion of a robot car-worker. 'Everybody needs a good start to their day.'

'I am invincible,' I said perfunctorily.

The bacon was laid on the grill. I went back to the Apple glow of my MacBook and Dad continued his warm-down stretches, looking about twenty years younger than I felt. The bastard. The jogging, the swimming, the vitamin-supplements stacked up in the kitchen cupboard. Burn your Ramones T-shirts, Dad. Your punk dream is over. It was almost easier when he was still depressed, slumping around the living room smoking old Clash songs down to the filter, the way he did for years after Mum disappeared. Now he's like some ex-gambler who has gone all Praise the Lord, attempting to make his every utterance a motivation to others.

'I mind,' he said, arms stretched back, holding his right foot up and pulling, 'the first day I dropped you off at that uni. How feart you looked. Like ye were about tay cross the rope bridge in a film or somethin.'

'I was only seventeen.' I tutted. 'I was terrified.'

'Look at ye now. Typin away.'

'That's right,' I said. 'I can type. That degree wasn't a complete waste, then.'

He sipped his orange juice, leaning back against the counter, taking in the sight of me sitting there, and I shuffled about in the spotlight and tried to look magnificent.

'That you lookin at nudie sites?' he said, gesturing towards the laptop.

'Dad!' I said, embarrassment tingling. 'I don't do that.'

He gave me a disbelieving look. 'Aw, cos ye're gettin so much ay it in real life? I ken whit these unis are like, by the way.'

Just tell him. Just open your mouth and say the words. Tell him, and once the first domino falls you can tell Dolby and

Frannie and Brian. And yourself.

'I'm not going to talk about my love life, okay, Dad?' I said, blushing and not really understanding the role of a son in the modern world, the appropriate levels of sarcasm or acceptance with which to underlay one's voice when speaking to one's *pater familias*. 'That's private. And . . . complicated.'

From this tiny chicken-scratch of a clue, I was expecting him to extrapolate the meaning.

'Oh, well,' Dad said, his cheeks burning lightly, 'ye can tell me anythin, son. I'm yer dad.'

'I'd rather not, if that's okay.'

'No ma business. But I'm here if ye want tay talk.' He gave me a meaningful nod and I inhaled, but before I could say anything else he went, 'Whit is ye're writin?'

'It's about Mum,' I said, mainly to shut him up.

Dad frowned. Then he set the kettle on to boil, downed the handle of the toaster. 'Well, whitever helps ye. Is this something ye're gonnay try and . . . publish?'

'No,' I said immediately. 'I want to publish Horror or Sci-Fi.' Even I noticed the tone of grandiosity enter my voice. 'This one's just for me.'

'Sci-Fi!' he said, as though I'd just told him a joke, 'Since when did you want to be a Sci-Fi writer?'

And, for some reason, this one sentence seemed to encapsulate how far me and my dad had drifted from each other since my birth, like continents connected now only by flight paths.

'Since always.'

'Reckon ye're good at it, likes?'

'I should be,' I say. 'After all, Iain Banks went to my uni and look what he's done.'

'Who's he?'

'He's a famous Sci-Fi writer,' I said, even annoying myself with how teenage I sounded, but I couldn't help it. There was something about being back in that house which brought it out of me, a Pavlovian response to regurgitate awkwardness in my speech. Dad is talking, thus I whine. Maybe, in our own families, we're all just salivating dogs. 'One of my professors, Rory Watson, he actually taught him.'

. . . which made him a virtual celebrity in my eyes, especially when he answered with patience my questions about what Banks was like each time I cornered him at the end of a tutorial . . .

'And whit if the writing doesnay work out?' Dad said. 'Whit's yer Plan B?'

'Well, I thought about doing a postgraduate degree in Gothic literature.'

'Ooh,' Dad said, waving his fingers in the air. 'Spooky!'

'Uh, yeah. But I'm already five thousand pounds in debt, so I can't afford it.'

'Oh.' There was a brief silence. We were both well aware that there were many parents who could afford to pay postgraduate fees for their sons, and that my dad wasn't one of them.

'I just need to get out of the university system,' I added, to try and draw the venom from the puncture wound.

He nodded solemnly.

'I need to get a career job, basically,' I said, projecting Everyman at him, before realising that this gifted him an opening.

'Soooo,' he said, rolling his hand and shepherding me through my own thoughts, 'what kind of jobs will you be applying for?'

This was exactly the question I'd avoided asking myself all the way through uni – content to just jump from square to square on the chequerboard of modules and essays as they came at me – and the very question I'd feared he'd ask me if I returned home, after Alvin's Big University Adventure. Now people were expecting the sequel. Bigger. Better. More celebrity cameos. Even more ambitious in structure and design. But done with the same minimal, psychological resources.

Strip it back to the basics: what was it exactly that I was trying to *become*?

The only answer I had was: the same thing Dolby was trying to become when he changed his name to Uriel back in the day. I wanted to be something *more than*, something beautiful and unique and splendid and real. But I couldn't think of a job that would fit this remit, or one that would accept my perfectly respectable 2:1 in English and decent reference from Rory Watson as entry requirements.

'Well,' I said, leaning back in my seat, 'I have to confess, uh, I don't know, Dad. I don't have a plan for that yet.'

'Right,' he said, and we both knew that he didn't have

a plan for that either. He'd never met a graduate before who hadn't either been handing over his disability benefit, back when he was depressed, or strolling through the building site with a clipboard. So the conclusion was inconclusive. All I could do was just take the next corner in the maze and hope it was the right path. Pac Man ma ma mamama ma ma mamama.

'You could come back to Falkirk!' he said brightly. 'I could say to the gaffer and see if he'd get you some labouring work on the site. You could move back in he—'

'That's not going to happen,' I said, while thinking: That's probably going to happen.

'Well,' he said, and tried not to show his disappointment, 'good luck out there, son. Just remember—'

Those words always made my back stiffen, partly because they opened the bridge to the chorus of (I've Had) The Time Of My Life by Bill Medley and Jennifer Warnes, but partly because they always preceded the final stage, the *endgame*, of every father-son conversation: career advice. How could I have known, though, that it'd be then, standing in the kitchen, five days before me, Frannie, Dolby and Jack left for Manchester, halfway through his stretching exercises, that my father would choose to deliver me the most perfectly articulate speech of his life.

'No matter how things go, son, it's not always about yer income or yer debt or yer status or yer lack ay it, but what happens in here.' He tapped his head and nodded at me. Then he placed a hand over his heart. 'And in here.'

I looked at him. He was staring back at me with an expression of simple sincerity.

'That's all ye have tay worry about.'

I didn't know what to say to this, but for the briefest of moments he was a senior wizard who'd taken down a huge dusty book and told me to incant a spell, by candlelight, word for word, that would guarantee eternal life.

'Dad,' I said, tantalised by this breakthrough, sensing more there, beyond barricades I'd just decided to storm. 'What's the worst thing you've ever done?'

Did you do it? Did you hit her? Is that why she ran?

His forehead wrinkled at this, but he answered: he stepped with me into the depths.

'We aw do things we're no proud ay,' he said, before rolling a boulder of a memory to the front of his mind. 'There was this one time, back when I was first wi yer mother. I think Derek had just been born. Greetin aw night. Couldnay sleep.'

'Sounds like Derek.'

He smiled faintly. My brother had moved to Aberdeen some time after Dad had discovered vitamin supplements, but Dad and I were still able to bond over his faults (forgetting birthdays, forgetting to pay back money, an inability to get over Mum), just as Derek and I bond over Dad's faults (self-absorption, laziness/manic-energy/laziness, an inability to get over Mum), just as, I'm sure, they bond over mine (oh-so-numerous, but including an inability to get over Mum). 'Aye,' he continued. 'So it was ma turn, and I was haudin Derek, rockin him, tryin tay get him tay shut up, when the door goes.

So I answers it.' He stopped, as though he'd just opened the door again to be confronted by the same past. 'And it's this auld guy. Says his car's broke doon and can I come out and help him have a look at it, cos he doesnay know anythin about cars. The bairn's screamin in ma ear and this auld guy's wanting me to fix his motor? "Sorry, mate, cannay help ye," I says, shuts the door on him. Just like that. And I comes back intay the kitchen and I looks oot this winday—'

He pointed to the same kitchen window, and I even got up from the breakfast bar and peered through the blinds to picture the scene: the grass outside and the main road, where cars shot past on their way to Falkirk town centre, and it's the early 1980s.

'And he can hardly walk. He's like this.' Dad did a stooped, slow hobble. 'And it takes him about a year tay get tay his car and he opens the door and he just sits in it, like this.' Dad did the old guy, hands locked on the wheel, staring passively out of the windscreen. Then he shook his head and ruminated on his own utter evil.

'And what happened next?' I said.

'Nothin,' he said. 'Yer mum came into the room and I started talkin to her about Derek – we were still tryin tay get him tay stop cryin, ye see.' He glanced out of the window, through the blinds, as though the old boy was still sitting out there in his car, hands on the wheel. Dad sniffed. 'But I mind thinkin: that guy will be me oot there wan day.'

Night has descended over Manchester. The air is cold now on

our bare arms as we walk in silence. Some lights from office blocks are on, perhaps guys trapped at work, seeing the chaos unspill below them and staying put.

Cowards.

Dolby holds a shivering Jack against his chest, his face tight. The wee man's crying and Dolby's saying, 'It's okay, pal, we're going to the bus now.' Frannie's striding purposefully, topless, his T-shirt pressed against his bleeding head. Bruises thud all over my body. We don't say anything, just breathe the nullity of our thoughts, as a helicopter chops the night sky above.

Back at the bus, the rest of the guys are waiting for us, their eyes wide and stunned at our bedraggled appearance, at Frannie's wound, at sniffling Jack.

'They can tell yese,' Dolby says, setting Jack into the front and clicking a seat-belt over him. 'I just want the fuck ootay here *the noo*.'

Frannie takes the stage at the head of the bus and starts the story from the point of the second goal going in and us leaving the bar, but misses out the detail of why we left the bar, and I scan the heads and see Cage and Chrissie nestled together on the back seat. Cage has his huge arm around her. She's cuddled into his chest, moving her cheek against it, purring. He's stroking her hair, oblivious to everyone else, to Frannie's story, to Manchester, even to Rangers. They are somewhere else, on a yacht in the Pacific, beneath a tropical sun, at peace.

Taylor and Burton.

The bus shunts away from its parking space, and as

Manchester slips past us, every so often there's a glance in my direction, and I wonder what they know.

The journey back up to Scotland is quiet, an endless, spectral line of dazed cars forcing themselves up the motorway. Everyone on our bus is asleep or half asleep or trying to sleep, except Frannie, who is leaning into the front seat, Rangers top still pressed to the wound on his forehead, listening to the radio. News of the riot starts to enlarge, fill up the night like a thick black cloak, smothering all other conversation. Pitched battles. Police injured. Shop-windows smashed. Horses.

'They're gonnay have a field day wi this,' he mutters.

He doesn't need to specify who 'they' are.

Jack is curled and sleeping in the front seat, having cried all his panic out. I rub the ugly bruise on my elbow and check it occasionally. 'Ow,' I say, to no one in particular.

'There has been widespread violence,' says a police spokesman, 'which our officers are continuing to combat, although we do want to make it clear that the majority of Rangers fans were good-natured and behaved themselves.'

'As if the press'll care aboot *that* the morra,' Frannie grumbles. 'Like the front pages will be fullay "good-natured fans" behavin themselves.'

A text from Brian comes through:

Shit result, boys. ☹ Hope yese wereny caught up in the trouble?

We pull into a Little Chef, but it seems the whole convoy has had the same idea. It's two in the morning, but the car park is full of buses. Some of our lot disembark and stretch and roam towards the building's glow. Jack stirs and Dolby says, 'Do you need to go to the toilet, son?' and Jack nods sleepily. 'Alvin,' Dolby says, 'can you take him? I needtay phone her – she's worried sick.'

'Sure, man,' I say, exiting the bus, opening the front door and lifting Jack's soft weight out.

The bright lights dazzle us, attacking our eyes with banality, and Jack screws his fist into his face. Little Chef goes about its midnight business. Everything has the slow, unreal feel of a night-shift. A drowsy hive of Rangers fans drip towards coffee machines, stare disconsolately out of windows, queue for toilets. A photocopier-bright glare from the panels above. The plastic plants. The burble and whir of arcade games no one's playing. Cashiers intone, 'Fivepoundsfortysevenplease,' to punters holding filled rolls.

I take Jack to the toilet and he stumbles over to the children's urinal, has a pee in a line of weary, grumbling punters.

'Shockin fay the polis.'

'Poor shout fay the City ay Manchester.'

'They werenay ready for us.'

We werenay *fuckin invited!* I want to scream. But what's the point?

Then Jack clops back towards me, eyes half closed, and I direct him to the sink and he runs the tap and holds his hands under it for a second, then just pads to the exit door. I take his wet hand and we head back to the bus. He doesn't even glance at the beeping arcade games. We shuffle back through the midnight air, the hugeness of the day nestled now as a sharp little pith inside me, and I am thinking this:

No one knows what it is to be in the mind of anyone else. No one but me knows the terrain of me; no one but you knows the terrain of you. We are all roughly crenellated land in there, and time is both gouging and building us. We are *becoming* things we don't know we are becoming, each of us, in our private selves, in the dark. And yet we have no way of telling each other what it feels like, beyond simple, useless, shopworn words. All we have is time together on this earth, to try and pierce through the crowd of lies we surround ourselves with, into the truth of each other. It is only then that we know we are not alone.

In the front seat, Dolby is pinching the top of his nose, his eyes closed, talking into the phone. But when he takes his fingers away from his face I can see he's sobbing. 'I want ye back, honey. I need ye and miss ye. I don't care what ye've done, let's just wipe the slate clean please, eh? I'm nothin withoot ye.'

I lift Jack up into my arms and walk a few feet from the bus. He leans his head into my shoulder sleepily.

'Hey, ma wee pal?'

'Mmp?' he mumbles.

'Look up.'

He lifts his head and with all his will makes it face up.

'Look at the stars,' I say. 'Amazing, eh?'

His gaze clambers from one star to another and he moves his head, approximating a nod.

'Would you like to be a spaceman one day? Would you like to find new planets?'

He considers this, halfway towards dreaming.

'You be anything you wantay be, pal,' I say, kissing his head. 'Don't let anybody tell ye what kinday man ye have tay be.'

He drops his eyes from the stars and inspects this advice. 'Unless it's a spaceman,' he says. 'Cos for that you have to do basic training.'

The door of the bus opens and Dolby steps out. He looks at me, then his eyes dart away, embarrassed. He takes Jack from me and makes an exaggerated 'Och!' sound as the weight shifts and says, 'Is he awright?'

'He's fine, man. You awright?'

Dolby nods and I pat his arm supportively and he carries Jack, who seems to be already asleep again, back onto the bus. The rest of the crew trudge back from the service station, Bex and Jeff helping Auld Alfred's stiff limbs into his seat. There's a tap on my arm.

'Listen, mate,' Frannie says, 'I wantay apologise for what I said earlier.'

'Naw, it's fine,' I say, 'I needed tay hear it.'

Frannie shakes his head, not prepared to let himself off the hook. 'Nay danger. I wis ootay line. Ye made it away, mate. You got that degree. I've never respected that, and I should've. I'm sorry.'

'Aye, but you're right,' I say, and exhale the last of my defences against him. 'I've done nothing with it. I'm nothing. But I've acted like youse are nothing.'

Frannie cocks his head like a stand-up comic inviting a heckler to take him on. 'Haw, let's just presume there's none of us are nothin.'

I weave my head, acknowledging this, and glance towards the bus. They're all staring at me. Every one of them. As though I'm a bizarre species.

'Ye'll never be nothin, mate. I'm proud tay call ye ma pal.'

I breathe and hug him.

'Same goes, man.'

We release each other and Frannie holds up his phone, with the crooked smile on his face I recognise from Falkirk nightclubs – Rosie's, Storm, the Martell – as he stood poised to approach a group of girls and tiptoe through their defences. 'It's three in the afternoon in California. Brian'll be halfwey through a shift. Mon, let's phone him and tell him ye've had a cock in yer mooth.'

I sigh and try to say something, but he raises a finger to halt me. 'Hey, dinnay fuckin push it. Don't say something stupit like, "I love you, man."'

'Awright,' I say, and just think it.

We step back onto the bus, through their curious gazes, and take our seats. Dolby turns the ignition, wrenches the vehicle into gear, and moves along the slip-road back towards the motorway. While we sit at the junction, Frannie cues up Brian's number, presses speakerphone, and there is a crackling silence before it starts to ring. Cars rush past us on the motorway, none with Rangers scarves. Civilians. Ordinary people going from place to place, job to job, oblivious to me, my life, the life of my friends. We are nothing. We are everything.

Frannie holds up the phone, waits, grinning. 'Hello?' Brian says, and I glance at Dolby and he sees me in the rear-view mirror, and whatever it is, it's understood.

I wish there'd be a meteor shower. Something to stun us all with beauty. Everyone in these cars, all along the motorway back to Scotland, slouching home – they'd look up and stare at the trailing lights, the magic of it, and it would tingle in our minds for the few hours that it takes us to reach the sign that says

YOU ARE NOW ENTERING FALKIRK

You may have heard of the following obscure, arthouse films, or late-night, barely watched television programmes, some of which were quoted very briefly in this novel:
Star Wars (p.9), Jaws, (p.58), The Naked Gun (p.107), Friends (p.166), Apocalypse Now (p.206)

I should also acknowledge the following songs, which you may have heard the milkman whistle:
p.7 – 'My Generation' by The Who, written by Pete Townshend (1965)
p.81 – 'Magical Mystery Tour' by The Beatles, written by John Lennon and Paul McCartney (1967)
p.99 – 'If' by Pink Floyd, written by Roger Waters (1971)
p.101 – 'Total Eclipse of the Heart' by Bonnie Tyler, written by Jim Steinman (1983).
p.115 – 'Club Tropicana' by Wham!, written by George Michael and Andrew Ridgeley (1983).
p.120 – 'Another Brick in the Wall pt.2' by Pink Floyd, written by Roger Waters (1979).

Awards For All: Redux

It's worth saying straight away that, while I was in Manchester on that particular day in May 2008, neither myself nor anyone I was with were involved in altercations with the police. That's not our style. Like the Monkees, we're just trying to be friendly.

Some extracts from this book were first published in the magazine *Gutter* and the online journal *From Glasgow to Saturn*, under the titles 'Loyalist Travelling Blues' and 'Screw the Nut'. Thanks to the editors Colin Begg and Adrian Searle in the first instance, and Alan Gillespie in the second. Between you, you're keeping the blood flowing round the body of Scottish literature. It's aliiiiive!

Grateful thanks are also due to the following:
For their crucial, timely and honest feedback (phew! made it!): Rodge Glass, Neil Cocker and Kirstin Innes.

For allowing me to, frankly, pinch some of their material: Elaine McKergow, Neil Cocker and Kirstin Innes.

For some peaceful time to focus on the project: Moniack Mhor Creative Writing Centre. Rachel, Cynthia, Lindy and Nicky indulged my 'mountain man' beard and cardigan combo.

For being good mates and cool as fuck: Thomas Tobias, Colin Armstrong, Kevin Saunders and Allan Mann. I am particularly grateful to Colin, for his support, his ever-insightful views on Rangers, and his excellent chapter on Maurice Johnston in the book *Ten Days That Shook Rangers* (edited by Ronnie Esplin), which distils much of the sectarian debate in its pages. Thanks also to Professor Willy Maley for his views on Celtic and his continual generosity of spirit. For any readers interested in the wider context of the sectarian issue in Scotland, I can recommend the following intelligent and informed books that were useful to me: the *Celtic Minded* series edited by Joseph M. Bradley and *It's Rangers For Me?* edited by Ronnie Esplin and Graham Walker.

For their ever-high production values: Leah Woodburn and Hazel Orme at Hachette, Chris Hannah and my man Bob McDevitt, the Gandalf to my Frodo, ever patient and willing. I'm also grateful to Sarah Morrison and Vikki Reilly at Polygon for reissuing the prequel to this book, *Boyracers.* If you want to see what these boys were up to before, have a look.

Thanks also to my agent, Victoria Hobbs, Magi Gibson, Ian Macpherson, Mark Buckland, Adam Stafford, Gylla-Fiona Swinney, Irvine Welsh, Des Dillon, Greg Easton, and my mother, father, brother and sister for their ongoing support. We're all still here, getting on with it.

For her tireless suffering of me during the writing of this novel: my lovely partner, Kirstin Innes. You fought the war with me.

For the the illustration 'Floyd Day in Falkirk' on p.32, for her incredible hard work and patience, and for making Art at school enjoyable: Nancy Brown. Flick your hair, Miss.

And thanks also to you, dear reader. You're one of my kind.

Death of a Ladies' Man

'*F*cked up, funny and fantastic*' Lauren Laverne

By day, Charlie Bain is the school's most inspiring teacher.
By night he prowls the stylish bars of Glasgow seducing women.
Fuelled by art, drugs and fantasies of being an indie star,
Charlie journeys further into hedonism, unable to see the
destruction his desires are leading everyone towards . . .

One of Scotland's dazzling young writing talents tackles
the modern phenomenon of sex addiction. Dark, funny
and deliciously erotic, DEATH OF A LADIES' MAN is an intense
portrait of male vanity, written with verve and emotional rawness.

'Bissett's third novel is delivered with invention and flair'
Esquire

'He has pulled the sheets back on Lothario men and shown them
lying there wriggling, pathetic and bare-bummed. Bissett proves
himself to be a fresh and compelling literary talent'
Scotland on Sunday

'Devilishly funny and disturbingly accurate. A real gem'
News of the World

'This is a very funny book . . . a complex, nuanced take on the
sexual and social behaviour of a certain kind of man.'
Sydney Morning Herald

ISBN 978 0 7553 1942 8
£7.99 PB

Also available as an ebook

The Incredible Adam Spark

A dazzling performance (think *Forrest Gump*, think *Curious Incident*, think Anne Donovan's *Buddha Da*) from one of Scotland's brightest new talents.

Adam Spark. Eighteen going on eight-and-a-half. Fast-food worker. Queen fan. Last in the queue for luck. On waking from an accident in which he saves a child, he has the distinct impression that all is far from right. What are these curious lights that seem to surround people? Why are animals and machines trying to speak to him? And can he really control time? Is it just his imagination, or has Adam Spark been chosen to become Scotland's first, and only, superhero? This, however, is the least of his problems. The local gang is luring him into deeper and darker peril. His sister and lone carer, Jude, is giving all her love to another woman. And if Jude abandons Adam – or Adam drives her away – all the superpowers in the world won't be able to save him.

'Sparky is a terrific character'
Sunday Herald

'Sparky is a virtuoso literary creation . . . a fresh and exciting read'
Scotland on Sunday

'Bizarre, hilarious, moving'
Big Issue

ISBN 978 0 7553 2646 4
£7.99 PB